Heaven's Mountain

The first book of the

Heaven's Mountain trilogy

JACALYN WILSON

ISBN-13: 9781477443972
ISBN-10: 1477443975

Dedication

To my dear daughters, Rebecca and Laura,
for your consistent encouragement and constant love

Prologue

*A*ll day long the snow fell, coming down pure and white and untouched by the disputes of men. Sadly, the unsoiled beauty lasted only until the moment the flakes touched the earth. Then the pristine fluff became a filthy brown muck, covering combat boots, uniforms, and gear. Jesse Brittain had come to hate the cold, the snow, and the raw discomfort of war in the winter.

He was hunkered down in the trench next to Buggar, the only other Georgia boy in their unit. Back in the states neither of them would have been aware of the other's existence, and becoming friends would have been inconceivable. But here, surrounded by a company of "yanks", they were drawn to each other, to the familiar feeling of home. So, in spite of their dissimilar backgrounds, they became buddies.

Jesse was the taller, more muscular of the two. He had neatly trimmed fingernails and, even here in the midst of battle, his hands were clean and his hair was combed. When he opened his mouth, the voice of a refined southern gentleman poured out slow and rich, bringing to mind crocheted table toppers and Sunday afternoon church picnics. One could easily assume Jesse Brittain had survived a proper southern upbringing.

As insinuated by his name, Buggar was decidedly less polished. The last time his fingernails were cut, he'd used a pocket knife and the dirt still showed under the rough edges. Peeking from underneath his helmet, a wild thatch of wheat-colored hair framed a surprisingly gentle face and, even in the dark, every soldier in the trench could recognize his voice instantly by the strong southern twang and the mutilated grammar.

The sergeant's signal was passed down the line. Time to move. After a long boring day of frozen misery, a strange feeling of relief and excitement swept through the ranks. In less than a minute, backpacks were hefted, rifles were checked and prayers were said. Their gear clanked as they went over the lip of the trench out into the open field, moving in a slow belly crawl, then graduating to a low crouch.

Ignoring the order for absolute silence, Buggar tugged on Jesse's sleeve and whispered, "Here, Jess. Keep this for me." He poked a small bundle into Jesse's chest.

Jesse shot him an exasperated glance. "Again?" he whispered. "Every time the fighting starts you hand me that letter, and every time I end up giving it back to you."

"Yeah, but this might be the night the Reaper calls my name," the boy shuddered, envisioning the deathly spectre.

"Don't say that! Do you want to jinx us?" Relenting, Jesse held out his hand. " Here, give it to me." He tucked the envelope inside his shirt. "There. You satisfied? Now, keep moving. Sarge is looking at us."

"Thanks, Jess." Buggar again grabbed his comrade by the arm. There was just enough moonlight for Jesse to see his buddy swallow hard, his eyes watery bright . "Jess, you know, I…uh… I've never had a friend as good as you before."

Jesse pushed Buggar back down to a crouching position. "Get down, boy. You want to give 'em a clear shot?" Falling silent, they moved quickly to catch up with the line, until Jesse halted again. Reaching out, his hand squeezed Buggar's shoulder tightly and he spoke softly. "I'm glad you're my friend, too." Then, louder, "Now, get your scrawny butt in gear, you crazy ole' Georgia cracker. We got an appointment tonight with our Nazi neighbors." With a friendly nudge, the boys from Georgia trudged on toward the enemy line, side by side.

Ten minutes later the sky exploded in streamers of light as the ground rocked and rose and sprayed dirt. And then, after a while, the screams and the moans gradually died away to nothing.

One

May, 1968

"Just where do you think you're going?" The regal tones of Augusta Brittain echoed up the attic stairwell. On the top step, Grace turned, letting her hand fall from the doorknob of the attic door. Their eyes locked in a childish staring contest as seconds ticked by.

Augusta was the first to break eye contact. After fidgeting with the graying hair which had escaped the tight bun at the nape of her neck, she resumed the battle. "Young lady, I asked you a question. Where are you going?" She lifted her chin and fixed her eyes on Grace. This time her gaze did not flinch.

All of her life, until a few months ago, Grace had feared this arrogant, haughty, bitter woman. She couldn't remember a kind word ever being directed her way from that hateful mouth. Grace had to stifle a laugh now, at the thought that this "genteel" southern lady was actually her grandmother.

"I am going to the attic," Grace replied coolly. "I want to go through my great-uncle Zachary's belongings." She watched Augusta for any reaction. There was none, so she added more fuel to the fire. "You know, all of his personal things, which he left to me." She pivoted on the top step and inserted the key in the lock. "Along with this house," she added softly, as she turned the key.

At those words, Augusta drew herself up to her full height and closed her eyes for a moment, as if to shut out something painful. Then, with her eyes wide open but her brows drawn tight together, shoulders back and spine straight, she sailed away down the hall.

As her grandmother's footsteps grew fainter, Grace felt her tension subside. She pushed open the attic door. She hadn't been up here in years, not since the last time she accompanied her mother, the family's housekeeper, to dust and sweep. Nothing had changed. Nothing in the attic, anyway. But everything had changed for her.

She wandered among the old furniture and sheet-covered paintings, peeking and touching and opening, but not disturbing. Tucked under the dormer window, a dilapidated steamer trunk caught her eye. Pushing aside several crates of books, she cleared a space in front of the trunk then hesitated, rubbing her fingers across the brass initial plate. "Z B". Uncle Zachary would have been ashamed of her for the way she had spoken to her grandmother just now. "I won't do it again," she promised herself. "I'll be respectful to the old biddy, even when she's horrible to me. I'll do it for you, Uncle Zach." Her guilt thus assuaged, she lifted the lid.

There wasn't very much inside. Handwritten journals of farm receipts and expenses. A moth-eaten sweater with his college letter. A couple of trophies and some framed awards from his younger days. Then, she pulled a fat photo album from the bottom of the trunk. The late afternoon sun coming through the dingy window was barely sufficient, so she wiped the panes with an old rag and sat down on top of the trunk.

Flipping through the pages, she recognized only a few faces. Uncle Zachary as a young man, looking a little goofy in his golf attire, knickers and all. Augusta with her husband, Grace's grandfather, who died from injuries sustained in the Great War. Neither of them looked very happy, she thought. Turning the page, there was Augusta again, this time holding a toddler in her lap. Fascinated now, Grace studied the little boy's features, delighted to discover a definite resemblance to her own baby pictures. She decided to take the whole album home with her, to peruse at her leisure. Disappointed with the meager results of her work thus far, she surveyed the attic, searching for anything that would connect her with this family, especially her father. Her gaze came to rest on a small, military trunk in the far corner. Military. Maybe…

Hoping, hurrying, she shoved aside furniture and boxes until she was kneeling in front of the trunk. She found a key hanging from a string attached to the carrying handle. Inserting the key, she turned and felt the lock give. The lid creaked with age and rust when she lifted it.

Clothes. She saw nothing but clothes and some old boots. Irritated but determined, she emptied the chest item by item, looking for anything that might link the contents to her father. Finally, in the bottom under some binoculars and an old pistol, she found several manila envelopes.

One contained the "We regret to inform you" letter from the U.S. Army, notifying the family of her father's death in December, 1944. Another contained his personal effects: a watch, a ring, a dogtag, some questionable sticks of chewing gum, a key, and a wallet. Grace opened the cracked leather wallet and found identification cards and two photographs. One was of her mother. Why, she was beautiful! And she looked so young and carefree, Grace marvelled. She picked up the second photo, which was of Augusta and Jesse in his dress uniform. Checking the back, she read the inscription, "Jesse, I am so proud of you, son. Know that I am praying constantly for your safe return. Love, Mother." Hmmph. Imagine that. Augusta Brittain used to have a heart.

Keeping out the ring, the dogtag and the two photos, she began replacing the uniforms in the trunk. As she picked up one of the shirts, she felt a crackle in the pocket. Running her hand inside, she retrieved a small envelope. It looked as if it might have gotten wet at some point in the past, judging by the smeared and washed away look of the address. The addressee's name was completely gone, but the address line was mostly clear and appeared to read "Heavens Mountain Goergia". Hmph. Terrible handwriting and he misspelled "Georgia", whoever the writer was.

Heaven's Mountain. She had heard of that place. Somewhere in north Georgia, she thought. Intrigued, she carefully opened the flap and slid the pages out. Some of the parchment crumbled immediately into a powder and fell through her fingers, but she was undeterred. Grace had never been able to resist the allure of a mystery yet to be unraveled, so she slowly peeled apart the sheets which were stuck together.

Much of the ink had disappeared entirely, but there were some legible phrases, mostly at the top and bottom of each page. She set about deciphering what was there. At the top of the first page, she read:

"To the shurif at Heavens Mt

Yuve gott the rong man in the jale"

A few more words here and there on that page,

"…my daddy…."

"…church yard…"

"…his nife…."

The second page was a little clearer:

"cut him bad then throed the nife"

"put him in the truck"

" I climed up in that tree and yankd owt that nife I hid it in the …."

"I am truely sorry I did not tale you. I am scairt I mite die so that is why I must set the rekird strait now before I die"

There was nothing more. Where the signature would have been, the paper had disintegrated.

Grace's mind was racing. Surely this was not an eyewitness's account of a murder. Was it? She read it again. What was her father doing with this letter in his pocket? Nothing made sense. She'd run it by Ed, her boss, in the morning, she decided. Maybe a fresh, objective pair of eyes could clarify this sketchy missive.

Checking her watch, she realized she had to get home for supper. She hadn't even noticed the waning light, so engrossed was she in her plundering. Gathering up the photo album, the few personal items of her father's and the Heaven's Mountain letter, she left, locking the door behind her.

"Do you want some more tea, honey?" asked Nan, Grace's mother.

"Yes, please." She held out her glass.

Grace was expecting the next question. She was simply surprised it had taken her mother and her grandmother this long to get to it. "What were you doing over at the Big House for so long?" inquired Granny Annie.

Concealing her irritation at her lack of privacy, Grace replied, "I thought it was time I went through some of Uncle Zachary's personal things. Up in the attic."

"Oh," was Granny Annie's only comment.

Grace was thankful that seemed to be the end of the interrogation. She wasn't going to offer more, but then she remembered the letter. Curiosity won out over privacy. "I went through a trunk that belonged to Jesse, too." Grace had never grown accustomed to calling him her father. "There was an old letter, not in his handwriting, addressed to Heaven's Mountain, to the sheriff. Do you know anything about that?"

Her mother thought for a minute. "You know, now that you mention it, your father had a buddy from Georgia in his unit. I think they became good friends."

Looking over her bifocals, Granny Annie's fragile voice demanded, "What did the letter say, dear?"

"I'm not sure. Most of the ink had faded away, but whoever wrote the letter was telling the sheriff that he had the wrong man in prison." She paused for effect. "Maybe for murder."

"Goodness gracious!"

"Lawzee mercy!"

Oops. Grace had momentarily forgotten how innocent and sheltered their lives were. Murder, prison, violence, these were subjects that never came up in their quiet home.

She reassured the ladies, "That was a very long time ago. I thought I'd ask Ed to read it tomorrow. I'll see what he thinks. Besides, whoever wrote that letter probably told the sheriff the truth as soon as he got home from the war."

Nan and Granny Annie looked at each other. Then, Granny Annie whispered, "Honey, there were no survivors at all in that battle where poor Jesse was killed. Not a one."

It was a night for remembering. In her room, long after the older women slept, Grace found herself unable to resist touching and examining each article from the attic. She tried hard to imagine the young man, Jesse. Her mother always used certain words to describe him. Handsome. Intelligent. Tall, slender, strong. Kind and gentle. Stubborn. A man who was unfailingly faithful to do what was right. It still wasn't enough; it didn't come close to actually meeting someone, talking to him, knowing him. And even though she had lived with it all her life, Grace couldn't shake the little thread of bitterness over the fact that her parents were never married.

When she was very little, she was often hurt and bewildered by the slightly different treatment she and her mother received, at the department store, at school, even at church. By the time she was ten years old, she knew the stares and snickers had something to do with the fact that she didn't have a daddy like the other children.

Finally, when she was fifteen, she confronted her mother, respectfully, of course, but with the same fierce determination that was evident whenever her mind was made up about something. Grace wanted to know the truth, the whole truth, and she was not giving up until she had it.

Her mother was taking laundry off the clothesline in the backyard while Grace sat on the porch steps, watching and waiting for the right moment. A little nervous, she was pondering the best way to broach the subject when Nan started back into the house. Grace was right behind her.

"Are you following me, Grace?" asked Nan, as she placed the clothes basket on the table and pulled out a towel to fold.

Grace leaned against the screen door and sighed. "Momma, you know I'm fifteen now." She ran her tongue over her braces, a habit she had just developed.

"Yes, you are becoming quite the young lady. On that we can agree. But I know you want something, honey, and I'm running behind today. I'm late getting up to the Big House to get dinner going. So, what is it, Grace?"

"Momma, I… I want you to tell me about my daddy." Grace hurried on to say, "I'm old enough to know, and I know how to keep a secret if

I have to, and also," Grace looked at her mother defiantly, "I think I'm old enough to understand the reason you never married, whatever it is."

"Yes." Her mother was very still, staring back into her daughter's eyes. "You're absolutely right, Grace. It's time you were told."

So, with a light breeze wafting through the screen door, lifting the loose hairs away from their faces, they sat at the wobbly old kitchen table and folded clothes. And Nan answered all of Grace's questions.

Nan and Jesse were high school sweethearts. Secret sweethearts, that is, for it would have been improper for the daughter of Annie, the cook, to become romantically involved with the only son and heir to the Big House and the two thousand acres of surrounding farmland. According to Nan, Jesse wanted to make their relationship public, but she was more cautious and urged him to be patient. He finally agreed to wait until Nan finished college and he came back from the war. Only he never came home.

Within days after he left, she discovered she was pregnant. She refused to place that burden on him, knowing there was nothing he could do from overseas but worry and feel guilty. So, she faced it alone, except for the support of Granny Annie, who stood by her through it all. Finished with her confessions, Nan said, "I'll be right back." She returned with a handful of yellowed letters, Jesse's letters to her, written during the war. "You keep these as long as you want, Grace. I know them by heart," she said.

After that, Grace began to pay more attention to their rich neighbors. When Augusta was condescending or unkind, Grace now took it personally. But with regard to Zachary, who she now began to think of as "Uncle Zachary", she realized that he must have known all along. He had always been unfailingly kind and loving and generous to her, and that did not change. Her newfound knowledge only strengthened the bond between them.

Two years ago, when he found out he had cancer, Grace had quit her entry level job at the newspaper in Savannah, and had come home to be his primary caregiver. She took a part-time job at the little weekly paper in Jackstone. It wasn't exactly the career path she would have chosen for using her brand new college degree in journalism, but she didn't regret it.

She would never have consigned her dear Uncle Zach to the insensitive care of Augusta Brittain.

Grace was still amazed that Uncle Zach had left everything to her. Of course, Augusta had married into the Brittain family, and Jesse was the only child, so Grace had to admit it was a logical decision since she was the only direct descendant. But the thing that touched her heart most was Uncle Zachary acknowledging her publicly as his great-niece.

After his will was read, Augusta had reluctantly given her access to the big house. Which brought Grace's thoughts back full circle to the faded letter she had found there earlier today, and the gravity of the circumstances it suggested. If an innocent man had been imprisoned for murder, something had to be done.

Two

"Well, if it ain't Lois Lane, come all the way down from that big city paper just to join us country bumpkins."

Grace rolled her eyes good-naturedly and slapped Ducky's arm with the back of her hand. There was an on-going competition between them, as the small newspaper's only two employees, to best each other with smart-aleck greetings. Grace considered herself to be in the lead at the moment, so she let Ducky have his moment of glory.

"Where's Ed?" she asked, as she put down her things.

"He's in his office. Said for you to come see him as soon as you got here."

Hurrying to the back office, she knocked, then stuck her head in and grinned. She and Ed got along just fine. He was old enough to be her grandfather, and if it weren't for the fact that he was such a darn good journalist, she might dismiss him as an old has-been. As it was, she considered herself lucky to be working under him.

At this moment, though, she had caught him in one of his whimsical interludes. He was listening to the classical radio station, singing and twirling to Madame Butterfly. She closed the door behind her, crossed her arms, and watched.

The aria ended, Ed bowed low and Grace applauded, laughing. She hoped she still wanted to dance to opera when she was seventy-five. She plopped down in her usual chair. "So, Ed, what's going on this morning?"

"Good morning, Ace. Not too much, but I thought I'd send you down to City Hall today. Might be some fireworks later on, from that argument between the chief of police and the fire chief. They're supposed to address the issue at the city council meeting this morning."

"Oooh, yeah! That sounds like fun. I'll head down there in about an hour." Grace laid something on his desk. "Read this and tell me what you think. Careful. It's old and crumbly."

Ed put on his spectacles and picked up the envelope. He opened it gently. Taking his time, he read the letter several times, turned it over, inspected the envelope, then looked inquisitively at Grace. "Where did you get this?"

After filling him in, she asked, "What do you think it means?"

He shrugged slightly. "Could be nothing. Water under the bridge and all that. Even if it is what it seems to be, the poor fellow in jail could be dead by now. So many unknowns…."

He perused the letter again, then peeked over his bifocals with a mischievous sparkle in his eyes. "Then again, Ace, this could be your big chance to get out there and do some real investigating. Break a major story. Maybe get picked up nationally." He raised one eyebrow. "What do *you* think, Gracie?"

Grace opened her mouth, then closed it again. Finally, she found her voice. "I think I'm ready to do something, something different, something challenging. Not that I don't love my job, boss!" she said with a smile. But the truth was, for the last several months, she had begun to feel smothered. Smothered with mothering! With three adult women, of whom she was the youngest, living in one house, she guessed it was inevitable.

She chewed on her bottom lip, thinking, then gave her considered opinion. "I like the idea of digging up the truth." She wiggled her eyebrows and gave him a lopsided smile. "You always say I'm like a dog with a bone. Once I get hold of something, I don't let go 'til I've gotten all the 'goody' out of it. You know something, boss?" her voice grew more excited. "I think I'm ready for this!"

"You can't go all that way by yourself!"

"Why, you don't know a soul, and besides that, it's just not proper for a young lady, not proper at all!"

"Granny, come on now," Grace tried to respond calmly. "There is nothing improper about a woman traveling on her own. It *is* 1968, and lots of women travel all over the world by themselves every day…"

"But, Grace, you don't have any experience, staying in a motel, driving all that way… What if your car breaks down on some remote mountain road?" her mother wanted to know.

"There are some bad people in this world, honey," said Granny, in her most somber tone.

"Oh, Grace!" Nan gasped. "What if the real killer is still there and finds out you're looking for him?"

Bracing her elbows on the table, Grace put her hands over her ears and closed her eyes, attempting to block out their voices, if only for a moment. After presenting her plan to her mother and grandmother, Grace had expected an uproar, but not this overwhelming barrage of negative comments that had been coming at her for the last thirty minutes. The remarks fell short of an actual denial of permission to travel to Heaven's Mountain, but the persuasive quality of their discussion was having the desired effect. It was so hard to argue with these two. Two against one. What chance did she have?

Now, the older ladies had reached the point of promising a family trip to Heaven's Mountain sometime during the summer when, they assured Grace, she could spend the entire time researching to her heart's content. Weary from the battle, she finally agreed to consider that alternative, but she wasn't feeling happy about it and took herself off to bed with a most disgruntled attitude.

Perhaps because she was agitated, Grace's sleep was troubled that night. In her dreams, she saw her father, Jesse, in full parade dress, marching around the veranda of the Big House, as a young Augusta came out the front door with a tray of iced tea. Stopping directly in front of her, he reached into his jacket and pulled out a shiny key, which he offered to her. She took it, and placed a glass of tea in his hand, whereupon he drank the tea, clicked his heels and saluted, then disappeared around the corner of the house.

Standing at the edge of the porch, Augusta threw the key high into the air, where it twirled and glittered and became a blue butterfly. Grace saw it in her dream, circling high then coming to rest in the magnolia tree between the Big House and their cottage. Wanting desperately to hold it, she ran to the tree and cautiously held out her hand.

But it flew away again, to where Augusta stood on the porch, beckoning it to return. The vibrant blue wings lit on her finger. With a piercing look of disdain for Grace, Augusta glided back into the Big House, cradling the butterfly close. Grace sat down in the grass and cried, heartbroken.

The tears on her cheeks disturbed her slumber, and she woke, feeling sad and irritated. She knew she'd never get back to sleep again that night, so she took a blanket to the summer porch and waited for the sun to rise. It wouldn't be long, for the songbirds were already warming up. Wrapping the blanket close she leaned back in the rocker and closed her eyes, wishing she could slip back into sleep.

The previous night's "discussions" were heavy and swarming in her thoughts, and the fresh dream-feelings kept mixing in with reality, confusing her, making it impossible to organize her thoughts logically. When the sunrise snuck up on her and the rays shot through the clouds hovering on the horizon, she had to admire the magnificence of it. Maybe there really was a God, somewhere up there. She didn't think he lived at the church though. Not at their church, anyway.

Across the way, a light came on in the Big House. Her house. How very strange that was, to think that she, Grace Turner, was now the owner of the Big House. The interested parties had agreed that, for the time being, all would continue as before, and Grace, wanting nothing beyond access to certain personal effects and one small bedroom to use as her office, was satisfied with that for the time being. Though Grace had no affection for Augusta, she knew that her mother deemed her worthy of respect and consideration, and in fact, Nan had shared several instances when Augusta had gone out of her way to be generous and kind. Grace had yet to experience any of that kindness herself.

Up at the Big House, a slice of dim light revealed Augusta coming out the front door then being absorbed into the darkness of the porch. When Grace saw a pinprick of red light, fluctuating from bright to weak, it took her a moment to realize that her grandmother was smoking a cigarette. So, Grace mused, her grandmother had a secret bad habit. Interesting. Grace continued to watch, as the sky lightened. Augusta finally stood, pausing in front of the door, and the dream-vision of Augusta stealing away with the butterfly became superimposed on the moment. Against all logic, the resentment and hurt Grace felt in her dream flooded through her. For too long, Augusta had hidden away the key entrusted to her by Jesse, never sharing it, never fulfilling the duty that it represented. With new urgency, Grace was consumed with a desire to perform that obligation for her father, and thus become a part of his life and legacy. The key to finding the answer was hers now. She was claiming it, and nothing was going to stop her from unlocking the truth.

Three

*N*ausea. Even with the VW Bug's windows down and brisk mountain air blowing in her face, Grace was fighting it. After almost an hour of negotiating hairpin curves, her head ached and her internal organs seemed to be floating, swaying, with each change of direction. She wanted to pull over but, unfortunately, the narrow road had no shoulder. At least she was in the descent mode now and within a few miles of Fairmount, a small mountain town situated in the valley below Heaven's Mountain. Her plan was to find someplace quiet and sit absolutely still until her head and stomach were back to normal.

When she reached the outskirts of town, the roads became congested, and pedestrians were everywhere. She was mystified by the amount of activity until she spotted a hand-painted banner, hanging between the street lights, proclaiming, "Welcome to the Fairmount Centennial Celebration". The worst part was, there were no empty parking spaces close to the center of town and Grace realized she would have to park a couple of blocks away and walk to the town square, which was roped off. As she searched for a spot, her departure from home this morning, amidst a clamor of maternal objections, was beginning to seem a little impulsive. With the clarity of hindsight she wondered if she should have prepared more carefully for this trip. With all the festivities, she might not even be able to get a motel room, and wouldn't her mother and grandmother have a hissy if they knew about that? She decided that was something about which those genteel ladies never needed to know.

She whipped into a space just vacated by a station wagon loaded with kids. With a sigh of relief, she switched off the car, let the seat back and closed her eyes. No, that made the nausea worse. Sitting up, she swallowed hard and tried to ignore the growing lump in her throat. Straight ahead she could see all the vendors' booths lined up around the courthouse square. Maybe one of them had an ice cold Coke. That might help.

Gingerly, she eased out of the car and made her way to the square. She was scanning the half-dozen nearby food booths when she felt someone watching her. There, at the other end of the square, behind the counter in the Fairmount Community Church barbecue booth, a pair of piercing blue eyes was fixed fast on her. Being well aware of her own charms, she was used to a certain amount of male attention and adoration, but she was not so accustomed to this instant attraction on her own part. The blue eyes were only part of the entire intriguing package, topped off with sun-streaked hair and dimples. She noticed the dimples when he smiled and raised a hand to wave. Nausea momentarily forgotten, she timidly raised her hand in an answering wave.

"Hi there, Ethan," came a shrill voice just behind her. Turning slightly, Grace saw a blond pony-tail swishing past. Pony-tail girl was waving at the blue-eyed hunk and jogging in his direction. Grace quickly lowered her arm and headed in the opposite direction from the barbecue booth. Waiting for her drink at the hotdog stand, she sneaked a peek down the square. Yep, they were still there, talking enthusiastically. Sheesh, did she feel foolish, for thinking that a perfect stranger would be staring at her and waving. Taking her drink, she found a bench by the trunk of a gigantic oak and sat down to watch the passersby. She felt better – for about thirty seconds.

Fighting back a new wave of queasiness, Grace leaned forward, holding her head in her hands. Maybe she could make it into the courthouse before embarrassing herself, she thought. Steeling her stomach muscles for the short walk, she stood and began walking quickly around the oak tree toward the closest entrance. Looking down to keep from tripping over the roots, she didn't see the person coming around the other side of the huge tree's trunk, so when the impact of their collision shattered her fragile concentration, her stomach convulsed, Grace gagged, and then proceeded to puke all over the unfortunate recipient's shoes. As she was bent over, heaving, she felt a steadying hand on her shoulder. Finally, totally emptied and totally humiliated, she wiped her mouth with her sleeve and straightened, her eyes widening in shock. For there was Mr. Blue-Eyes, his expression emanating his concern, the heat of his touch now burning through her blouse.

"I'm so sorry," was all she could manage before bolting for the courthouse. Had she turned around to look, her embarrassment might have been eased somewhat, to see that the handsome stranger was actually chuckling to himself and calmly scraping his shoes in the grass.

With an ample supply of soap and paper towels, Grace was soon able to make herself presentable, with the exception of the wet spots on her clothes. Thankfully, the nausea had subsided, and the embarrassing cleansing seemed to have washed away the headache, too. Waiting on the damp spots to dry, she wandered the halls of the courthouse, exploring and snooping, feeling more like her usual self. She was in the courtroom upstairs, contemplating the almost dry condition of her shirt, when she looked outside and saw Pukey Shoe Guy, formerly known as Blue Eyes, sitting on the bench she had vacated. She had planned on going out that same way, but now reconsidered, for she was still completely mortified and didn't feel quite up to facing his shoes again this soon. And why was he still sitting there? Surely he wasn't lying in wait for her. Maybe he wanted her to pay for his shoes. Anyway, shouldn't he be at the booth selling barbecue with Pony-Tail Girl? With that resolved, she skipped down the marble stairs and went out the exit on the opposite side of the building.

Ethan didn't know why he was still sitting here on the bench when he needed to be working in the church's food booth. Actually, he did know why. When he had first looked across the square and seen the young woman, he had found himself captivated by a total stranger. How strange and uncharacteristic of him was that? And then…waving at her! What was he thinking?

Maybe he should be thankful that Margaret had been standing right behind her. But when Margaret came running over, much to his frustration, with a million typically teenage questions about Billy, Ethan's younger friend and her current boyfriend, he was effectively trapped. Ethan just hoped he hadn't said anything stupid, considering his intense preoccupation at that moment with trying to keep track of the whereabouts of the lovely new arrival. When he finally spotted her, sitting on the bench under the big oak tree, he disengaged himself from the conversation with Margaret, only to see the young lady rise and start around the other side of the huge tree's trunk. And that's when he blew it. In his eagerness to introduce himself, he had probably forever ruined his chances of making her acquaintance, for she was evidently never coming out of the courthouse. He waited a few minutes more then, finally resigned, he gave up and ambled back over to the barbecue stand.

On the other side of the courthouse, Grace was entering the offices of the Fairmount Chronicle. A boy was sitting on the floor beside a stack of newspapers, busily inserting flyers, folding the papers and wrapping them with rubber bands. "We're not open," he said, as he slid a rubber band onto a paper and tossed it to the side. When he finally looked up and saw Grace, he simply stared for a few seconds, then grinned and scrambled madly to his feet. With the air of a much older gentleman, he extended his hand. "My name is Jack Wilson, miss. My daddy owns the paper."

Grace responded with equal gravity. "It's a pleasure to meet you, Jack Wilson. I'm Grace Turner from the Jackstone Gazette. I was hoping to speak with your father about an article I'm writing."

Jack smiled shyly now. "Well, miss, I'm sure he'd be happy to talk to you tomorrow. He usually gets here around eight-thirty. Can you come back in the morning?"

"Yes, I can. My plans are to be here in Fairmount for at least a week. Speaking of which… Jack Wilson, I need somewhere to stay. Is there a nice hotel here in town?"

Jack's forehead wrinkled in thought. "There is one hotel, but my momma says it's roach infested."

"Oh, dear. Well, I guess I could drive back to Gainesville...." Grace thought of all the switchback curves if she had to go back over the mountain, then said quickly, "But I don't really want to. Isn't there any other place?"

"Oh! Oh, yeah!" Jack's eyes lit up and he grinned from ear to ear. "There's a boarding house in Fairmount. I'll be glad to walk you over there. It's just a couple of blocks."

Pictures of shared communal bathrooms and rough characters reaching rudely across the table to grab their food filled Grace's head. This was not enticing. Maybe she could make it to Gainesville without getting carsick. She tilted her head and was about to say no.

"It's a good place to stay," Jack added persuasively. "My aunt stayed there a while when her house burned down. And my momma says you can eat off of her floors."

Well, then, thought Grace. Eating off the floors. You never knew when you might need to engage in that practice. And as any southern woman could tell you, that was a trusted gauge of a home's cleanliness and decency. "Let's go, Jack."

Four

ven Granny Annie and Momma couldn't find fault with those accommodations, thought Grace, as she strolled back toward the middle of town. Now, at mid afternoon, the crowd had grown even larger and the vendors' booths were doing a brisk business. Stopping at one, she pretended to examine the homemade wares while secretly checking the barbecue area for Pukey Shoe Guy. Seeing no sign of him, she continued to cross the square in the general direction of her parked car.

Rounding the corner of the courthouse, Grace saw that a stage had been erected over the courthouse stairs, where a bluegrass band was warming up. There was a banjo, a guitar, two fiddles, even a set of spoons and a sawblade. When they began to play, she stopped to listen. Their opening song was unfamiliar to her, but the audience chimed right in as if they'd been singing it all their lives.

Up on Heaven's Mountain, sitting by the throne,
With my blessed Savior, calling me his own.
O, to be so happy, not a tear I'll see.
Up on Heaven's Mountain for eternity.

Then the rumbling basses led off in the chorus...

(I'm climbing up..) I'm climbing up to Heaven's Mountain,
(Where his face..) Where his blessed face I'll see.
(I'm climbing up...) I'm climbing up to Heaven's Mountain,
Heaven's Mountain for eternity.

She was waiting for the second song to begin, listening to the band members introduce themselves, when she heard a friendly voice in her ear.

"Feeling better?"

Oh, foot! That had to be Pukey Shoe. She had hoped to avoid this but she forced herself to turn and smile graciously at him. "Yes, much better. Again, I'm so sorry for that ...accident. I'll be glad to pay for your shoes. They were probably ruined...."

"Nah, see?" He pointed to his feet. "These are my oldest loafers. I figured I'd probably get filthy today, working with the grill, so I wore my rattiest clothes." He seemed unreasonably pleased with himself for some reason.

"Well, if you're sure..." Grace purposely directed her attention back to the stage as the music recommenced. There, she thought. She handled that just fine. Of course, it would have been easier if his eyes were a little less mesmerizing and his manners a little less friendly and open. Was he gone yet? Nope. Still there. She could feel his nearness.

He was saying something to her but she couldn't hear him over the music. Not wanting to appear rude, she leaned closer. "What?"

"I said, are you a visitor to town?"

"Yes. I'm here for a few days on business."

"Not for the Centennial?"

"No," Grace shrugged. "I didn't know about the celebration."

"Well, speaking for the town, we're glad to have you here, whatever the reason." He extended his hand. "My name is Ethan...."

"Ethan, where've you been?" A grinning teenager wiggled his way in between the two, then openly stared at Grace in obvious admiration.

Shaking his head at his besotted protégé, Ethan made the introductions. "Miss, this is my friend, Billy Lucas. Billy, this is…I'm sorry, I don't know your name…" He looked to Grace for help.

She realized she was behaving childishly, remaining aloof only because of her embarrassment, first with the awkward hand waving, and then puking on the poor guy's oldest shoes. And then, she had to admit, there was also her disappointment at finally finding herself attracted to someone, only to discover he was already taken. So, squaring her shoulders, she stuck out her hand to this newest admirer. "My name is Grace Turner. It's very nice to meet you, Billy."

Billy held onto her hand quite happily, until he remembered the reason for his errand. "Oh, yeah! Ethan, they sent me to get you. They need some more hickory wood for the fire." Billy let go of her hand but kept right on smiling at her.

"Guess I'll have to go,= then," said Ethan. "Billy, maybe you could play the hospitable host to Grace." Billy tore his eyes away long enough to give Ethan a puzzled look. Ethan realized he needed to break it down into smaller words. "You know, Billy. See if she needs any help with anything while she's in our fair city…" Ethan gave them a quick salute, then jogged away

Billy smiled. "Yeah, sure, I can do that." He put on his "grownup" face. "So, Grace. What kind of business could you have in our little town?"

Ah, the transparency of teenage boys, Grace thought with some amusement. But, as Ed always said, you never knew which person might be the one to give you that key piece of information….. "I'm a reporter. I work for the Jackstone Gazette."

Billy's eyes grew big in disbelief. So much for the grownup act. "And you came here to little bitty Fairmount, to work on a news story? Did something finally happen here and I missed it?" he laughed.

"No," she laughed, too, then explained, "I'm researching an article, though it's still in the early stages. In fact, maybe you could point me in the right direction. I'm interested in any murders that took place around Heaven's Mountain between 1900 and 1950." Billy's face grew serious as he thought on the matter. Grace continued, "I'd like to interview anyone who knew the victim, or the killer, or who might know details about the crime."

"I'm not sure, but I think I remember my daddy talking about him and my grandfather finding a body one time. Do you want to talk to them?"

Bingo. "Sure. When do you think I could do that?"

"Would you like to come to Sunday dinner at our house? I know my grandma won't mind," Billy's words tumbled out quickly. "I'll ask her, but I'm sure it's all right." Seeing the doubt on Grace's face, he hurried to convince her. "If you really want to talk to them, that's about the only time you're gonna catch 'em. They stay out and about all week. Seeing about business and all." Billy waited expectantly.

What could it hurt, she thought. "All right, Billy. It's a date."

That evening, after settling into her room, Grace went downstairs hoping to meet the other boarders. Two Asian girls were writing at the table in the spacious living area. When Grace approached, they introduced themselves as sisters Mia and Babs Villanueva, recent immigrants from the Philippines. Listening carefully to compensate for their very pronounced accents and their frequent interruptions of each other, Grace grasped that they would be working at the textile mill in Fairmount through the summer, with plans to relocate to Atlanta in the fall to attend the university. Their cheerfulness was refreshing and Grace found their conversation fascinating, especially their description of their home life back in the Philippines. She would have been content to chat longer, but she excused herself when she noticed Clare on the far side of the room settling into the corner of the sofa with her crocheting bags.

"May I join you?" Grace asked.

"Why, I'd appreciate the company. I usually can't do but one thing at the time, but talking and crocheting are the one exception to that rule, which is good, because I tend to do a lot of both!" Clare's merry laughter bubbled over, she grabbed a breath, and continued, "I'm real glad you've come to stay with me a few days, Grace. If I do say so myself, there just isn't any other nice place for a young woman to stay in Fairmount. And

I told you, didn't I, that breakfast is served buffet style from seven until eight-thirty every morning, and I serve a family style supper at six-thirty every evening."

Grace nodded, but didn't attempt to break in. Clare's crochet hook dipped and twisted, moving rapidly, as she picked up the threads of the, so far, one-sided conversation. "We missed you this evening, but one of the boarders told me she saw you in the park, listening to the band." Clare looked up from her work. "Do you want something to eat now?" Grace shook her head and Clare went on.

"The town has really gone all out for this centennial celebration. They've got all kinds of things going on all day tomorrow, then a big square dance in the middle of town tomorrow night. You ought to go to the dance, a pretty young thing like you. I can promise you won't want for partners." She giggled. "Sometimes, just for mischief, I'll ask one of the young men to dance with me, and they always go along with it, just to be polite. But you should see their faces by the time I get through with them! Their tongues are hanging out, and honey, you've just about got to mop them up off the pavement, they're so tuckered."

Clare stopped to count her loops and Grace jumped in. "You're not that much older than me, are you, Clare?" She couldn't be more than thirty-five, she thought, not with that perfect petite body and her auburn hair in that cute page boy cut.

Clare simpered just a little. "Honey, you have just made my day! I'm forty-seven. But I work like a dog every day, running this place all by myself, so I stay in good shape."

"My mother's forty-three and she can work circles around me," commented Grace. "So, do you have any children?"

"No, no children. I've never been married. Roger, the love of my life, and I had planned to marry, but he was killed in the war."

"So was my father," said Grace.

"Oh, I'm sorry, dear." She sighed. "There just never was anybody after Roger but that's all right. I'm happy. God is good and he takes care of all my needs."

"There was never anybody else for my mom, either. I think you two would get along, Clare."

"I bet we would, too." There was a pause in the conversation. "So, what brings you to Fairmount, Grace, if you don't mind my asking?"

" I don't mind. Actually, I wanted to talk to you about it. I'm a reporter. I work for a small newspaper in Jackstone and I'm here doing research for an article I'm writing. In general, I want to learn all I can about any murders that took place in this area in the first half of the century." Grace finished her spiel, taking care to present it in the way she and Ed had agreed would give her access to the information she needed, without revealing too much and possibly exposing her to the killer's scrutiny.

"Well, I declare!" Clare exclaimed. "That seems a strange thing to write a story about. But, on second thought, you know how people are, always wanting to hear the worst things. I guess that's just what most people *would* want to read a story about. But... won't it be right hard to find out about some murders that happened such a long time ago?"

"It could be. I'll use the old newspapers and courthouse records, of course, but my main source of information, I hope, will be people who were actually involved in some way, or who were related to one of the primary characters, the murderer or the victim. How about you, Clare?"

"Me?"

"Sure. You probably know someone who was involved in some way with a murder. Maybe it was their relative that was murdered or was a murderer. Or maybe they witnessed a murder?"

"Hmm. Back where I used to live, a lady down the street from me had a son that was killed on the railroad track. Oh, but he wasn't murdered. He just got drunk and fell asleep on the track."

"So, you haven't always lived here, Clare?"

"Gracious, no. I only moved here about five years ago. This was my aunt's place. She never married either. No children. She left this establishment to me in her will. I guess she figured this would be a way for me to always have my own place." Clare thought a minute. "You know I think I remember someone saying that this lady who goes to my church had a brother who was murdered a long time ago. She doesn't come every Sunday. She's sort of a nursemaid to someone, so she can't always get away."

"You see, you do know somebody! Do you think you could introduce me to this lady?" Grace asked.

"Well, she might be at church Sunday. Would you like to go with me? Maybe you could meet her and talk to her there."

No, she wouldn't like to go to church, but this was business and she was a professional. Grace hesitated only a second before saying, "Sure. I'd appreciate that, Clare."

Clare began putting her crocheting needle and thread away. "Well, I've got to get myself to bed. Don't want to be late with breakfast in the morning. Good night, Grace. Sleep well, and let me know if there's anything you need."

As Grace sat alone in the living room, she realized she was exhausted, but overall pretty pleased with herself. It was her first day in the field and already she had two leads. Not too shabby. Lois Lane would sleep well tonight.

Five

*G*race liked to dress well. She had never really been able to indulge her tastes before, but Uncle Zachary had changed all that. Over the last six months, she had taken her time and used what she felt was a reasonable amount of money to build a fashionable wardrobe for herself. Now, getting dressed every morning was an adventure. And today, though she would never have admitted it, she was dressing to impress a lovely young man.

Today's ensemble, highly stylish, consisted of a heather green Villager skirt and matching cardigan, a crisp white blouse with front tucks, finished off by John Romaine loafers, bag and belt. Her chestnut hair was in a perfect flip all the way around, thanks to the curlers she had slept in, and her makeup was tastefully applied to enhance without being flashy. Whatever happened today, she would look good doing it.

In the dining room, Grace was enjoying a last sip or two of coffee when Clare popped in and began clearing.

"You look like you stepped out of a fashion magazine, Grace! You must have a big day planned."

"Mmm. Big enough. I hope I'll make some progress on the article today," said Grace as she rose and pushed her chair back into place.

"Well, don't forget the dance tonight. We can walk down town together if you like."

"I'll think about it," she promised.

The short walk to the town square was invigorating, thanks to the refreshingly brisk mountain air. Grace checked her watch. Almost nine-thirty, so the newspaper office ought to be open by now, she thought. Within a few minutes, she was pushing open the door and shaking hands with the owner.

"Good morning! I'm Joe Wilson, owner, manager, editor, you name it! My son, Jack, told me you'd be coming by this morning. He was quite taken with you, you know. Miss Turner, isn't it?"

"Grace Turner, yes. And I was quite taken with your son, Mr. Wilson. He's a charming young man. Very polite and well-spoken," she complimented.

"Takes after his momma!" he joked, motioning her to follow him into his office and be seated. "Now, in what way can I help you, Miss Turner?"

"Please, will you call me Grace?" she asked.

"Only if you call me Joe."

Grace nodded. "Joe, I was hoping that you could help me with some research. I work for a small paper in Jackstone. The Gazette?"

"I've heard of it. I don't know the owner, but he's reputed to be brilliant."

Grace grinned. "He is."

"Ed...?"

"Ed Broadman."

"Ah! I'm terrible with names. Not the best trait for a journalist, eh?" he chuckled. "Anyway, I'm happy to be of service, Grace. What do you need?"

Grace considered giving Joe the more general spiel, but she had a gut feeling that she could trust this man. She plunged in.

"Joe, we're both reporters, so I'm going to trust you with the real story. I'm trusting that you won't repeat this." She looked at him inquiringly. He nodded and she continued. "I'm searching for a murder that happened here in the Heaven's Mountain area before 1944, probably between 1932 and 1944. The victim was a man, not a woman. And that's about all I have to go on. I'd like to have access to your stacks for those years, and, if you have any personal knowledge you could share, I'd be grateful."

"Hmmm. I moved here and took over the paper about three years ago, but my uncle had the paper before me, and he remembers every detail from every story he ever ran. I'll talk to him tomorrow at Sunday dinner. I can just about guarantee you he can give me the date, place, name of victim, how they were murdered,, name of the accused, whether they were convicted and every detail of every murder trial during those years."

Grace spent the rest of the morning wandering around town, strolling by the booths, stopping to examine the handmade crafts. Several times, when she spotted an older person sitting alone, she walked over and started a conversation which she guided into a casual set of questions. Two of the older ladies mentioned a young woman caught with another man, both of whom were killed by the woman's jealous husband. Another old woman remembered a young man shot in a honky-tonk back in 1937. And an old gentleman mentioned a drunk by the name of Amos Canfield who was found stabbed to death. That one was a definite possibility, she thought.

Excited that she might be on to something, she went back by the newspaper to tell Joe, but the office was locked, with a closed sign on the door. She would just have to wait until Monday.

It was long past lunch time, Blue Eyes was nowhere to be seen, and Grace's fashionable look was beginning to feel a little confining. With a quick trip back to the boarding house, she remedied the situation by changing into flowered jeans, a white button-down shirt and a long sweater vest. And her Keds, of course. Comfortable at last, she made a bee-line for the Methodist Women's booth, where she had spotted some tempting fried apple pies. She bought two.

She noticed a number of folks were headed down a side street, so she followed the flow. Along the path, signs pointed the way to "Field Day

Games, Kids of All Ages Welcome." She was still humming, the sun was shining, the air was bracing. She felt …. thankful! Of course, that was a little absurd, since she did not believe in God, so who did she think deserved her thanks? Quit analyzing, Grace, she admonished herself, and just enjoy this beautiful day. So, she did.

At the community recreation football field, there must have been a hundred or more children and teenagers, scattered among a dozen activity stations. She watched the group closest to her, then moved on down the field to see them all. The final group was split into two teams, racing back and forth with an egg in a wooden spoon. Lurching awkwardly toward Grace was a little red-haired girl, trying most unsuccessfully to keep her egg in the spoon. Grace held her breath each time the egg hit the ground, but the tenacious child just kept putting it back in the spoon. Finally, the little tousle-head made it to the chalk line, gave an ear-splitting grin, and turned the spoon and the egg over to her teammate.

"I was hoping to see you again today."

Dear old Pukey Shoe. He sounded awfully glad to see her. Maybe he and Pony-Tail Girl weren't really an item after all. All this flashed through her mind as she gave in to the moment and allowed her delight to shine full on for him to see. She wouldn't know until much later the effect the undiluted joy on her face had on him that day. "Hello, Ethan," she managed.

"One of our workers got sick, so I've been filling in here at the ball field all day. You look as if you've had a good day."

"Yes, I…"

A commotion at the other end of the field halted their conversation. Shouts and a couple of wails could be heard over the murmuring crowd. Ethan and Grace both began running. As they got closer, Ethan called out, "Where's Janet? Wasn't she assigned first aid duty today?"

"She said she'd be right back," someone answered.

"Excuse me." Ethan pushed his way through, followed closely by Grace. "What happened?"

"Climbed up the goal post, lost his balance. Looks like his leg's broken," one man yelled over the child's sobbing.

"Everybody move back a little. Has anyone called the ambulance?"

"I'll go," said the same man, and tore out at a fast run.

"He-e-ey, he-e-e-y. Calm down, now, buddy. I know it hurts, but you've got to calm down a little, so we can help you." Ethan took the child's hand in one of his, and with his handkerchief, started drying his tears with the other. Grace had knelt further down the child's body and was examining the leg that was broken. Ethan turned his head quickly,

"What are you doing?"

A little taken aback by his tone, Grace replied, "I'm checking his leg to see where the fracture might be."

"Well, maybe you ought to let it be until the paramedics get here," he said.

Grace stopped moving her hands, and looked up at him. Under different circumstances she might have told him to go jump in a lake, but since the boy was really in no apparent danger, she decided to let it go. "Fine. We'll do that."

The tone of the day had suddenly shifted. Grace rose and backed away a little, as Ethan continued to soothe the boy. She was going to slip through the crowd and leave, but little Jack Wilson had seen her and had immediately run over to talk to her. So, she stood there for several minutes, as he called several of his friends over to meet her, too. The ambulance had come in the meantime, and Ethan was already helping to get the boy loaded up. As soon as the doors closed, he came over to where Grace was laughing with the boys.

He waited until all the lads had said goodbye and drifted away, and only the two of them remained. "Grace, I am so sorry. I shouldn't have spoken to you that way. I should have shown more faith in your judgment and your ability."

Grace tilted her head to the side and gave him a one-sided half-smile. "Yes, you should have. But, on the other hand, you don't really know me. I might be a perverted lunatic out to torture little boys with broken bones by practicing witch-doctor medicine on them."

"Hmm. I can see right now it's going to take major crawling and begging to make this up to you. Am I right?"

"Totally. But I think you're going to have to wait a while. Your egg-spoon teams are getting restless over there."

"Well, I tell you what. I have a tremendous idea. Why don't you.…..come and help me.…..and then later.…..we'll see what we can do about finding me some crow to eat?", he said as he took her hand and pulled her back across the field, faster and faster, until they were running.

"Okay, okay." she laughed, breathless now.

They spent the rest of the afternoon together, guiding youngsters through the intricacies of the egg-spoon race, then switching over to the three-legged race, which, of course, they had to try for themselves. Grace couldn't remember the last time she had played this way, and had such pure, innocent fun. She knew it wasn't just because of the beautiful day and getting to "play" right along with the kids, though that certainly was part of it. There was something about being around Ethan that brought out a joyfulness in her. Maybe it was the way he made her feel secure, as if nothing too terrible could happen while he was at her side.

They were herding children off the field, picking up paraphernalia, closing up shop, when a gentleman motioned Ethan over to the side. Crossing his arms over his chest and with a very serious expression, Ethan conversed with the man for a few minutes, then came back over to Grace. "I've got to leave, Grace." He held out his hand. She took it and he enclosed her hand within his. "Today was special," he told her, with a gentle squeeze.

The gentleman asked Ethan if he was coming. Ethan turned his head towards him and nodded. "I've got to go," he told Grace. He released her hand and began walking away. "Maybe I'll see you at the dance tonight. Not sure if I'll make it or not," he said as he got into the car. Grace waved and watched them drive away, wondering what was so important.

Six

"Grace, it's almost eight o'clock. You 'bout ready?"

"Almost." Grace opened her door and beckoned Clare to come in. "I just need to decide which earrings to wear. What do you think?" She held up to her ears first a pair of gold rope studs, then a pair of silver hoops, and finally a sparkly dangling blue pair.

"Oooh, I'd wear the blue ones. They go great with that skirt I loaned you. And you know what? You can have that skirt, honey. I'm *never* gonna get into that again."

"Why, thank you, Clare. I'd love to have it, if you're sure...?" Grace glided her hands down the royal blue and white striped satin skirt. Unlike the skirts she had brought, which were all straight or A-line, this one was perfect for dancing, very full, swirling straight out when Grace spun around. The white chiffon blouse, with wide soft ruffles around a scooped neck, was a perfect balance against the simplicity of the stripes in the skirt.

Grace quickly slipped the earrings on. Checking her reflection one last time, she was pleased with what she saw. Her shiny chestnut hair was drawn into a French twist, her skin was glowing from being outside all afternoon, and the blue earrings were a perfect complement to the lighter blue of her eyes.

Satisfied, she held out her arm to Clare. "Shall we go, miss?" she teased.

In spite of the difference in their ages, Grace found that talking to Clare was surprisingly easy. She had such a cheery, optimistic way of looking at everything, you couldn't help but laugh and feel good when you were around her. As they walked, the two women compared notes on which dances they knew, which ones were most fun, and which ones were the most likely to get your feet stepped on. They even stopped along the way for Clare to teach Grace the basics of buck dancing, a favorite in the mountains.

As if by magic, the town square had been transformed by all the Chinese lanterns hanging everywhere - in the trees, on the light poles, and from the awnings and overhangs on the stores and offices on the square. All four of the streets surrounding the square were now roped off for dancing. The band was already playing, the caller was calling, and square dancers galore crowded the street. Many were dressed in their square dancing best: for the ladies, checked skirts, crinoline petticoats, and shiny black patent Mary Janes, and for the men, starched stiff and sharply pressed jeans, white starched shirts and shiny pointy-toed boots.

Standing on tiptoe, Grace searched the nearby faces for Ethan's. If he was here, she hoped he would try to find her. Clare had already been asked to dance. Waving to Grace while talking a blue streak to her partner, she danced with him out into the street. And it didn't take long for the younger men to zero in on the new young lady in town, either. Before she knew it, Grace was whisked away into the midst of the dancers. She was charmed by the politeness of the shy mountain boys and the courtly gentlemen who treated her as if she were a royal princess. They usually didn't have much to say, but Grace didn't know if she would have had enough breath to carry on a conversation anyway, for their energetic clomping and stepping were a challenge for her to keep up with.

With just a few necessary breaks to rest her feet and get something to drink, Grace, and Clare too, for that matter, danced away the next two hours. The two of them had just sat down to compare notes on the evening when Billy Lucas came charging up.

"I just saw you out there dancing, Grace! I didn't know you were here or I would have asked you to dance before now," Billy said, the words almost tripping over one another.

"Hey, Miss Clare, how are you?" he added, remembering his manners.

"Hey yourself, Billy. I saw you dancing with Margaret Dennis a minute ago. You two made a pretty couple," Clare commented.

Ignoring Clare's remark, Billy went on, "Well, uh, would you like to dance, Grace?"

Seeing the anxious look on his face, Grace couldn't bring herself to say no. Handing Clare her soft drink, she held out her hand to Billy and let him pull her up off of the bench. While Billy's movements were perhaps a little smoother than her mountain courtiers, they were no less energetic. In fact, she was getting a little dizzy, he was spinning her around so hard. After a couple of dances, she pleaded exhaustion, and he reluctantly took her arm to walk her back to the bench.

And there was Ethan, talking to Clare. He smiled and said hello. Then Clare whirled around, grabbed Billy by the arm, and said, "You don't look worn out yet, young fellow. Let's see if you can keep up with an old lady like me." And, giving Grace a wink, she dragged him back out on to the street.

"Did you just get here?' she asked.

"A little while ago," he answered. He took another moment to stare at her. "You look absolutely beautiful, Grace. Our mountain air must agree with you, because it looks like there's a light shining inside of you tonight."

"Thank you," she whispered. She looked down and ran her hands across the satiny skirt, then raised her eyes to his," You look very handsome, too, Ethan." Just then, the band began playing "The Tennessee Waltz".

"May I have this dance, Grace?"

She didn't answer, but simply nodded and held out her hand. He took her hand and began moving slowly backward towards the dance floor. They didn't speak; they didn't even hold each other tightly. In fact, they kept a very proper six inches between them, but that was all the better, for they were able to gaze into each other's eyes and study each other's faces the whole length of the slow sweet ballad. This was a wonder to her, this powerful attraction to a member of the opposite sex, a feeling she had never experienced before, not once in high school or college. She didn't quite know what to make of it. It was exciting but scary at the same time, as if she wasn't quite in control of things anymore.

The song was over too soon. "Would you like to sit and talk for awhile?" Ethan suggested, guiding her back to a bench. Grace agreed readily, thinking perhaps some casual conversation might make her feel normal again.

"Your friend Billy seems like a nice young man," she commented.

"He's a great kid," he agreed. "His mother died when he was two or three years old. His father runs the family businesses, which is a full-time job, considering the Lucases own about a quarter of the businesses and property in this area. Unfortunately, when Bo, that's Billy's dad, isn't busy with business, he's usually drunk or well on his way to being drunk."

"So, I guess he doesn't spend much time with Billy, huh?"

"Nope. But Billy does have his grandmother, Sadie. She's a good woman, and one of the few good influences in Billy's life. Her husband Beamon, on the other hand, is about as mean as they come. He built the Lucas' fortune, doing whatever it took to get it. And, from what I've heard, it took some fairly nasty doings."

"Well, gee… I may be having lunch at the Lucases tomorrow…" She looked questioningly at Ethan.

"Oh. No need for concern about that. I probably shouldn't have said so much, it's just that you asked about Billy."

Grace decided to change the subject. "So, have you lived here all your life?"

"Except for the years I was away at college. I love it here. Love the people, love the place – the way this little valley sits up here, almost hidden away, with Heaven's Mountain sort of standing guard over us. "

"It is beautiful here," she agreed.

"So are you," he said. Then, his eyes got a mischievous twinkle in them. "By the way, when you travel for business, do you always pack your square dancing outfit?"

Laughing, Grace was explaining how Clare had given her the skirt, when the same gentleman who had come for Ethan at the ball field showed up in front of them.

"I'm truly sorry to disturb you, Ethan. But, can I talk to you?" he said.

Ethan looked at Grace. "I'm sorry. I have to go."

"It's all right. I understand." But she didn't. She wondered what was the matter with this man, that he had to be at everyone's beck and call.

"Will I see you tomorrow?" he said.

"Probably," she answered, thinking that they would probably run into each other as the celebration continued tomorrow.

"Good night then," he said as he hurried away.

Not feeling much like dancing anymore, she decided to go on back to the boarding house. She stood up on the bench to see if she could spot Clare's curly brown hair. She didn't see Clare, but Billy saw her. He immediately made his way over to her. Before he had a chance to ask her to dance again, she jumped in. "Billy, I think I'm going to call it a night. Dancing with all you fiery young guys has got me beat. Have you seen Clare? I need to tell her I'm leaving."

Billy stood on the bench and located her right away. "I'll go tell her, if you want me to."

"Would you please? My feet are starting to hurt. Thanks, Billy. I'll wait right here until you get back."

Within a minute Billy was back. "She said to tell you that she's going to dance until they turn out the lights, and that she's cooking breakfast for the seniors at the church in the morning, so she can't walk with you to church, but for you to be there by eleven o'clock, and she'll see you there tomorrow. And she said to tell you to let me walk you home." Billy finished, proud that he had remembered everything.

"Okay, then. I guess you are my escort, Mr. Lucas." Grace stuck out her arm in an exaggerated manner. Billy took it and played along with her, thrilled that she would include him in her charade. Grace kept up the antics until they reached the porch of the boarding house.

"Thank you, Mr. Lucas. You were an excellent escort, in that you kept all the wild animals and the bad boogey men at bay, and delivered me safely to my very own doorstep," she joked.

"You're welcome, Grace. Oh, I almost forgot! You're invited to Sunday dinner tomorrow at my house. I told you I would fix it so that you could talk to my daddy and my Grampaw, remember?'

"And you're sure it's all right for me to come, Billy?"

"Yes, ma'am. I could come by here and pick you up if you want me to. We eat about one o'clock, so I could pick you up about a quarter 'til?"

Grace would have preferred to drive her own car, but could tell it was a big deal for Billy to be the one doing the driving, so she agreed. "That will be fine, Billy. See you tomorrow at a quarter 'til one then, right?" Grace turned to open the front door.

Billy didn't answer. Grace looked back to check on him, and found him directly behind her. She hadn't even heard him come up the steps. "What....." was all Grace was able to say before he swooped his head in and kissed her on the lips. "Billy, you shouldn't have...."

"See you tomorrow, Grace," he sang out as he swung himself quickly down the steps and into the darkness.

Seven

*G*race was not very comfortable about going to church on Sunday morning. She hadn't even been inside a church for at least six years, maybe longer. Being there under false pretenses was not what she wanted, but as a professional she did need to be accommodating when someone offered to help her get the information she needed for a story, provided she wasn't required to lie or hurt anyone.

True to her word, Clare was waiting for her outside on the steps leading up to the sanctuary. "Don't worry, you're not late. They actually started the service a few minutes early! And believe me, that's a miracle!"

When they entered, the congregation was already standing to sing the opening hymn, a lively old-time gospel song. Clare guided Grace inside, down the far right aisle, and some folks moved down to make room for them in the pew. Clare found the place in the hymnal and they joined their voices with all the others. Grace couldn't see very much. In the pew directly in front of them were several members of an unusually tall family. When the hymn was over, and they were all seated, the song leader and a lady from the choir sang a lovely, contemporary song, which Grace actually found herself enjoying. She surreptitiously glanced around the sanctuary, noting that there were very few empty seats. They must have a pretty good preacher, if he could pack them in like this, she thought to herself. From her vantage point, all she could see was one of his legs sticking out from behind the pulpit, as he was seated to the left and behind the pulpit.

The duet had come to a close, followed by sustained applause. The singers went back to their places, and the congregation "rustled" as the service paused for a moment between the special music and the morning prayer. Grace was looking down to accept the bulletin Clare was handing her, when she heard the next speaker say, "Let us join our hearts together now and approach our dear Father's throne. Let's give him our thanks and praise, and share our burdens with him. Will you pray with me?"

That voice was unnervingly familiar. Grace listened, unmoving, while his voice rolled on and on. That couldn't possibly be Ethan, could it? Surely not. She would have realized it if he had been acting like a religious man, wouldn't she? Her thoughts were whirling, racing through every word, every gesture of the past two days, seeking to discover any telling remark, any strange mannerisms. Nothing stood out in her mind as unusual.

Then she realized what the answer must be. Other people, besides the preacher, prayed in church all the time. That had to be it. Ethan had just been asked to say the prayer, and great guy that he was, he had agreed to pray. Okay, she could deal with that. She no longer attended church herself, but she could be tolerant of the beliefs of others. Calmed down now, she cracked her eyelids slightly so that she could try to get a look at him. Of course, that meant that in order to actually see through the little slit of an opening between her eyelids, she had to raise her chin to an entirely unnatural level. Giving up, she lowered her head again. She'd just have to wait until he finished praying. Finally, she could tell he was winding things up. Just a little more. Now. There it was, "Amen".

She punched Clare. "That was Ethan?" she whispered. Clare smiled and nodded, looking back at her bulletin.

"The preacher asked him to pray?" Grace persisted.

Now, Clare stopped and gave Grace her undivided attention. "He *is* the preacher!" she whispered back, staring at Grace as if she had lost her mind.

Grace tried to compose her face. "Oh. Oh, okay," she said, attempting to smile at Clare. Failing that, she turned and faced forward again, trying to maintain a nonchalant demeanor. Inside, her emotions were churning. How could she, a reporter and journalist, have been so unobservant? Hadn't the food booth at the festival been sponsored by the Fairmount Community Church? And Ethan was "in charge" as he had openly told her. She guessed that explained why he seemed to be at everyone's beck and call, too.

Now that this information had surfaced, continuing their fledgling relationship was totally out of the question. When she left home for college at eighteen, she had made her own choice to sever all ties with the church, and with the God who was supposed to transform his people into good, kind, and loving folks. Even if Ethan didn't mind being romantically involved with a "heathen" (which he probably *would* mind as soon as he discovered her lack of faith), this particular heathen had no desire to get roped back into a religion that preached one thing and lived another.

Her mind was absolutely adamant on this, and she determined she would not waver. She would not be false, to herself or to Ethan. But even though she knew she had no choice, she couldn't help but grieve over what might have grown up between them, given a little time and opportunity. Grace had never had more than minor crushes on any of the guys she dated, but she had always been open to the idea of romance, and had looked forward to the day when she and a special man would fall in love and build a life together. She was honest enough to admit to herself that, in the back of her mind, she had begun to entertain the notion that Ethan might be the one. It was disappointing and crushing and it hurt her feelings, but she would just have to get over it. She had a job to do here in Fairmount and she was not leaving until it was done, but there was no reason to make herself even more miserable by seeing Ethan again. She would end it now, and that would be that.

By the time Ethan finished his sermon, and they all rose for the invitation hymn, Grace had reconciled herself to the new situation. As soon as the benediction was said, she planned to tell Clare that she couldn't wait on her, that she needed to get back to the boarding house to get ready for dinner with the Lucases. She didn't want to risk getting caught and having to face Ethan, not yet. The reason Clare had invited her in the first place had completely slipped her mind, until Clare pointed down toward the front of the church, almost directly in front of where they had been sitting. "That's the woman I was telling you about, the one whose brother was killed. Let's see if we can get through this crowd." Before she could stop her, Clare was weaving in between the folks who were "stalled" in the aisle. All Grace could do was try to follow her. But by the time they reached the front of the church, the woman was gone.

Grace was relieved that she had been able to slip out the side door of the church. It was better this way, she thought. Easier on both of them if they didn't have to see or speak to each other. She had only a few minutes before Billy was to pick her up, so she brushed her hair and freshened her make-up. If the Lucases owned half the town, they must be fairly wealthy, and she always liked to make a good first impression. It was easier to persuade people to open up to you if they respected you, rather than pitied you.

She remembered Billy's little shenanigan from last night and shook her head. Teenage boys! She wasn't uncomfortable or worried about the kiss or what he meant by it, however she intended to make it clear to him that it was not going to happen again.

When Grace was ready, she went out on the porch and rocked while she waited on him. Right on time, he pulled up, bounded up the steps and offered her his arm. When they got to the car, he was quite the gentleman, opening the door and helping her in. She complimented him on his manners, and his chest puffed up right away. Evidently on his best behavior for her, he drove at a sedate speed all the way, through the small town, across the valley a couple of miles, then winding a few more miles partway up Heaven's Mountain.

The large, hip-roofed home was situated almost at the top of a ridge. The land was a little less sloped in the area surrounding the house, so there was a nice grassy yard, interspersed with some beautiful old hardwoods. Inside, the house was even larger than it appeared as they were driving up; Grace guessed at least five thousand square feet. There was no one to greet them as they came in. Billy led the way to the dining room, where they found the whole family already seated at the table.

Neither of the two men bothered to rise as Grace and Billy came in, though Billy's grandmother smiled as soon as she saw her grandson. Her face lit up even further upon Grace's entrance, and she spoke excitedly in a kind, but frail voice, "Please, please, come in and have a seat. Billy, dear, show our guest to her seat. Hold the chair out for her, Billy. There, now that's lovely. We're so glad you could join us, dear. Miss Turner, isn't it? May I call you Grace?" Grace nodded her acquiescence. "And would you just call me Sadie, dear?"

"Yes, ma'am. It was very gracious of you to have me over for dinner today. Billy has been a wonderful ambassador for Fairmount ever since I arrived on Friday, but an invitation to Sunday dinner is certainly more than I expected." Grace said, laying her napkin across her lap.

"Well, now, let me introduce you around. Opposite me, at the other end of the table, is my husband, Mr. Beamon Lucas. Beamon, dear, Miss Grace Turner, a new friend of Billy's, is joining us for dinner today."

"Hmph. Welcome to our home, Miss Turner." With a most unwelcoming tone and demeanor, Beamon spoke in a low, unemotional voice. His eyes, when they lit on her for just a moment, gave her a very uncomfortable feeling, as if, had they met under different circumstances, he might be someone to fear.

"And there, sitting across the table from you is our son, Billy's father, Beauregard." At an impatient gesture from him, Sadie corrected herself, "I mean, Bo, of course. I'm the only one that ever uses the old-fashioned name any more."

"Nice to meet you," was Bo's gruff greeting.

"Now then, we'll all just bow our heads for grace, and then Thelma can begin serving." Sadie gave a simple blessing, and the meal began.

Grace recognized Thelma as the woman that she and Clare had just missed at church that morning. As Thelma came to serve her, Grace thanked her, and commented, " I believe I saw you at church this morning, Thelma."

Thelma didn't pause from her serving, but merely nodded and answered in a strong, unemotional monotone, "Yes, miss, that was me.

Welcome to Heaven's Mountain, miss." There was something about her gruff, no-nonsense manner that made Grace believe that this was a woman she should interview. Whatever her story was, she would tell it exactly as she knew the truth to be. She would make it a point to pursue that story as soon as she could.

Through the efforts of Grace, Billy and Sadie, they were able to maintain an acceptable level of conversation at the dinner table, without any participation from Beamon or Bo. It was obvious that Sadie had been brought up as a true Southern gentlewoman, in the best sense of the word. Her concern was always for the comfort and pleasure of the others around her. She saw to it that everyone's plates were filled, and that Grace's needs were anticipated before she even realized them herself.

Sadie handled every aspect of the meal so graciously and without fanfare, that it seemed as if it were nothing. Grace, however, noticed all those little things, as a woman would, and marveled that Sadie was able to carry it all off when she was apparently not well physically, and, even more difficult, had to deal with two such ill-mannered fellows as her husband and her son.

Eventually, as everyone's appetite became sated, and Grace found herself mostly playing with the pear dumpling in her plate, Sadie asked the question that Grace had been dreading. Though she wanted to give the appearance of pursuing not just the Heaven's Mountain murder, but all murder leads in order to back up her cover story, she was having second thoughts about trying to discuss anything with Beamon and Bo. What a miserable pair to have to live with. She truly felt sorry for both Sadie and Billy.

"Your work as a journalist must be so interesting, Grace. What a wonderful thing, that a woman can now go into any field of endeavor she wishes. Billy was trying to explain to me yesterday all about your research here on Heaven's Mountain. You're trying to find out all about murders, is that right, dear?"

"Yes, ma'am. Basically, I want to get an overview of the murders that happened in North Georgia in the last fifty or sixty years. My final story could end up being about all the murders in general, or perhaps murders that were related to feuds the mountain people may have had with their neighbors, or I may choose one particular murder that I find interesting enough to write an article about."

"Oh, my goodness, I don't think I could do that at all, my dear," said Sadie.

Billy, who had been busy with his pear dumpling up to this point, broke in now. "Daddy, I told Grace that you and Grampaw found that fellow who was killed, and that she could talk to you and ask you her questions," Billy finished proudly.

Neither Bo nor Beamon spoke for a moment. "Well, Daddy?" persisted Billy. "Tell Grace about finding that guy." Still no response.

"It's all right, Billy," Grace said, trying to smooth things over. "Sometimes people would rather not talk about something gruesome or disturbing like that, and I absolutely respect their wishes. That's fine, Mr. Lucas, Bo. I understand completely."

Beamon looked straight at Grace, his eyes boring into her, and ordered his son, "Tell her about it, Bo."

Bo shot a quick, stunned look at this father, then looked up at where the wall met the ceiling directly in front of him. They were all quiet, waiting for him to speak. Finally, he began, "There's not really that much to tell. We just happened to be the ones to find 'em. Amos and Preacher James." He stopped, as if that was all he had to say about it.

Grace couldn't make any words come out. Amos? The murder victim was named Amos? It had to be the same man. How many murder victims named Amos could there be around these parts? And to think she had considered pleading a headache so she could leave as soon as the desert was eaten. Finally, the reporter in her took over and she managed to speak. "If it's not too hard on you, Bo, could you tell me a little more about how it came about? Where were you and your father going, where did you find the victim, what was the situation when you got there - that kind of thing." She had gone from expecting only a Sunday dinner to wanting it all -- the story, a confession, everything.

Bo glanced over at his father, who gave him an imperceptible nod, then resumed his focus on the ceiling. "Me and Paw had been up in the hollers around where we lived back then. We'd been huntin' through the night and early morning. We didn't kill anything, but wild pigs got hold of both of our dogs. We carried 'em back to the truck, loaded up, got back on the road, and ran out of gas. Gas gauge on that old truck was broken. We got out of the truck, just standing there, trying to decide whether we should wait for somebody to come by, or just walk back home up the mountain. We saw old lady O'Dell coming from town with her mule and wagon. Decided we'd ask her for a lift to the house. Figured she wouldn't mind if we loaded the dogs on the wagon, too. She said that'd be fine. So, we did. We rode about twenty minutes, about two miles down the road, half a mile past the church, and we saw 'em off the side of the road. Amos and Preacher James. Amos was dead, stabbed in the gut and his throat was cut. Preacher James was leaning over him. When he heard us coming, he raised up and waved for us to come over. Old lady O'Dell got the mule moving as fast as she could, and when we got close, me and Paw got out and ran over to 'em. Like I said, Amos was dead."

"What happened then, Bo? Why was it assumed that Preacher James killed Amos? Maybe he had stopped to help him," Grace pointed out.

Bo ceased his study of the ceiling, and turned to Grace, glaring at her with a defiant gleam in his eye. "Because Preacher James had blood all over him, and it was in his car, too. And when the sheriff got there, he found the knife underneath the body, covered with blood."

"I see," was all Grace said. She didn't want to get into an argument with Bo over the relative value of circumstantial evidence, not when he clearly did not wish to have his story questioned. She summoned up her courage and addressed Beamon. "Mr. Lucas, do you remember anything else that might be important?"

"No, *my dear*," he said, with a sneer that was so slight, you had to wonder if you were just imagining it. "I think Bo has covered everything."

Eight

$\mathcal{A}$s Billy drove her home, Grace tried to organize her thoughts - and her feelings - not only about Bo's reluctant eyewitness account, but also about the strange dynamics in the Lucas household, particularly Beamon's almost hypnotic control over the entire family. Next time she saw Ethan, she would ask him again about the Lucases. Then she remembered, her plans were to avoid the preacher for the remainder of her visit. Well, she would just have to suffer through being in his presence once more – for the sake of the story. After all, she was a professional journalist.

Billy was unusually quiet on the way home, whether by coincidence, or due to some embarrassment over the somewhat cold reception she had received from Bo and Beamon, she couldn't tell. When they pulled up in front of the boarding house, Grace jumped out before Billy could again play the gentleman. "Thanks, Billy, for inviting me to dinner today. The interview with your father was good. Maybe I can use it somehow. Got to run now. I'll probably see you around town this week. Bye, now!" And Grace hurried on into the house.

In the living area, the Philippine sisters were watching a football game on TV, but the older one beckoned Grace over to the telephone to show her some messages. "Mees Grace, you have phone call from

Meester E-then, and you have phone call from Meester Joe Weel-sahn and phone call from Meester Brotmun and phone call from you mudder."

Grace thanked her and picked up the slips of paper. Hmmm, Ethan. That was one problem she wasn't ready to tackle right now; better to save it for later, even tomorrow, if possible. She was still feeling so unsettled about the whole situation; she just needed a little more time to get her thoughts in order before trying to explain to him her strong feelings against both God and the church. On the other hand, she was anxious to call Joe Wilson. He must have discovered something of interest, to be calling her on a Sunday afternoon instead of waiting until Monday morning. She put her curiosity on hold, however, long enough to return the calls to her mother and her boss.

Her duties being fulfilled (amidst heavy reassurances that all was well and she was extremely safe), she turned her attention to the business of advancing her story and dialed the number the newspaper owner had left for her. "Hello. This is Grace Turner, returning a call from Joe Wilson."

"Hi, Grace. Let me just try to find a quiet corner here." Grace could hear quite a commotion of children laughing and talking in the background. "Now, that's better. I talked to my uncle today, and he definitely knew which murder it had to be. He said there were only two murders around here during those years, and the other one was a jealous husband deal. So, it looks like the one you want has to be the murder of Amos Canfield. In 1940, he was found by the roadside stabbed to death. Apparently the murderer and the knife were still at the scene when, of all people, two of our most (ahem) outstanding citizens, Beamon and Bo Lucas, came upon them. Actually, Uncle George said there was one other person with the Lucases, an older woman who he said was a real character. The most unusual thing about this murder was who the murderer was. Preacher James was convicted of the murder, but there was a good bit of controversy over that verdict. George said lots of people believed he was innocent, in spite of the fact that he was seen in Fairmount earlier that day threatening to kill Amos. I'm afraid that's all I could get today. My uncle generally takes a nap right after lunch, so I was lucky to keep him awake long enough to get this."

"Joe, I can't tell you how much I appreciate your help. I did hear a couple of things since I talked to you yesterday that made me think the Canfield murder might fit the bill, but this just pretty much clinches it. I hope your uncle didn't mind having his nap delayed."

"Oh, not at all. It's a pleasure for him to pull some of those old stories out of his stockpile of memories. I think he enjoyed it."

"I'd like to meet him, if I have a chance while I'm here. I'm sure he'd have some good advice to give a novice like me. Anyway, now that I know which murder, I'd like to look at your stacks tomorrow, if I wouldn't be in your way." They talked a few more minutes making arrangements for the next day, then Grace went on up to her room, declining the sisters' invitation to stay and watch the game with them.

Clare usually spent Sunday afternoons resting in her own private rooms, leaving the guests to prepare their own simple supper, normally sandwiches and chips on paper plates. Since she always liked to finish anything she started, she had called a friend and found out who it was that Thelma worked for. She had then proceeded to telephone Thelma at the Lucases, to see if there was a time Thelma could meet and talk with Grace. "Thelma Canfield? This is Clare White. I don't know if you know me, we haven't actually met, but I go to Fairmount Community Church with you. I tried to catch you this morning, but you got away from me!"

"Yes, ma'am, I've seen you at church. I try to get back pretty quick to help with Sunday dinner. Is there something I can do for you?"

"Well, yes, there is, if you don't think you'd mind doing this. I have the sweetest little young lady staying with me who wants to meet and talk to people who know someone who was murdered. She's doing some kind of newspaper article on it, and anyway, she's not pushy or anything, and I wondered if you would mind telling her about your brother?" The line was silent for a few seconds, and Clare was mortified, thinking that she had probably offended Thelma by asking her to discuss such a personal subject with a stranger.

"I guess that would be all right, Miss Clare. Uh, I tell you what. I don't have very much free time, I try to stay pretty close by Miss Sadie most of the time. But every Sunday evening, I drive her to see her sister over in Bitterspring Holler. Do you know where that is, on Treeback Road?"

"Yes, I do."

"We get there about 6:30, usually stay until about 8:00. If Miss Grace wants to come over there and talk to me, I don't mind."

"Oh, thank you, Thelma. I know she'll appreciate it. We'll see you about 6:30 then." Clare realized when she hung up that Thelma had called Grace by name, and she didn't remember mentioning it during the conversation.

Neither of them heard the click as Beamon hung up the phone in his office.

Nine

"I'm really grateful you set this up for me, Clare," Grace said as she maneuvered the small VW around the curves on the narrow road. Just a few minutes before, they had left the main road that wound up Heaven's Mountain, and were now hugging the side of the hill as they travelled through Bitterspring Hollow. They had already passed three small cottages - "houses" would have been a little too grand to describe them - and now the road had turned to dirt.

"There it is. The log cabin where the road ends," Clare pointed. "I think that's Thelma's car beside that old truck." It was just past 6:30, but Grace guessed it had been full dark in the hollow for at least an hour. She and Clare walked up on the front porch that was across the front of the tiny abode, and knocked. Thelma came to the door and beckoned them in.

Inside, the room was small and dark, with just a couple of inexpensive dime store variety table lamps to throw yellow light on the few pieces of living room furniture. There was a small couch, a cushioned rocker, and two straight back chairs situated on either side of a large coal burning stove, window glowing bright. Directly beyond this room was the single bedroom and beyond that, a tiny kitchen.

Sadie was sitting in the rocker, close to her sister who was sitting in one of the straight back chairs. Thelma introduced them to Sadie's sister, Mrs. Walker, to whom Clare handed some lemon squares she had brought.

"Law, you'uns didn't have to do that, Miz Clare. I sure do thank you, though. Wouldn't you'uns like to have some coffee and eat some of these right now? Sadie brung me some coconut cake, too, that Thelma made, and we can have that, too." Mrs. Walker had already headed back to the kitchen, with Clare following, insisting on helping her.

"It was so lovely to have you at the house today, Grace. Such a pleasure for me," mused Sadie.

"And for me, Sadie. Maybe we can do it again while I'm here in town, maybe just us girls next time."

"That would be a treat, dear. But now, I know that you came especially to speak to Thelma tonight, and you two probably need some privacy. I was wondering if you thought the front porch might be a good idea?"

"I think that would be perfect, if that suits you, Thelma," Grace addressed her for the first time.

"Suits me just fine," she answered, and led the way back outside. There were two rickety wooden rockers on either side of the door, so they pulled them both to one side and sat down. "Now, what do you want to know?"

"I'd like you to tell me about your brother. What was he like? And I'm also interested in your thoughts about his murder. Why do you think he was killed?"

"Well, Miss Grace, I wasn't living here then, but I wasn't really surprised to hear what happened to Amos. He wasn't a bad man, he just wasn't a very good one. He might've done better with himself if he could have left the 'shine alone, but he never could. It had ahold of him for a long time, and he didn't know any other way to live, I guess. You want me to tell about him growin' up?"

"Please. I'd like to hear about it."

"Me and Amos were pretty little when our parents died. It was a bad winter for influenza, so they say, and we lost both of them. I was about six or seven, Amos was maybe two, when we came to Heaven's Mountain to live with Granny and Paw. We lived between here and the top of the mountain, way back in another holler. Granny and Paw were good to us, within their means. What I mean is, we never really went hungry, but there were some lean years, if you know what I mean."

"Things must have been a lot different back then, living way up here on the mountain. Pretty isolated, wasn't it?"

"That it was. Me and Amos went to school a few months every year, but when it started getting cold, Granny didn't want us walking that far. Most of the time, we couldn't have gotten through because of the snow, anyway. It piled up in the hollers, and would stay 'til spring got here. In the winter, that's when Granny taught me how to quilt. And Amos learned how to hunt, skin, dress out an animal. Paw thought he was teaching Amos a livelihood when he showed him how to make the 'shine. That was how Paw saw it.

"We had a hardscrabble garden to grow some vegetables, and a few chickens, couple of pigs, and Granny sold a quilt or two most years, but about the only other way to make money here in the mountains was to make 'shine. Paw had to watch for the Revenooers from time to time, but they never found his place. He had it hidden away in the next holler, a long ways from the house. It was on our land, though. Granny used to tell us about when they first came to Heaven's Mountain. They had a little stake, not much, but enough to buy two or three acres with a nice clear stream running through it. They were still clearing the land and building the cabin when one day, Paw went to the stream to fill up the pail for Granny, and you won't believe what he found, Miss Grace." Thelma turned her head and peered at Grace through the darkness.

"What?" Grace found herself intrigued.

"A big old chunk of gold. He sure did. They thought life would be easy from then on. Paw went and spent every bit of the money he got from the gold to buy all the land around them that he could buy. He didn't want anybody else to find any of the gold. But he never found any more, not a flake. He spent the rest of his life looking, trying to find the vein that chunk of gold came from, but he never did."

The screen door squeaked open, and Clare came out bearing coffee cups and cake for them both. "Here you go. Don't let me interrupt you ladies. You just keep right on talking." And she scooted back in the house.

"Did you make this coconut cake, Thelma? It is out of this world!" Grace exclaimed.

"Yes, ma'am, I did. I'm glad you like it. That's one of Granny's recipes she taught me. Coconut was a luxury, so I only helped her make it a couple of times, but I kept all her recipes written down, and I'm sure glad I did now."

"I am going to get so fat, they'll have to roll me out of Fairmount when I leave!" Grace laughed, and heard Thelma chuckling softly.

"I guess you need to hear more about Amos, not me," said Thelma, getting back to the task at hand.

"No, everything you're telling me is interesting, and it's his background as well as yours, so please, just keep going," Grace truthfully replied.

"Well, like I said, Paw was sort of obsessed about that gold. He drug Amos around with him all over the mountain, looking for it. I guess it sort of infected Amos, too. That's probably why he always wanted the easy way out of everything." Thelma stopped talking, and they sat in silence for several minutes.

"Granny had the sight." Another pause ensued. "Do you know about the sight, Miss Grace?"

"No, not really." Grace waited for Thelma to explain.

"Sometimes Granny could see things before they happened. She called it her premonitions. I remember one Christmas. It was one of the lean years, when all we got was a cookie on Christmas morning, and we were grateful to get that. Granny was quiet all day, every once in a while mumbling to herself. We were still snowed in from a big storm the day before, so we just stayed by the fire all day. That evening, Amos was playing on the hearth with his wooden carved animals, when Granny started trembling, sitting there in her rocker. You could see the veins in her hands she was holding onto the arms so tight. Her eyes were rolled back in her head, too. Then, she stopped trembling and looked straight at Amos and said, 'Through you all will be lost', and then she looked right at me, and said, 'Through you all will be made right again' and then she just keeled over, right out of that rocker. We put her to bed, and she woke up the next morning just fit as a fiddle. "

"Wow. Didn't that scare you when she did that?'

"Mmh. No. I guess it just seemed normal to me. I remembered what she said later, though. I told you Amos liked the drink. Well, Granny, she died when I was about sixteen, and Paw, he passed a couple of years later. Amos was almost grown, but not quite, so I stayed and cooked for him, kept his clothes washed, tried to keep body and soul together, though I didn't get much help from him. He had quit going to school at all when he was about twelve. By the time Paw died, he knew how to make 'shine, so he made it, but there wasn't much to sell after he drank it all up. Well, I stayed til he was almost nineteen. But I finally got my fill of taking care of a grown man who wouldn't try to do his part, so I up and moved to Gainesville, got a job at the hospital, and I felt real happy for the first time in my life. I had me a little room, and a couple of girlfriends I went to the movies with every week or so. Those were good years for me. Back then there was supposed to be a depression, but things never seemed too bad to me. Especially after I met Nathan."

"Who was Nathan?"

"Nathan was my husband." An uncharacteristic softness crept into Thelma's voice. "I was already an old maid when I met him, but he didn't seem to care. He was even a few years younger than me, but he said it didn't matter. We didn't ever have any kids. I guess I was too old. But we both wanted 'em. He died in the war, on the Bataan march."

"I'm sorry, Thelma."

"Ah, it's okay now. At least I had my happiness. Anyway, while I was living in Gainesville, Amos was still here on the mountain, making 'shine and getting drunk. I guess he probably didn't ever eat right after I left. He started gambling, going to the honky-tonks. He gambled away everything that was left at the cabin. Then he started selling off the land, a little bit at the time. Whatever he got, he used it to gamble with. From what I heard, he still had about half of the land left when he was killed. But, to get some gambling money, he had signed a I.O.U. to

Beamon Lucas a few days before he was killed. After Amos turned up dead, Beamon demanded payment on the debt, so he ended up with the rest of our land."

"Why didn't you claim a half interest in the land, Thelma?"

"Well, I figured it was a family debt, needed to be paid."

"Did you think there was anything strange about Mr. Lucas coming up with the I.O.U. after Amos' death?"

"Yes and no. Amos had done the same thing lots of times before, so they said, but never for that much. But even if I did think it was odd, it didn't matter. I couldn't have done anything about it. Besides, my home was in Gainesville, with Nathan. And that's all I cared about, was going back home to him."

"Had Amos had a falling out with anyone? Was there anyone who had a grudge against him?"

"He could be a terrible aggravation, and that's a fact. But he wasn't usually mean, except occasionally when he was drunk. I wasn't living here, so I don't know for sure if anyone had a reason to kill him. After I left, he sort of took up with my second cousin, Betty, who was Preacher James' wife. She would feed him a few times a week, wash his clothes every once in a while. She and Preacher James were both good to Amos. Better than he deserved, for sure."

"I'd like to talk to Betty. Does she still live around here?"

"Betty died from cancer about five years ago."

"Oh. I'm sorry again, Thelma." She waited a few seconds before asking, " Did you talk to Betty about what happened the day your brother was killed?"

"Some. She was having such a rough time, what with Preacher James being accused of the murder and everything, and I didn't want to hurt her even worse by talking about it too much. She said that Amos had come up to her on the street in town, begging her for money. She told him no, but he kept on. He was drunk, and you couldn't talk to him when he was that way. Finally, he tried to grab her purse, and she wouldn't let him have it. People were heading in their direction to help her, so I guess he got desperate. He took out his knife, grabbed the kid, and threatened to cut him if she didn't give him some money. That's when Preacher

James showed up and got into it with him. He took the knife away from him and yelled at him to leave his wife and son alone, and if he bothered them again, he would kill him."

"How old was the little boy when this happened?"

"I guess he was about four years old."

"Did you ever ask him about that day?"

"No, I never did. But you could ask him yourself, see if he remembers anything."

"Oh, that's great! He still lives in Fairmount then? Would you mind introducing him to me, Thelma?"

"Well, no, I mean, I don't mind, but you've already met him."

"Really? Who is he?"

"Preacher Ethan. Ethan MacEwen. He's Preacher James' son. Preacher James MacEwen's son."

Ten

*G*race felt like screaming on the way back to the boarding house. Could things get any more twisted together and confused? And, once again, she had to ask herself the question, what kind of reporter was she to have failed to uncover the fact that Ethan MacEwen was the son of "Preacher James" MacEwen, convicted murderer? It was embarassing to think that perhaps she was too smitten with the son to bother to get all of her facts straight on this story. So, what was she supposed to do now? How could she possibly continue to work on the story if Ethan was a central character? And how could she possibly not continue if it could mean freedom for his father? Already, she dreaded having to explain to Ethan why she couldn't be personally involved with him. Now, in addition to that, she was also going to have to explain to him why he needed to talk to her about his father's murder conviction.

Her life had become a soap opera since arriving here, she thought to herself. Good grief! Things were so tangled up, it was actually sort of comical. Mentally, she threw up her hands and said "what the heck". There, that felt better. She just needed to get a little perspective on things. She could handle this. She had handled lots worse, like when the other kids had whispered "bastard" to her when the teacher wasn't around. Or when Augusta had snatched her from the fellowship hall when she wouldn't agree that her sweet mother had sinned, just like the woman caught in adultery. Oh, yes. She could handle this. She would be a professional, and do her job, and keep a professional distance from *Preacher* MacEwen at all times.

"Grace, are you all right?" Clare asked.

"What? Oh, yeah, I'm fine. Just a lot of information to process. Thank you again, Clare, for getting in touch with Thelma. Tonight was invaluable, really."

"You're very welcome. I'm glad it turned out well. I have to say, I was a little worried about you at church this morning, honey; you seemed a little uptight. I was afraid you were upset that we didn't catch Thelma this morning. Or maybe you were uncomfortable being in a church other than your own?"

"We-e-ell, Clare, I have a confession to make. I don't actually go to church, not since I was a teenager, living at home."

"Oh. Oh, well..., were you afraid to tell me, Grace? Because I wouldn't have been upset with you, or anything. I'm disappointed that we can't share that bond, but I still want us to be friends." She looked away from the road to smile kindly at Grace.

"Oh, I am so glad you said that. Me, too. I've never had a friend who was so much older than me, but I've had a lot of fun being around you." Grace popped her hand over her mouth in embarrassment. "Ooo, that sounds so tacky, doesn't it, as if it was a shock to me that you would be fun to be around, just because you're older. You know what I meant, right?"

Clare couldn't breathe, she was giggling so hard at Grace's discomfiture. Then, she spoke in a shaky voice, "Eh? Eh? What's that you're saying, little girl? You'll have to speak up, I don't hear so good anymore. And my rheumatiz has been acting up lately, too...." And then, they were both giggling and tearing up from laughing so hard.

"Stop, now, you've got to stop so I won't run off the road!" Grace complained, still hiccupping with laughter, and wiping her eyes again.

"Oooh, that felt good. I haven't laughed that hard in a long time," said Clare. "Grace, if you don't want to answer this, it's okay. But why did you stop going to church?"

Grace didn't answer right away. Clare spoke again, "I shouldn't have asked you. I'm sorry. Don't answer."

"No, I just... It's been a long time, but I think I'm ready to talk about it to somebody. Hmm. Why did I stop going to church? I stopped going to church because I didn't like being there. There were people who said mean things at my church, and nobody ever stopped them. And it made me angry that the preacher said we should all be good and kind, and the Bible said we should all be good and kind, but there in God's house, people weren't always being good and kind. Hypocrites. There were too many hypocrites and too many unhappy memories at my church."

Clare took her time answering. "You poor baby. I don't know what happened to you at that church, and you don't have to tell me. But I want you to know that you are absolutely right, that it is not supposed to be that way. Someone should have stepped up and put a stop to whatever meanness was going on. Jesus was probably crying over what was happening to you in that church. And crying for those other folks, too, that they could know so little about him and his ways. But the fact that they caused a little one like you to fall away from him, that would have made him very angry, too. Jesus never put up with anyone being unkind to a child; he always defended them and protected them. That's what he would have wanted his people in your church to do, too. So, I don't blame you for wanting to get away from that."

"You don't? I thought you'd tell me I needed to go back. Wait, you are going to say that, aren't you?"

"No. No, I'm not. You shouldn't go back to that church unless and until they have a change of heart. God will take care of that, in his own good time. In the meantime, you know what I think you should do?'

"What?"

"I know it probably sounds impossible, and it's definitely going to be hard, but you need to start working towards forgiving those people that were mean to you."

Grace started to protest, but Clare continued. "Wait, wait, now, hear me out, honey. All that anger that you've got inside of you for what they did to you, who do you think that anger is hurting? It's a bitterness that's eating away at the inside of *you*, not anybody else. If you could get rid of that feeling of anger, and not have it in your heart anymore, wouldn't your heart feel better, lighter, freer? And another thing that you've forgotten. Every person on this earth is still just human, Christian or not. Every person has had hurts and disappointments in his life, and has had some bad things happen to them, some much worse than others. To lay all those hurts aside and walk every day with Jesus and show people all that love he's put in your heart every single day, that's what he wants us to do. But most of us fail at it, at least sometimes, and some of us have a lot of problems to work on, and we fail at it a lot. I guess what I'm trying to say is, those people, who hurt you, are probably themselves hurting and miserable inside because they haven't relinquished to Jesus some bad, hurtful things that are in their heart."

"Hm. Maybe." Grace was not convinced.

"And one other thing for you to think about. You know, our church is open to anyone who wants to come on Sunday, or anytime. Yours was probably the same way. That means that at any given time, you might have inside your church a few people who know God and love him with all their heart, a few people who love God, but don't know him very well, a few people who say they love God, but don't know him at all, a few people who are there truly seeking God, and a few people who really don't care to know God at all. The church lets them all in, anytime they want to come. The point is, just because you're in church doesn't mean that everyone around you will be a good, loving, kind person, but a lot of them will be. I wish you'd try again to give us a chance."

"Well, that's a new thought, too. I'll think about all the things you've said, I really will. Clare, I wouldn't have guessed you could argue your points so clearly and so logically. What, were you on the debate team, or something?"

Clare went back into her routine with the old-timer's voice, "Why, you young whippersnapper! Sometimes I lose my glasses, and sometimes I lose my nerve, but so far I haven't lost my mind!" And once again, the little VW was filled with peals of laughter.

Bo was running down the road as fast as he could. Behind him was his father. He looked back, but didn't see him. Maybe he had lost him.

He could still hear him breathing, though, huffing, getting closer. Now he could see his shadow coming around the curve in the road. Only he was in the truck now, their old truck. It was no use, he couldn't outrun him.

Beamon pulled up beside him. "Get in. You've got some work to do." Bo got in and slammed the door shut. Beamon changed gears and drove on. Bo tried to open the door and jump out, but the door wouldn't open. He put his head in his hands and wept.

"Get out." They were at the church now. There was Amos standing under the trees. Bo followed Beamon to stand in front of Amos. "I want the gold," said Beamon. Amos didn't move. "Give it to me *now,* " Beamon said gently. Amos held out a large ornately inscribed sheet of parchment with "Deed" written across the top. Beamon took it and said, "Bo, you know what you have to do."

Bo's arms and legs felt like they were weighted with lead. He was moving in slow motion. He took the knife Beamon was holding out to him. He reached for Amos, but when his hands closed around him, Amos' body slipped through his fingers, it was so slick and red with his blood. His body slid to the ground, and there was no more breathing.

Horrified with all the blood on his hands, Bo took the knife and threw it as hard as he could, but it was stuck to his hand. He threw it again, over and over, but he couldn't get rid of it.

"Ow! Bo, dadgum it, wake up! You're hitting me again in your sleep!"

"What? Oh, mmnnh. Sorry. I'm sorry. Go back to sleep." Bo's forehead was dripping with sweat, and his heart was racing. The dream again. After all these years, he thought he was through with it. But here it was again, reminding him that he was a murderer. And almost worse, reminding him that he still did whatever his father told him to do.

Eleven

Thelma was refilling the coffee pot in the dining room. Beamon had been reading the morning paper, but now he laid it aside neatly and removed his reading glasses as he spoke to Thelma. "Come over here and sit down for a minute, Thelma. Freshen up my coffee first."

After filling his cup, Thelma pulled out a chair, leaving an empty chair between them. She never allowed Beamon to intimidate her, but she still didn't like being any closer to him than she had to. "Yes, sir?"

"I heard you had a little visit with Billy's new friend last night," he began in an almost pleasant conversational voice.

Thelma wondered how in the world he could know that already. It was amazing, the things he knew, with him not even leaving the house much anymore. "Yes, sir, I did."

"And what was it you talked about?"

Thelma's first impulse was to tell him it was none of his business what they talked about, but Grace was making no secret of her investigation so there was really no point in trying to hide the subject of their conversation from Beamon. "She's writing a story about murders, so she asked me about Amos."

"I see. And what did you tell her about him?

"Well, she wanted to know about how he grew up, what kind of person he was. She asked me what I knew about the murder."

"And you told her....what?"

"I told her I didn't live here then, so I only knew what I had heard from other people."

"Which was?"

"I told her about the fight in town with Preacher James, told her about how good Betty was to Amos." Thelma considered whether to refrain from making her next statement, but went ahead. "I told her how Amos lost our land, gambling and drinking it up."

"Ah. A sad thing for your family, that was. But a debt is a debt, and must be paid. Right, Thelma?"

"That's pretty much what I said to Miss Grace." Thelma rose from her chair. "If that's all you wanted, I need to take Miss Sadie some breakfast now."

"That's all, Thelma. But I want you to tell me if Miss Turner contacts you again or asks you any more questions. After all, a stranger like her really has no business coming into our little town asking a lot of personal questions and getting people upset with old, painful memories."

Thelma made no answer, just stared back at him for a second or two, then went on about her business in her usual methodical manner.

After a night of tossing and turning, Grace woke up feeling sluggish. Yesterday had been a turbulent day for her emotions. She knew she needed to focus, make some decisions, and get on with the business of investigating the murder. Her mind just didn't want to cooperate. Maybe after some coffee she would be able to maneuver a little better. Grace threw on her robe, snuck downstairs and fixed a cup of coffee, relieved that she made it without seeing anybody except the two sisters.

It was still early, only a few minutes after seven, so Grace didn't feel any necessity to get dressed yet. She had left her bedroom window open just a crack the night before; now she opened it up wide, hoping the fresh air would help clear her mind. There wasn't much activity out there yet, just the occasional car, the sound of a door slamming, a dog barking. The weather was a little murky yet, sort of like her brain, she thought. It was foggy, with a slight drizzle coming down off and on. She hadn't heard what the forecast was for today. She hoped it wasn't going to rain, because she had a lot of places she needed to go today to do her research.

After allowing herself some time to simply sit and be quiet, Grace forced herself to pick up a pad and write down the issues that were bothering her.

Number 1. Telling Ethan she wasn't a Christian, and therefore couldn't see him anymore.

Number 2. Getting Ethan to tell her everything he knew about the murder (which might not be possible unless she told him about the Heaven's Mountain letter).

Number 3. Wondering if she was capable of being professional when she had all these uncomfortable issues going on with Ethan.

Number 4. Giving consideration to the things Clare had said last night about forgiveness, and giving the church another chance.

Grace reviewed the list. As far as Number 1 and 2 were concerned, she would just have to prepare herself mentally, say what had to be said, remain professional at all times, and stay away from Ethan as much as she possibly could. With regard to Number 3, she was making up her mind right here and now that everything would be strictly business from now on. No more dancing or flirting or staring at handsome preachers. She would focus only on her story. And number 4. Well, she could just put that on the back burner for now. Later, when she had more time, she would take it out and examine it more closely.

Satisfied with the disposition of all her problems, Grace got herself dressed and went out to face the new day.

Sitting straight and demurely, as a lady should, Sadie waited patiently on the little patio outside her bedroom for Thelma to bring her coffee and toast for breakfast. It was getting harder and harder to get out of the bed and get dressed by herself each morning. Old age was a test of patience and fortitude, she had decided, and she would do her best, as she always had. Still, she thanked God every day that her mind was still sharp, as well as for the many other blessings she had in her life. One of those blessings was definitely Thelma. She was friend, companion, and, more and more frequently, nursemaid to Sadie, whose days would certainly be empty and dreary otherwise.

"Here we are, ma'am," said Thelma, as she set the heavy tray down on the table. The tray would have been fairly light, but Sadie always insisted that Thelma bring her own breakfast also, so that neither would have to eat alone. And Thelma's breakfast was usually a good deal heartier than Sadie's light fare.

After saying their blessing, Thelma, who was always one to say what was on her mind, began talking. "Miss Sadie, I haven't figured out what's going on, but something is going on. And it has something to do with Amos' murder. It has to do with Miss Grace, too, since she's the one that's asking questions. And Mr. Beamon's got something to do with it, too. "

"Why, what makes you say such a thing, Thelma dear?"

"Well, I know you noticed how Mr. Beamon acted yesterday at Sunday dinner when Miss Grace asked about the murder. I know you noticed, so it's no use pretending you didn't. And then this morning, when I was getting your breakfast, Mr. Beamon wanted to know what all Miss Grace asked me about last night. Said I should let him know if she asked me anything else. Now, I ask you, how did he know we saw Miss Grace last night?"

"My goodness, that is strange. I've not talked to him myself since right after dinner yesterday."

"Well, we'd best keep our eyes and ears open, for Miss Grace's sake, anyway. You know how Mr. Beamon can be sometimes, and I don't want that girl to get hurt."

"No, no. We certainly don't want that to happen, Thelma."

Thelma whisked their breakfast dishes away to the kitchen, and came back to do her morning routine, straightening and cleaning Sadie's rooms. Moving slowly and carefully, Sadie situated herself comfortably in her sitting room and began reading her daily devotional. As she opened her Bible, several papers floated to the carpet. She moved as if to retrieve them, but Thelma, waving her to sit back, picked them up first.

"Oh dear, I meant to put those back in my treasure box yesterday." Sadie murmured. "I was thinking about Floyd and how old he would be, had he lived. That's the picture he had taken right before he joined the Army. He looks so young. Too young to be a soldier." She sighed softly, "I was able to protect him from Beamon's influence, but I couldn't protect him from dying. I wish you could have known him, Thelma. He was such a sweet boy."

"He took after his momma, then. Do you want me to put these up for you?"

"Yes, dear. Please put the picture and all the letters back in my box for me."

"'Mornin', Preacher."

"Good morning, Emmett. You doing all right today?" Ethan said as he signed the guest register at the visitors entrance to the prison.

"Can't complain. You and your dad having services today?"

"No, that's usually just on Sundays and Thursdays. I'm here for some counseling today."

"Some of these guys sure need it."

"No, not them. Not this time. I'm the one being counseled today. I came to get some advice from my dad."

"Oh, ho! I get it. Well, we could all use some wise words from our fathers from time to time. Go on back, Preacher. He's in the chapel."

After walking about halfway down the corridor, Ethan went through a door on the left. The chapel was really just a large room with four rows of chairs and a small wooden podium. On the floor against the wall were a stack of Bibles and a stack of hymnals. On a chair in the front row sat a man with an open Bible in his lap.

"Dad?"

"Hi, son." James MacEwen jumped up immediately, smiling, and came to hug his son. "Come have a seat. Now, what is it you wanted to talk to me about?"

"Dad," Ethan said with a wry smile, "I've met a girl."

"Well, Jiminy Cricket! How did that happen? Who is she?"

"Hmm, actually I don't know a lot about her, yet. She's a journalism major, works for a newspaper in Jackstone, and she's here in Fairmount on business of some kind. She's smart and funny, fun to be around, and... pretty easy on the eyes, too, Dad. I feel a strong attraction to her, and I think she feels it, too, even though we haven't made it past the very first stages of getting to know one another yet."

"All that sounds great. What's the problem, son?"

"I'm not sure there is one. She came to church on Sunday morning, but slipped away before I could speak to her. I called a couple of times Sunday afternoon, but haven't heard back from her. Surely my preaching didn't scare her off - I mean, I'm not that bad, am I?" Ethan was half-joking, half-serious.

James chuckled, "No, son, I don't think that was it. She probably was busy with something, and just hasn't had a chance to call you."

"I know. That's not really the reason I wanted to talk to you. One thing that concerns me is that she hasn't mentioned her faith at all. She may not have had a chance yet, because we've only been together a few times. But Dad, what if she's not a Christian? If that's the case, what should I do?"

James squinted his eyes shut and sighed. "I think you know the answer to that question. You just want me to affirm it for you." He opened his eyes and smiled at his son. "You know that we should not knowingly become 'unequally yoked' in a romantic relationship with a nonbeliever. God doesn't want that for us, because it makes life so much harder - harder to pull together on things."

"Yes, I know that's right. But if that is the case, what do I say to her, so that she'll understand?"

"You have to explain the difficulties as best you can and with as little hurt to her as possible, and then you have to walk away. Hard as that may be, you have to trust God's judgment and not your own feelings. You have to walk away."

"Right. You're right. And I will do it, if I have to, because I know God knows what, or who, is best for me. But that's not my biggest concern. Dad, I am certain that God is telling me to be in continual prayer for Grace."

"God's grace is given to us all, freely and abundantly."

Ethan burst out laughing, as James looked on in total bewilderment. He managed to squeak out, "No, not God's grace, my Grace. The girl's name is Grace."

"Oh! Oh, I see. Great name! Now, repeat what you were just saying."

"I said that God has put a heavy burden on my heart to pray for Grace, well beyond my normal prayers. I am to pray for her safety. And for her to show wisdom. And I feel that I should pray very hard for her relationship with God, that there is a spiritual battle going on in her life, and she needs a prayer shield over and around her."

"Then, consider me your prayer partner in this, son. We will wrap her in our prayers day and night."

"I was hoping you'd say that, Dad."

Twelve

*G*etting up early had at least one benefit, Grace decided as she served herself from the sidetable, and that was having your pick of the scrumptious variety of breakfast food Clare provided. The sisters were still at the table, and Grace enjoyed the challenge of conversing with them in their not-quite-perfected English. After they left, she remained at the table for several more minutes, but finally, she could put it off no longer.

Pulling out the piece of paper with Ethan's number on it, she reluctantly went to the phone and dialed his number. She was granted a temporary reprieve when the answering machine picked up. She left him a message. "Ethan, this is Grace. I'm going to be out and about most of the day, but I have some things I'd like to talk to you about. Could you give me a call later today? If I don't hear from you, I'll try you again. Thanks." There, that was professional, non-emotional. Good girl, Grace.

With that taken care of, Grace headed off to the first place listed on the schedule she had created for herself, the Fairmount Chronicle. Joe had very generously gone ahead and pulled the stacks she needed, as well as clearing out an area for her to spread out her materials.

"Joe, you're a great guy! Thanks for doing all of this," said Grace, smiling her thanks.

"No big deal. I was happy to do it. No sense in you having to crawl around in all that dust and dirt. Come to think of it, maybe I did that to avoid the embarrassment of having you see our non-existent housekeeping back there!"

"Well, for whatever reason, thank you."

"Okay then, I'm going to let you get to work. If you need anything, have any questions, I'll be up front or in my office. Just give a yell."

"Thanks, Joe," she murmured, already engrossed in the stacks. Shaking his head in amusement, Joe retreated to his office. Fairly quickly Grace zeroed in on the initial reporting of the crime, and began making her notes. Within thirty minutes she had perused all of the pre-trial articles, and was now studying the stories covering the trial. So far, the newspaper reports, with a few minor exceptions, fairly well matched the information she had received from Joe's uncle, Bo Lucas, and Thelma Canfield. She noted the name of James MacEwen's lawyer, and planned to contact him as soon as possible. Lawyer-client privilege would probably come into play, of course, but perhaps he would know of certain "publicly known" facts or circumstances about which he could speak freely to her. She finished reading the articles describing the trial, and felt the first wave of doubt wash over her. The evidence was certainly compelling. The fight on the street indicated motive. And even though no one witnessed the murder (except, allegedly, the writer of her letter), the fact remained that James was found bending over the body, there was blood on his clothes, there was blood in his car, and the murder weapon, which witnesses testified they saw James snatch away from Amos earlier that day, was found at the scene. All circumstantial, but very incriminating, especially twenty eight years ago, when forensic science was non-existent.

Grace scanned the remaining stories regarding the verdict and sentencing. Nothing of note there. Next she moved forward a few years to the obits for 1944 and 1945, and began searching for the names of soldiers who died in combat. She made a list, being careful to note the branch, company and unit of each. None of them looked very promising. Feeling she had squeezed everything she could from the old papers, she carefully replaced the yellowed sheets, packed up her notebooks, and went to the front of the building. "Joe, I'm finished."

"Already? You're a fast worker, Grace! Wish I could talk you into coming to work with me." Grace smiled and rolled her eyes. Joe continued, "I'm serious. This county is growing like crazy - almost 25% since I bought out my uncle and moved here just three years ago. We're just a small county newspaper, but we're busting at the seams, just like every other business around here."

"Sounds like one of those "good" problems to me," she replied. "And I'm extremely flattered, Joe. If I should decide to make a move, I promise I'll keep it in mind. By the way, did your uncle say anything else after he woke up from his nap?"

"Hey, you know, he did say one other thing, and I apologize. I intended to pass this along. He mentioned that the preacher at the Fairmount Community Church, Ethan MacEwen, is James MacEwen's son."

"Right. I did become aware of that fact yesterday. Thanks anyway. I really appreciate everything you've done, Joe. And, if and when the time is right, and after I've satisfied my other commitments, I'll want to fill you in on how this story turns out."

"I can't wait. Let me know if I can do anything else to aid the cause."

"See you later, Joe."

"You're late. Again," said Beamon, without looking up from his work.

"Sorry," Bo mumbled as he slumped into the high backed chair in his father's office.

"I have no interest in where you spend your nights, only in how you perform your job. See that you make an appearance here each morning by 9:00 a.m., no later. Do I make myself clear?"

"Yeah," Bo replied, looking out the window, wondering why Billy was coming home from school in the middle of the morning. "What do you want me to do today?"

"Today you're beginning a new project. I want you to watch that little idiot reporter, and don't let her or anybody else see you doing it. I want to know where she goes, who she sees, what she talks about."

"I don't see why it makes any difference. There's nothing she can find out."

"There's always something to find out. You never know which little string someone might pull that will cause all sorts of things to unravel."

"All right, all right. I'll watch her."

"Bo. Listen carefully. First and foremost stay out of sight. Don't let her see you. But if the opportunity arises to put a little fear in her mind, do so. Nothing messy. Do you understand?"

"Got it," said Bo as he rose to leave the room. Just outside the door, Billy saw the movement and moved quietly back down the hall toward the kitchen.

Beamon held up his hand to stop him. "Bo, if you handle this situation well, I'll make arrangements for you to take a nice vacation, maybe Hawaii. How does that sound to you?"

"There's nothing I'd like better than to get away from here."

The next stop on Grace's list was the county sheriff's office. Unfortunately, as she discovered upon her arrival, the sheriff and chief deputy had left just that morning for a seminar at the state capitol. The other deputies on duty were all out on patrol, so only the old jailer was available to answer her questions. As she soon realized, this may have been a fortunate turn of events, because Deputy Diggs, who was actually retired and only worked part-time now, had been working as a deputy since 1937, and was, in fact, the first official to arrive on the scene of Amos Canfield's murder.

Since there were currently only two prisoners in the jail, Deputy Diggs, or Diggy, as he preferred to be called, had no problem taking time to answer Grace's questions, and in fact, was happy for the diversion . "That's a good man, Preacher James. Not a mean bone in that man's body. I know they convicted him, I know the evidence pointed to him, but I won't never believe it." Diggy paused to place a chew of tobacco into his mouth. "And that Amos was a sorry rascal. Never did an honest day's work. He purely aggravated Miss Betty to death, and her always good as a saint to him. "

"What do you mean by that, Mr. Di.." Diggy held up his index finger and smiled a warning to Grace. "I mean,...Diggy," she corrected herself.

"Well, y'see, Amos wanted her to give him some money that day. To buy his liquor, no doubt. And she wouldn't give it to him. She'd feed him and wash his nasty clothes, treat him like family, which I guess he was, but she didn't condone that liquor. So he threatened her and her little'un. Had a dadgum knife to the boy's throat, if you can believe it. Well, that's when the Preacher come up, grabbed that knife away, knocked him plum off his feet, and told him he'd best not come around again, bothering his family, or he'd kill him. Half the town was watching and heard every word. So when Beamon and Bo come across 'em up on the old Mountain Church Road, well, that's just what was fresh on everybody's mind."

Interrupted by a knock at the back door of the jail, Diggy ceased his story-telling, which he was obviously enjoying, to receive a large cardboard box from which some delicious smells were emanating. "Ma'am, I've got to feed these prisoners now, and take care of a few other chores. Gonna keep me busy til I get off at three o'clock. Would you like to come back after while? I don't mind answering some more questions for you." Diggy truly seemed eager to have someone listen to him reminisce some more.

"I can do that. In fact, Mr... uh, Diggy, do you think if I came back at three, that you and I could drive up to the old church road where Amos' body was found, and maybe you could actually re-enact how you first saw the body, what each person there was doing, that kind of thing?"

She could see Diggy's chest swelling, and his back straightening as she asked for his help. "Yes, ma'am," he said emphatically. "I surely can. I'll call my wife and tell her to keep my supper warm, 'cause I'll be a little late this even'."

With a couple of hours to fill before coming back at three. Grace decided she would try to track down Mrs. O'Dell. Clare had mentioned she thought the old woman was now residing in a nursing home on the far side of the valley. After calling to be sure Mrs. O'Dell was indeed a resident, Grace drove back across the valley the way she had first come in to Fairmount, and easily located the small facility.

The young receptionist told Grace she could find Mrs. O'Dell in the common room, probably watching TV at this hour. Upon reaching the room, Grace noted nine or ten residents, all in wheelchairs, all facing the black and white TV with a fuzzy picture which was flipping every few seconds. Grace looked around. No attendants were in sight. Feeling compassion for their plight, she went over to the television, and, after a few moments of searching, was able to adjust the horizontal control to stop the flipping. Several of the patients murmured their thanks, but one raspy voice stood out above the rest with "Hallelujah! Glory be! You're a angel, honey!" Grace spotted the speaker, a very old woman sitting in her wheelchair toward the back of the room. What made her stand out from the others was the lively glint in her eye, and her still erect posture. Grace nodded at her, then addressed the room in general. "I'm looking for Mrs. O'Dell. Is she in here?"

"That's me, honey," the woman in the back rasped out. "Come on back here." Grace walked to the back. "I don't know you, do I? Sometimes it's hard to remember anymore."

"No, ma'am, you don't know me. My name is Grace Turner, and I'm a writer." Instead of going into her usual cover story, Grace thought it would be best to keep it as simple as possible for the old woman. "I'm writing a story about the murder of Amos Canfield." Mrs. O'Dell began nodding her head. "Do you remember when that happened?"

"Course I do. I can remember those years a lot better than what's going on nowadays. You're gonna write a story 'bout it? Well, 'law! Imagine that. I was there when we found Amos," she asserted.

"That's what I heard, Mrs. O'Dell. And I wondered if you would mind telling me what you remember about that day?"

"Sure, I'll tell ya. I'm just glad to have somebody to talk to. All my folks is gone, 'cept a couple of nieces. It's lonely when you get old and can't get out and don't have nobody." Mrs. O'Dell's alert eyes filled with unshed tears. Wanting to comfort her somehow, Grace lifted the old woman's hand into her own, and kept it there.

"Well, I'm glad I'm getting to spend some time with you today, Mrs. O'Dell. I bet you've had an interesting life."

Perking up a bit, Mrs. O'Dell answered, "It was a hard life, but it was a good life. My man died when I was thirty. Left me with four little boys to raise on my own. Had to do all the farming, split wood, kill pigs and smoke the meat. Did it mostly by myself 'til the boys got up big enough to help me. 'Twas a rough life, but I always kept myself happy and busy. You know that, don't you, honey, that a whole lot of being happy in this life is just making up your mind to keep a happy outlook?"

"I don't know if I ever thought of it that way, but I promise I'll remember it. Where are your sons now?"

"They've all passed on. I outlived 'em all. Got several grandchildren and a few greats, but they all live a ways from here. But they're all coming for my birthday next month. I'll be ninety-five," she said proudly.

"How wonderful!" Grace did a few calculations in her head. "So, you would have been about fifty-seven when Amos Canfield was murdered."

"I was. Let's see now, you wanted to know about that day. I had been to Fairmount that morning. Started back home up the mountain about two, three o'clock. Only the old mountain church road back then, all dirt, full of ruts, and curvy as a corkscrew. They built that new road about ten years ago. Let's see, where was I? I was coming back from town, and the Lucases waved me down. Their truck had quit, and they asked me for a ride to their house. I was happy to oblige. Those two Lucases were a right mean pair, but neighbors should help neighbors, I believe. I recollect something had got hold of their dogs. They was both dead. They asked me would I mind taking the dogs, too, in the back of the wagon. So we loaded up the dogs and the Lucases jumped up in the back of the wagon, too. We were within less than a mile of the church when we all saw Amos and the Preacher. 'Course we didn't know it was them till we got close. The Lucases jumped right out and went to see. Preacher James had been kneeling down by the body, looked like he was holding Amos' hand. The Lucases started yelling and pointing their fingers at Preacher James then at Amos. Then Bo grabbed up Preacher James by the back of the collar, drug him away from the body. Beamon got down by Amos, looked like he was checking his breath, fiddling with him, lifting him up to look at his back, feeling in his pockets and such. I wasn't real close. I was still in the wagon but I knew what kind of thievin' scalawag Beamon was, so I tried to watch him best I could. I didn't ever see him take anything off of Amos."

"Hmm. So Amos was definitely already dead when you got there."

"Oh, yes. Preacher James said he was, and he wouldn't have lied."

"Did you know the Preacher well?"

"He was my preacher. I always went to Heaven's Mountain Church. Preacher James was only twenty when he started preaching, but you could tell, even then, he was filled with the Holy Ghost."

"How long did it take for the sheriff's deputy to get there?"

"It must have been an hour or more. We had been there with Amos about fifteen minutes, when Bertha Mulholland came driving along in her Model T, headed down the mountain towards town. She went straight on to get the sheriff. I'm glad, 'cause I didn't want to leave Preacher James alone up there to have to watch the Lucases by himself."

"Did anybody else stop to help you?'

"No, just right before the sheriff got there, a couple of folks stopped. But all of them stayed far away from Amos, though they were looking real hard at him. When the sheriff did get there, he said I could go on and leave. He kept the Lucases for a while though. I took their dogs on up to their house and throwed 'em up on the porch. I reckon Beamon and Bo walked on home later."

"Is that all you remember, Mrs. O'Dell?" Grace watched as Mrs. O'Dell nodded. "Well, this has been a great help to me. I really appreciate it. I'm only going to be here a few more days, but if I get a chance, I'll come back by to see you. Will that be all right?"

"Yes, honey, I'd sure like that."

As she was driving back to town, Grace's thoughts were on her own sweet grandmother. Having lived in the same house all of Grace's life, the two were very close. Grace hoped that, with her mother and herself close by, her grandmother would never feel the loneliness so evident in Mrs. O'Dell's life. Reluctantly, she allowed the thought to intrude that she had another grandmother who truly had no one, no family and few friends, to fill her empty life. Grace pushed the thought aside. If Augusta had ever been anything other than cold and cruel, she might not be so alone now. Still, the things Clare had said last night kept sneaking back into her mind. Who knew what Augusta's life had been like? Grace really had no idea, except for the fact that Augusta had lost her only son in World War II, after losing her husband only a year or two before. That was a lot of heartbreak in a short space of time.

Somehow, Grace's mother had forgiven her. Grace didn't know how Nan was able to forgive Augusta for the many slights and unkind words through all the past years, but she had. Her mother consistently treated Augusta with kindness and appeared to genuinely care about her. And Nan's attitude had remained the same even after Grace had inherited everything - house, land and family investments - from her Uncle Zach, leaving Augusta with not much more than her own personal belongings. Though Augusta's overt demonstrations of bitterness had ceased, she had never expressed any appreciation for being allowed to stay in the house, run the house as she saw fit, and continue to enjoy the house-keeping and cooking services provided by Nan. And it didn't seem to bother Nan at all. Despite Grace's urging her to give it up, Nan said she would rather keep busy and let things go on as they always had. Maybe someday she would be half as good as her mother, Grace thought.

Why couldn't they leave anybody alone? Billy's thoughts were resentful and bitter as he thought on his grandfather's instructions to his father. Grace was beautiful and sweet; couldn't they see that? He had to find out the truth first so he could show them that they were wrong. He knew how mean his grandfather could be. He didn't want Grace to have to face anything that Beamon might devise.

Sitting in his car a half block away, Billy watched as Clare pulled out of the boarding house driveway and drove towards town. When she was out of sight, he got out of his car and strolled down the sidewalk, passing by the boarding house, then turned back and walked up the driveway. At the back of the house, he went quietly up the steps, across the porch, and peeked through the window. No one was in the kitchen. He tried the door and found it unlocked. Going in, he padded carefully across the kitchen to the back staircase. He stopped a moment to listen. All he could hear was the sound of the television coming from the living room. His left hand was resting against the doorframe. Focusing on the wall beyond his hand, he saw a small blackboard, with hooks and keys, and something written below each hook. Bingo! Stepping back, he scanned the names until he found Grace's hook and key. Taking the key, he tiptoed up the stairs and began looking for room number eight. He hesitated only a second before inserting the key and opening the door. His reluctance was overcome by his desire to not only protect Grace, but also to prove his grandfather wrong for once in his life.

Inside the room, all was neat and orderly. If he had had more time, Billy would have liked to see and touch everything that belonged to Grace, but he knew he had to look for something related to her work. The desk. He should start there. He looked through the few papers on the desk. Just a letter to Grace's mother. He opened the drawer. Nothing but blank paper and pencils. He closed the drawer and looked around the room. A little boxy suitcase was next to the bed. He sat on the edge of the bed and opened it up. Inside were Grace's make-up, deodorant, toothbrush and toothpaste. Fascinated, Billy couldn't help but touch them, but self-preservation reminded him that he had to hurry if he didn't want to get caught. He put the case back down, stood, and looked around the room.

Staring at the desk again, he realized he had completely overlooked the tote bag leaning against the wall on top of the desk. Beginning to feel some urgency to find what he needed and get out, he emptied the contents of the bag on the desk. He quickly eliminated some of the items and replaced them in the bag. All that was left was a small ring binder with divider tabs, and a folder with pockets. He opened the binder and read the tabs. "Amos", "James", "Lawyer", "Thelma", "News articles", "Court documents", "Sheriff", and "Other". This didn't make sense. The only murder she was researching was Amos'. There was nothing in here about any other murders. Maybe Grampaw was right about what Grace was doing here in Fairmount.

After replacing the binder in the bag, he opened up the folder. Tucked in the right-hand pocket was a very old brownish envelope. He opened the envelope and pulled out a single piece of paper. The writing was illegible over at least half of the page. But there was something familiar about this letter. He couldn't remember why, but he felt that he had seen this letter before. Weird. He wanted to figure it out, but didn't want to risk staying any longer. He put the letter back in the envelope and thrust it into his jacket pocket.

Billy took a quick peek out the window, happy to see that Miss Clare's car was not there. In his haste to leave the room, he didn't stop to think about putting things back the way he found them. He brushed past the desk, pushing the blotter awry, knocking the folder to the floor and kicking it out of sight beneath the desk. After checking the hall, he slipped out of the room, being careful to relock the door, and down the backstairs. Encountering no one, he went out the back door, up the driveway and down the street to his car.

Thirteen

race pulled into the Sheriff's office parking lot promptly at three
o'clock. Only a moment later, Diggy shuffled out, digging in his
pouch for another chew of tobacco.

"Okay, Diggy. Do I simply head towards Heaven's Mountain?"
Grace asked, as he settled himself into the passenger seat.

"Yes, ma'am. I'll tell you when we get to where the old road starts."
Diggy was quiet for several minutes, but then, couldn't resist the chance
to talk some more. "They used to call the old road "Heaven's Mountain
Church Road". The new road they just call "Heaven's Mountain Road".
It goes clean over the mountain. The old one ran out just a couple of
miles past the church. That was Preacher James' church. Empty now.
Without him, there wasn't no church. Everybody's got cars now. They
all just drive here to town." Diggy looked over at Grace and grinned.
"Sorta fittin' that it's Preacher James' own son still preachin' at 'em after
all. Here's where we turn, Miss Grace," Diggy pointed to a narrow paved
road branching off to the right.

"Did Preacher James live up here on the mountain, Diggy?"

"No'm, he lived between here and town. During the week, he worked
in the office at the sawmill this side of town. Our little church couldn't
pay him enough to let go of his other job. He had his own car to get back

and forth to the church, though, so he said he didn't mind. Said he knew he was right where God wanted him to be." After a few minutes more of weaving around the curves, Diggy told Grace, "We're getting close to where Amos was. There. Just right up there, on the left side of the road." Grace slowed and pulled the VW off on the narrow shoulder of the road. They both got out. Diggy began laying out the scene for Grace.

"Amos was laying about right here, with his head up this a-way. Beamon was standing right beside the body, on this side. Bo and Preacher James were up the road about ten or fifteen feet, looking back towards Amos. And Mrs. O'Dell was sitting in her wagon, down below where your car is parked. There were a few other folks showed up, just to see what they could see, but they stayed on the other side of the road, didn't get in the way."

"So, Beamon and Bo, in Mrs. O'Dell's wagon, came the same way we did?"

"Yes'm."

"When you drove up here that day, did you see the Lucases' truck a couple of miles back from here?"

"Yes'm, I did notice it. They told me they ran out of gas. Waved Mrs.O'Dell down to give them a ride."

"What did you do when you arrived here that day?"

"First thing I did was walk over here to the body." Diggy was showing Grace how and where he walked, clearly enjoying his important role in re-creating the scene for her. Though slightly amused by his officious manner, Grace nevertheless appreciated his assistance and urged him to continue.

"I got down on my knees," Diggy demonstrated, "and I made sure he was really dead. He was already getting cold. He must have been dead at least a couple of hours, maybe three or four, And, you know, that didn't make sense to me, Miss Grace. Bo and Beamon found Preacher James here with the body just a little more than an hour before I got here. If he killed him, why would he just stay here with the body for two or three more hours, just to get caught?"

"How could you know how long Amos had been dead, Diggy?'

"Well, ma'am," said the seventy year old man, looking sheepish, "my daddy was the undertaker around here. I grew up knowing what dead folks look like and feel like. So, I don't have no scientific knowledge about it, but I know about what a body's gonna feel like after one hour, or three hours, or four hours."

"All right then. So what did you do next, Diggy?"

"Well, I looked over his body real good. Saw several stab wounds in his stomach and chest. Looked like he had been beat up a little, too, but not real bad. Didn't see no other injuries, though."

Grace remembered reading about a murder victim who had been killed with a knife in one location, then moved to another location where he was later found. According to the reporter, the police had known the murder was committed elsewhere because of the fact that there had been no bleeding at the location of the body, other than the blood on the victim's clothes.

"Was there a lot of blood on Amos' clothes, Diggy?"

"'Law, yes. The front of his shirt was completely red."

"So, he must have bled a lot judging from the way his shirt looked?"

"Yes'm, I'd say so."

"Was there a lot of blood on the ground?"

Diggy looked stumped. He closed his eyes, thinking. Then he looked up, thinking some more. "Do you know, I can't remember hardly any blood on the ground. I can't see any in my recollection of it. Maybe I've forgotten because it was so long ago, but I don't remember seeing blood on the ground, nothing beyond just the little bit that rubbed off his clothes."

If Diggy's memory was correct, then the murder could have been committed at the church as the Heaven's Mountain letter said. "Then what did you do?" Grace asked.

"Okay, let's see. I looked over his body. Then I checked his pockets, didn't find anything much, just the usual for a mountain man. A few coins, a box of matches, a can of tobacco, and his mojo. Then I looked underneath his body, and found the knife. It was the knife Preacher James took away from Amos that very morning. And that was another thing that made no sense to me. Why would Preacher James kill him and leave the knife there for anyone to find?"

"Why indeed? Anything else?"

"After I finished with Amos, I talked to Mrs. O'Dell, told her she could go. Then I talked to the Lucases. They didn't say anything different from Mrs. O'Dell, but I told them to stay, because they had been up here touching the body and such. Then I talked to Preacher James. He said he was on his way to the church when he saw Amos' body lying beside the road. He stopped, and was trying to see if he could revive Amos when the Lucases and Mrs. O'Dell arrived. He said he got blood all over him from leaning over Amos, trying to get him to breathe. Then he went to his car to get a blanket, said he must have leaned against the seat, for the blood to have gotten in his car. He said he didn't kill Amos, didn't know who might have done it, said all he did was stop to help."

"But the jury convicted him."

"Yes'm. The fight in town, and the knife, that part was just too hard to explain away. But I don't believe it, Miss Grace."

"I don't think I do either, Diggy. You did a great job showing me how it all happened. You wouldn't happen to have just a little more time this afternoon, would you?"

"I 'spect so. What can I do for you, Miss Grace?"

"I'd like to go on up to the church and look around for a few minutes. Can we do that?"

"Yes, ma'am. I haven't been up there in a long while. I'd kinda like to take a look at it myself."

The two of them got back in the little VW and headed further up the mountain, winding round the curves, back and forth on the northwest face. Now, finally, they were coming out of a curve and into a small mountain vale. There, directly ahead of them was the old Heaven's Mountain Church against a backdrop of bluegreen forest and the majestic peak of the mountain directly above, with curving shoulders formed by the ridges arching in toward the church, like a protective father's arms. Even with the whitewash long since faded, the simple stately structure sat with dignity among the hardwoods and pines. Grace slowed the car to prolong the moment. "I don't think I've ever seen a church more beautifully situated."

"It's a sight, all right. Makes you feel worshipful just to see it, don't it? But don't let the beauty in the lines of the building fool you. It's not exactly safe anymore, parts of it, anyway. We can walk in if you want, but watch your step."

The inside of the church was perhaps a little disappointing, when compared to the natural grandeur surrounding it. Simple wooden pews, surely built by the mountain men. A wooden pulpit in front, plain except for some lovely carving around the top. A large wooden cross on the wall behind the pulpit. Another door on the right wall in line with the pulpit. Grace walked through the tiny sanctuary, trying to imagine where her father's friend might have been standing when he viewed the murder. He could have been standing at the window, of course, but then he risked being seen himself. Grace strolled back toward the small vestibule. She stared up over her head.

"Diggy, is there a belfry up here?"

"Yes'm, we have a real fine bell up there."

"How do you get up there?"

"You can't see it, can you?"

"No, I can't see anything at all," Grace replied.

Diggy walked over to one side of the vestibule, pushed on one of the large boards running from ceiling to floor, and the whole board swung open like a door. Inside was a small space, no more than a foot and a half deep, with a series of two by fours nailed to the outside wall to serve as steps.

"How about that," Grace spoke with admiration. "How ingenious!"

"We only had to use this when the rope broke or we needed to clear out the bats. We rung the bell with a pull rope hanging down inside the sanctuary against the back wall."

As she admired the set-up, Grace was thinking that the writer of the letter, who would probably have been thirteen to fifteen years of age in 1940, would have had no trouble at all in climbing in and out of the belfry, and that he was probably hiding there during the murder. Grace decided that climbing up into the rickety belfry was not worth the risk.

She doubted that even the agreeable Diggy would allow it. Besides it really would serve no purpose, other than to allow her to see the view from above as the writer of the letter would have seen it.

As they were leaving, she asked the deputy, "Did the Lucases go to church here at Preacher James' church?"

"They did. They lived up here on the mountain back then, and all the mountain folks came to this church. The Lucases had a little piece of land just the other side of the vale. That was before they got rich and moved closer to town."

"What happened to the church after Preacher James went to jail?"

"Well, some of the men tried to carry on on Sunday mornings, but you know how things go. Then the war came and men started leaving the mountains. More folks got cars and could go to town and hear a real preacher. And that was all she wrote."

Grace noticed there were no locks on the doors, so she determined to come back at a later time, and, very carefully of course, take a quick look around in the belfry.

Supper was on the table at the boarding house by the time Grace arrived. Clare had outdone herself again, and Grace found, due to skipping lunch, that she was once again starving. The fresh mountain air certainly seemed to have an amplifying effect on her appetite.

Grace had just started up the stairs to rest for a few minutes when the phone rang in the living room. One of the sisters called out, "Mees Grace, the phone for you."

She knew it was most likely Ethan on the phone. Wishing she could just continue up the stairs and avoid this conversation, she nevertheless forced herself to turn around and pick up the phone. "Hello, this is Grace."

"Hi, Grace. It's Ethan. I guess you've had a busy day. How did everything go for you today?"

"Very well, actually. I still have several more leads I want to check out over the next day or two, but today was pretty productive. How about you?"

"I had a great day, a blessed day, in fact. Hey, I know you said you wanted to talk. I was wondering if you'd like to go downtown to the grill. Maybe have some pie and coffee?"

Better there than here in the boarding house, Grace thought. "That sounds fine, Ethan. We've just finished dinner here, but a cup of coffee would be nice. Shall I meet you there?"

"I could pick you up, if you don't mind riding in a truck?" Ethan sounded hopeful.

Grace decided to go with the flow. "Sure, that's fine. See you in a few minutes?"

"I'll be right there."

While she was waiting for Ethan, Grace found herself completely re-doing her makeup, and changing into one of her favorite A-line dresses, topping it off by knotting the sleeves of a cardigan around her shoulders. She was almost ready when Clare knocked at her door. "Honey, you've got a visitor. Ethan's here!" She could tell Clare was excited for her. Not wanting to disappoint her new friend, Grace answered, "Thanks, Clare. Would you tell him I'll be down in a sec'?"

"Sure thing, honey." Grace heard Clare going back down the hall. She took a final look in the full length mirror. There. Just the look she needed. Cool, calm and professional. Except for the nerves! After wiping her sweaty palms once more on the hand towel, she opened the door and went downstairs.

The hometown grill was almost empty on this weekday night. Sitting opposite Ethan in the booth, Grace felt a huge wave of loss wash over her. She truly felt a connection that went beyond physical attraction, beyond complementary personalities, beyond logical explanation. It was an undeniable yearning in her heart to be, with this vibrant, strong, and loving man, as intimate in every way as a man and woman could be. Lost in her thoughts, she didn't hear Ethan speaking to her.

"Grace, would you like some coffee?"

"What? Oh, yes, coffee, please."

After the waitress had filled their cups, Ethan smiled warmly at Grace, and she hated the words she knew she had to say. Ethan began with, "What did you want to talk about, Grace?"

"Several things, actually." Grace was looking down at her cup, slowly turning it around and around on the table. She realized she was doing herself and him an injustice by not facing him squarely and telling him how things stood, so she raised her chin resolutely, ran her tongue across the front of her teeth, and looked him in the eye. "Ethan, I...was very surprised to see you behind the pulpit yesterday."

"You were? I thought I had mentioned it at some point on Friday or Saturday. I guess there was so much going on this weekend, I didn't realize the subject hadn't come up. Why, ...is there a problem, Grace?" Ethan said the words kindly, but Grace could tell there was genuine worry in his tone.

"Yes." Grace looked down again, took a deep breath and looked back up. "Yes, there is. I'm not a believer, Ethan. Until yesterday, I had not been in a church since I went away to college six years ago."

Ethan was silent, waiting for her to continue. "I like you, Ethan. And under other circumstances, I would want to continue our relationship and see where it goes. But, I have strong feelings about this, and I'm sure your beliefs are equally strong, so...I don't see any choice other than to cut it off now. As I see it, there's no possibility of reconciling our views." Grace waited for his reply, hoping he might offer a solution.

He answered softly, "I have to agree with you, Grace. I admit that I'm very disappointed. I was anticipating the possibility of there being more between us. I like you, too. But you are very wise. On something of this importance there should be agreement between a man and a woman before they embark on a relationship that might join their lives forever. To do otherwise would mean a constant pulling in two different directions. You are perfectly right. Unfortunately," he said with a sad, lopsided smile.

Grace sighed loudly. "I know." She gathered her strength and her thoughts to tackle the second item on her list tonight. "There is something else, too, that we need to discuss. Totally unrelated," she assured him.

"I told you I'm here doing research for a story, which is true. But I've told only a few people the specifics, which I'm now about to share with you." Grace paused, searching for the best way to broach the subject.

"I'm listening," Ethan gave her an encouraging nod.

"I think it will be easier for you to understand if I start at the beginning." Grace proceeded to tell him about her inheritance and finding the letter in her father's belongings. She described how the letter had led her to Heaven's Mountain, and how the research so far indicated that the murder in question was that of Amos.

An excited look on his face, Ethan took Grace's hand on the table. "So, you're saying that you've got a letter written by someone who saw Amos being killed by someone other than my father? Well, why haven't you taken it to the sheriff?"

Reacting to his demanding tone, Grace raised an eyebrow and tilted her head. In a slightly irritated voice, she ground out, "Of course I considered taking it to the sheriff, but I decided against it. For one thing, the letter is smudged and smeared and faded, very faded. It's difficult to make out the words at all. If I were to take it to someone in law enforcement, I don't think a thirty year old murder would receive priority treatment. Besides that, the letter alone, by itself, hardly constitutes "sufficient new evidence" to re-try the case. We need a lot more. And, I admit, I want to break the story, if there is one. It could mean a lot to my career."

Ethan was quiet, considering her reasoning on the matter. It wasn't that he didn't trust her judgment, but that his father's release could depend on the decisions they made. There's "wisdom in the counsel of many", he thought. "Would you consider showing this letter to my father's lawyer? He's also a good friend. You can trust him."

"Absolutely. He was on my list anyway. I was planning on contacting him tomorrow."

"I can take care of that. I'll call him and set it up." Ethan offered eagerly. "And Grace, I'd like to see the letter. May I?"

"Absolutely."

Fourteen

race ran quickly up the stairs to her room. She went straight to the desk and began looking in her tote bag for the folder in which she kept the letter and most of her research notes. She didn't see the folder. She flipped through the bag again. Definitely not there. She was certain she had put the folder in there this morning before she left, taking only her pad with her on her travels today. Glancing around the room, she spotted something under the desk. There was the folder. How strange, she thought. Picking up the folder, she laid it open on the desk. She didn't see the letter. She began frantically thumbing through every paper in the folder trying to find it. She went through it a second time, then a third. Nothing. She stepped away from the desk and took a good look around her room. There, beside the bed, hadn't her nightcase been moved? And the blotter on the desk was crooked. She would not have left it that way. Tonight when she picked up the tote bag it was on the left side of the desk. She was certain she had left it in the middle of the desk leaning against the wall when she left this morning. And the folder had definitely not been on the floor, it had been inside the tote bag in its usual place.

Someone had been in her room, had fumbled through her things, and had taken the letter, she realized, slumping into the desk chair with a shock. Clare came in once a day to clean, but Grace quickly dismissed as ludicrous the thought that Clare would take even a single penny from any of her boarders. Who else? One of the other boarders? Grace jumped up from the chair, ran down the hall, then scurried down the back stairs. As she had hoped, Clare was still in the kitchen, tidying up.

"Well, hey, honey. You back so soon?"

"Clare, was anyone in my room today?"

Taken aback by Grace's abrupt manner, Clare replied, "Well, no. Just me, when I went in to clean. Why? What's the matter?"

"Someone took a letter from my room, a letter that was part of the evidence for my research. I've been gone all day, but I know where I left it this morning, and it's not there. Were you here all day?"

"Ooh, let's see," Clare was getting visibly upset. "I was here most of the day, honey. Oh, my goodness. Let me see, now."

"I'm sorry, I didn't mean to upset you, Clare. I just need to find that letter. Were you here all day?" she repeated.

"I was here until about one thirty or two o'clock. I had to run a few errands. I got back about three thirty, I guess."

"When you were gone, was anybody else here?'

"Gosh, I'm sure Mrs. Luther would have been here, watching her soaps. The sisters would have been at work. Mr. Gardner might have been here, too."

"Was anyone extra in the house today? A repairman, utility guys, anybody?"

"No, I don't think so. Oh, golly bum, how could someone go in your room and take something?"

"I don't know. The door was still locked when I came in this afternoon. I locked it when I left with Ethan a little while ago, too. Just be thinking about it, Clare. Maybe something will come to mind. Ethan's in there waiting on me, so I'll check with you later, I guess."

Grace circled through the dining room and motioned for Ethan to follow her outside on the porch. As soon as he shut the front door, she talked quickly. "The letter's gone. I know exactly where I left it, and it's not there. Certain items in my room are not the way I left them, either. I didn't notice before because I wasn't in my room much at all this evening, and I was busy with other things." Like primping so I would look good for you, she thought. She wished she had paid more attention earlier, instead of being so concerned with impressing Ethan. Fuming with frustration, she was getting close to tears.

Sensing her distress, Ethan took her arm and guided her over to the porch swing. "Hey. It's okay. You know what was in the letter. You can just tell me, and we'll see what we can figure out together."

Taking a deep breath, Grace nodded her head in agreement. Ethan waited for her to begin. "Like I told you earlier, the letter was very old, discolored. The writing was faint and hard to read, even in the clearer spots. It was in my father's personal effects when he died in December, 1944, in Europe, so it's logical to assume that one of his buddies wrote it. It's addressed to the Sheriff at Heaven's Mountain, Georgia. The next clear words were "wrong man in jail". When I looked at the letter this morning, knowing what names to look for, I could see where it *might* say 'James did not kill Amos'. It fit perfectly with the scattered letters I had already figured out. My interpretation of the rest of the letter could be wrong, but I think the writer may have actually witnessed the murder, possibly from the belfry of Heaven's Mountain Church."

"My father's church," Ethan murmured.

"Yes. And then there's something about the church yard and a knife being thrown. Then, this is sort of strange. Our witness retrieved the knife from a tree and hid it. I couldn't make out where he hid it."

Ethan was lost in thought. Suddenly, he looked up, and exclaimed, "Grace, we can just see who died in the war in 1944 from around here!"

Grace gave him a wry smile. "I already did that. This morning. I checked the old newspapers for names of soldiers who died each week, starting with January, 1944, and going through June, 1945. He probably would have died before or at the same time as my father, you see."

"Oh, I should have realized you would already have thought of that," Ethan said in a disappointed voice.

"I did," Grace said gently. "On each deceased, I checked the branch of the military, then the company and unit number. None were even close to my father's. There were nine deaths from this county during that period of time. Of course, there is also the possibility that he wasn't killed at all, but if he went through the war with this weighing on him, surely he would have gotten it off his chest when he got back. In that case, your father would already be free. So, I'm more or less working from the most likely premise, which is that he died in the war."

The two sat silently in the slowly moving swing. It was a comfortable silence, each lost in thought, minds working to solve the puzzle before them. "How about…" "What if….." They both spoke at the same time.

Chuckling, Ethan offered, "Ladies first."

"I was going to say, up until today, I've just been trying to get my background information and pinpoint the particular murder with which we're dealing. Now that I'm satisfied I have the right murder, the simplest way to identify the killer is to identify the writer. I think I'm going to concentrate on that from here on out. Now, what were you going to say?"

Ethan had been watching the way her hair shone and rippled as she moved her head for emphasis, as well as the way her facial expression switched to "all business" when she talked about her work. "Oh, well, uh, I was going to suggest that we cross check the newspaper list of the deceased against the monument in the city cemetery. There could have been a delay in reporting the death."

"Good point. I'll do that sometime tomorrow."

"Grace, I know this is your story. But it's my father's freedom that's at stake. I'd like to work with you, if you'll let me."

Grace hesitated. It was one thing to let him know periodically what was going on. It was quite another to be forced into close proximity to him for hours, perhaps days, at a time, knowing she had to keep her feelings hidden and clamped down. Still, she knew she would feel exactly the same way if it were her mother's freedom in the balance, so she let compassion rule over protecting her own heart. "Sure you can. It will probably be a big help to me, having someone who knows all the locals."

Ethan also had his own misgivings about seeing Grace so much. He knew he would follow God's guidance and avoid any romantic ties with Grace, but he would have preferred not to have to struggle with maintaining a friendly, caring relationship and at the same time not allowing it to progress any further. "Thanks. Right now, my schedule is pretty much open for the next few days. But, in my line of work, that can change unexpectedly. I do have one church member who's been fighting cancer for a long time, and we think the end will come soon. You know, the man who called me away from the dance, and the ballfield? That was her son. So, I'll just check in at the church a few times a day, to make sure I'm not needed. If nothing happens, I should be able to take as much time off as we need over the next few days. Will that work?"

"Yes. That will work," Grace replied. "Ethan, I was planning on interviewing your father soon, maybe tomorrow, but I was also thinking that it might be a good idea to talk to his lawyer first, just to see if he has any insights or suggestions for me. What do you think?"

"Sounds good to me. Martin Sawyer, Dad's lawyer, is a good friend. I know he'd be honest with me about the chances of Dad ever getting out of prison. It would be good to know what the odds are before we talk to my dad. I don't want to raise false hopes, you know? Not that Dad couldn't handle it, either way. You'll see what I mean when you meet him," Ethan said, pride and love clearly showing on his face. "He's steady and calm, like a rock. You'll love him. Everybody does."

"I'm sure I will, too. So, why don't I come by the church about nine in the morning? We can map out our day then."

"I'll be there," said Ethan, rising from the swing. Grace stood also, and moved toward the door. He opened the screen door and held it for her to walk inside. "Good night," he said with a smile. Grace watched him walk across the porch and down the steps to his truck. "Good night," she said softly, wishing that the evening could have ended in a much more romantic way. Oh, well, that wasn't to be. At least she had handled herself well tonight. She had been honest with him, and had remained true to her convictions. The trouble was, she was having difficulty re-kindling the anger and bitterness that had always kept those convictions strong. It was a little unsettling, like being adrift without a means of controlling where you were going. She remembered Ethan's description of his father, "steady and calm, like a rock", and wished her own heart could have such peace.

Fifteen

A misting rain floated around Grace as she ran to the church office entrance. Ethan's truck wasn't there, but it looked as if someone was in the office, maybe the secretary. The gray-haired matron sitting behind the desk was friendly without being overwhelming. She offered Grace some coffee while she waited, which Grace gratefully accepted, as the cool and damp morning had given her a little chill. A few minutes after nine, the phone rang. After speaking briefly with the caller, the secretary told Grace that Ethan wished to speak to her, and that she could use the phone in his office.

Grace stepped inside the simple but warmly inviting room, which gave her the feeling of being in a small library rather than an office. She stood by the desk and picked up the phone. "Hello?"

"Grace, hello, it's Ethan. I'm afraid I'm not going to make it for about another hour. One of our young people has been in an accident, nothing serious, but I need to be here at the hospital a little longer. But look, I went ahead and called Martin Sawyer at home last night. I didn't tell him why, I thought you might prefer to handle that. He said he'd be glad to see us this morning. So, why don't you go on to his office, and I'll meet you there as soon as I can. His office is on the square. Mrs. Pons can tell you exactly where."

"All right. I'll go on to Mr. Sawyer's office now, and I'll see you in a bit." Returning to her car, Grace happened to look across the parking lot as she was getting in. She felt an uncomfortable twist in her stomach at seeing Bo Lucas staring at her from the driver's seat of a dark blue Lincoln Continental. She realized it was the same car she had seen parked down the street from the boarding house as she was leaving this morning. This was not good. She must be getting close if they were watching her so openly. They just didn't know Grace Turner was like a dog with a bone, did they? She wasn't turning loose until she got what she wanted. The truth.

Mr. Sawyer was a gentleman who also happened to be a mountain man. While retaining the accent and some of the mannerisms of a mountaineer, he somehow managed to also project elegance, intellect and charm. Grace was thoroughly taken by him from the moment he graciously took her hand and twinkled his very bright blue eyes at her.

"Ethan attempted to tell me what a beautiful young lady you were, but even his eloquence could not do you justice, Miss Turner. It's such a great pleasure to meet you. Please, take this seat here by the window. And I'll just sit here opposite. Some of my flowers are beginning to bloom out back in my garden, and I enjoy sitting here so I can soak in their beauty, especially in the morning."

The view of the garden was simply stunning, framed by the window like a picture in a magazine. Soft blues, creamy white, butter yellow, and the occasional rosy pink were so arranged that the eye naturally followed the flow across the garden to a pedestal holding a statue of a woman carrying a pitcher on her shoulder.

Grace was awe-struck. "It's magnificent! Did you do it yourself?"

"I did. I'm delighted that you approve! My living quarters are above the office, so the garden serves to give me pleasure as I carry on my business and as I enjoy my leisure time. And, working in my little flower garden keeps me in touch with my roots. Perhaps you're too young to appreciate that concept now, but someday you'll understand. Would you care for some coffee or tea?"

"No, thank you. But please, go ahead if you do."

"Ah, these days, I reluctantly limit my coffee to one cup, which I consumed earlier. Now, I understand Ethan will join us a little later?"

"Yes. He hopes within the hour." Grace could tell that Mr. Sawyer was ready to get to the business at hand, whatever that might be. "Mr. Sawyer, I understand that you were Mr. James MacEwen's counsel when he was tried for the murder of Amos Canfield. Recently, I came into possession of a letter, written around December, 1944, which I believe was penned by a young man who witnessed that murder. The letter states, among other things, that the wrong man is in prison; it then goes on to describe how the murder was committed in the churchyard of the Heaven's Mountain Church. Unfortunately, the letter was stolen from my room at the boarding house yesterday."

"That is unfortunate. And were it not for Ethan's vouching for your veracity, I probably would not speak with you further. However, as he believes in your professional integrity, I can do no less. I assume there is a reason you have not already contacted the writer? Dead, perhaps?"

"Dead, we believe. The letter was in poor condition, with more than half completely faded away and illegible, including the writer's name and the victim's name, though I feel fairly certain that Amos is the one. We believe the writer is dead because this letter was found by me in my father's personal effects. He died in December, 1944, in the Battle of the Bulge. We're assuming, perhaps incorrectly, that, had the writer lived, he would have found the courage to tell someone the truth. In the last line of the letter, he said he didn't want to die without setting the record straight."

"Very distressing, that he did not find the courage before my dear friend James was convicted for a murder he did not commit. 'Twas the greatest failure of my career. Broke my wife's heart and my own to see James imprisoned. Each time I visit him, he reassures me that, except for missing the time with his family, he is content where he is, and is absolutely convinced that he is doing God's work ministering there in the prison. Have you met him, Miss Turner?"

"No, not yet. Ethan told me a little about him last night. I'm anxious to meet him."

"Simply a wonderful man. So wise and happy and full of love for everyone he meets. And Ethan is so much like him. Somewhat surprising since Ethan was only four when James was arrested, and didn't have the benefit of growing up with his father in his day to day life." Grace was listening intently, not moving in case that might distract Mr. Sawyer from his reminiscing about Ethan's childhood. She wanted to hear every word he had to say about Ethan. "But Ethan was always a good, stalwart lad. At school, he was often teased by the meaner-spirited boys. In fact, I remember stepping out the door of my office on several occasions to chastise them and run them away. Then Ethan would come in and we would chat a bit. It hurt his feelings, certainly. He was only a child, after all, but I think he always knew that it didn't really matter what those boys said. What mattered was that his father and his mother both loved him very much, regardless of where his father lived."

Mr. Sawyer seemed to be lost in his thoughts for several minutes. Grace waited patiently, hoping he would resume where he had left off. He continued, "Ethan's mother, Betty, was a sweet, gentle woman. Back then, most women were not equipped to support a family, manage the household and raise the children all by themselves. She managed to hold things together, but she never really grew into it as she might have. By the time Ethan was eight, he was the man of the house. He took on a great deal of responsibility, but he never complained. He simply took care of his mother, and tried to handle everything he possibly could so that her burden would be lighter. My wife and I always kept an eye on them, and I helped Betty with financial and legal matters, but it was Ethan who shouldered the day to day chores. Through the grace of God, they somehow managed to live those years with dignity. At graduation, Ethan received a full scholarship to the University of Georgia, earned his bachelor's degree, and had just completed one year of law school at Emory when his mother became ill. Cancer. He immediately came home, took a position at the hardware store, and took on the nursing of his mother. Never a complainer, that boy. Diligent to do his duty, no matter the personal cost to himself. After she died, he went back to Emory, but this time to study theology. When he determined to return here to pastor Fairmount Community Church, this town was indeed blessed."

"I wasn't aware of all those things," said Grace.

"I know. I just thought you might be interested." Mr. Sawyer now sat up higher and straightened his tie. "Now, what kind of information were you thinking I could provide with regard to the murder of Amos Canfield?"

"I have read the newspaper articles, and I've talked to Beamon and Bo Lucas, Mrs. O'Dell, and Thelma Canfield." Just then, Ethan entered the room. At Mr. Sawyer's request, he pulled another chair forward to join them at the window. "Mr. Sawyer, who do you think might have killed Mr. Canfield?"

Mr. Sawyer looked toward Ethan, who nodded. "You understand attorney-client privilege, I'm sure, Miss Turner. As he has power of attorney for his father, Ethan has just indicated to me that I may speak freely to you. I did have my suspicions about who the real murderers might be, but not one shred of evidence to support my theory. I always thought it strangely coincidental that the Lucases, who lived on the mountain on property adjoining the Canfield land, happened to be the ones who found Amos' body. And strange indeed that the persons who benefited the most financially were again the Lucases. You know, of course, that they claimed the land as payment on the I.O.U. Amos signed, and that no more than a year or two later, they found gold on the Canfield property."

"No, I didn't realize the mine was on the Canfield property, not theirs." Grace answered. "Thelma said that Amos had already lost some of the land prior to signing the note for Mr. Lucas. Wait, wait! I remember now in the letter, there were some phrases about signing, only it was misspelled, so it didn't make any sense. Maybe Amos was forced to sign the I.O.U. by Mr. Lucas! Maybe Mr. Lucas knew about the gold, but just waited until the controversy over the trial had died down to pretend to find that vein himself. It is believable that, with so much potential wealth at stake, he would be willing to kill to get his hands on it. What do you think, Ethan?"

"It certainly sounds plausible to me. But we have nothing but our own conjectures. We have no evidence at all. Certainly none to justify re-opening the case. Martin, would there be any benefit in going to the sheriff to tell him about the letter?"

"None at all. First and foremost, you don't have the letter. Secondly, the letter by itself means very little, without any corroborating evidence, of which you have none." Seeing the disappointed looks on their faces, he cajoled them, "Come, come now. We cannot have discouragement at this stage of the game. We have only begun to fight!"

"I won't give up. Not with this new hope of getting Dad released," Ethan assured him.

"I'm here for two weeks. I don't know if I can stay any longer, but while I'm here I will be working all day every day to try to find something substantial enough to merit re-opening the case," Grace promised.

"Thank you, Grace."

"You're welcome, Ethan."

Sixteen

"What's next on our list?" Ethan asked, rubbing his hands together in anticipation.

"Whoa, tiger! We don't even have a list yet. Let me see. I'd like to have a good long interview with your father. And you mentioned the monument at the cemetery. I went to the old church yesterday, but maybe we should go again, and also, while we're on the mountain, take a look at the old Lucas and Canfield places. I'd like to see where the mine is in relation to their property lines. The sheriff and chief deputy will be back in town tomorrow. I've not talked to them yet. I agree with Mr. Sawyer that we should not even mention the idea of re-opening the case. We'll just continue with my research into the facts of the crime as they are currently on record. I think they will be more likely to share anything they have with us, if they're not having to defend their position with regard to convicting your father. What do you think?"

"I think you are very good at what you do," he said admiringly.

Grace ducked her head, then cut her eyes back up at Ethan. "It's about time you noticed! Thank you very much. Now, what do you think we should tackle today?"

"Well, the warden at the prison is very lenient about letting Dad have visitors, even un-scheduled ones, but I try not to abuse the privilege any more than I have to. The most convenient time for them is between ten and eleven in the morning, so it's really too late for today. Let's plan on going there first thing in the morning. We could swing by the cemetery now. After that, maybe you could go get some lunch at the boarding house, while I run by the hospital, check my messages at the church, and grab a bite to eat somewhere in between. If you could meet me at the church around two, we'll go up the mountain in my truck. It may be rough going to get into those old homeplaces, and your little bug may not be able to cut the mustard."

"Hey, don't talk about the bug. It's like a member of the family! Come on, I'll drive us to the cemetery and you'll see what a sweet ride I've got." They continued the light banter all the way across town, each enjoying the conversational sparring with their intellectual equal. When they got out at the cemetery, the sun was trying to peek out, with blue sky beginning to show here and there between the clouds. The light drizzle of the morning had ceased, and the water droplets now had a different purpose, that of creating an awesome, clearly defined arc of colors stretching from the valley floor on one end to the foot of Heaven's Mountain on the other end.

"Ah," Grace's breath caught in her throat. "Oh, beautiful!"

"Wow! 'The heavens are telling the glory of God; and the firmament proclaims his handiwork.' Thank you, Father, for this glorious sight!" Ethan spoke simply and from the heart, with genuine wonder evident in his voice. Grace found herself gazing at him instead of the rainbow, feeling a slight sense of envy at his unashamed child-like enjoyment of nature's palette. Thus they stood as a minute, then two passed. Finally, he turned to Grace, "The monument is over this way."

There was a paved walk leading to the older, central part of the cemetery. On a circular concrete pad, there were several large granite stones, etched with line after line of names and dates. "This stone here has World War II veterans who died. The other stones are for the Revolutionary War, Civil War, World War I and Korea," Ethan spoke softly, for the very place commanded respect.

"I'll start at the beginning, you start at the end," Grace instructed. "Then we'll cross over so that we both will have looked at all the names." They began perusing the list.

"Here's one who died in December, '44." Ethan pointed at the name.

"I saw his name in the paper. He was either in the air force or the navy, I can't remember which. Dad was in the Army."

Ethan asked Grace about another name or two, but they were also ones she had previously eliminated. She was moving into the "M's", when something clicked and she ran her finger back up to the "L's". "Floyd Lucas. Who was Floyd Lucas? It says he died in November of 1945. I didn't see him listed in the newspaper anywhere. Wait, I only checked through June, 1945. This could be it, Ethan." Grace had already grabbed his arm and was pulling him back down the sidewalk towards where the VW was parked. "Come on, I'll take you back to your truck. I'm eating at the newspaper office today. I'm going to find out who Floyd Lucas was, who he's related to, what branch and company and unit he was in, and how he died. Hurry!!," she urged him with a grin. It was infectious, and Ethan found himself growing as excited as she was.

Grace did force herself to slow down enough to explain to Joe Wilson why she needed to go back in the stacks. He was happy to oblige, and even offered his assistance, which she declined, with thanks. "It shouldn't take too long this time, but I appreciate you, Joe," she sang out as she headed to the back room.

She pulled the papers for the months of November and December, 1945. She found what she was searching for in the first week of December. Under the "Our Fallen Heroes" heading, she read:

Lucas, Floyd C.,PFC, U.S. Army, Company L, 393rd Infantry,
99th Infantry Division

PFC Floyd Carey Lucas of Heaven's Mountain Community in Laurel County, Georgia, died November 23, 1945, after being wounded in action on December 20, 1944, in Elsenborn, France. PFC Lucas was the recipient of the Purple Heart for his heroic efforts which resulted in the rescue of many of his wounded comrades during the Battle of the Bulge in the Ardennes . PFC Lucas was the son of Mr. and Mrs. Beamon Lucas of Heaven's Mountain.

Oh, my goodness. Grace sat back in her chair so hard it almost tipped her over. Oh-my-goodness. The pieces fit. They all fit. Floyd Lucas was in her father's division. He was wounded on the day her father was killed. If he died from the wounds he received, chances are he was unable to retrieve the letter, and unable to "set the record straight" as he had wanted.

He was Sadie's son. And Beamon's son. Beamon was the "daddy" in the letter. That explained why Beamon and Bo acted so strangely when she asked them to tell her about finding the body. More important, she was now absolutely certain that Bo's crossing her path more than once this morning was no coincidence. He was following her, probably on Beamon's orders. They wanted her to stop asking questions. They wanted to scare her away, which meant that she and Ethan, and anyone else she had involved in her quest for information, could be in danger.

She may have figured it out, but they were still no nearer to coming up with actual evidence, which was absolutely necessary in order to make any real difference.

Ethan couldn't get a word in, Grace was so brimming over with facts and conjectures and possibilities and comments. He finally gave up in favor of nodding and responding with an occasional "un-huh", "oh", and "really?", all the while enjoying the way her eyes sparkled when she was excited, and the way the words tumbled out quickly but clearly, and the way she wrinkled her nose and squinched her eyes just slightly when she was talking about something with which she wasn't happy. They were halfway up the mountain before Grace stopped to take a good breath. Ethan saw his chance and took it.

"Grace, I'm concerned for your safety. Beamon and Bo have probably been watching you since Sunday. Beamon is smart, in an evil sort of way. He knows where you've been, so he has probably figured out how much you know. I think we can assume he somehow got his hands on that letter. So, he knows your original cover story was bogus. He knows the letter said the wrong man was in prison. He knows that you're looking for the real killer. It probably has made matters even worse by my joining forces with you. Now, he can figure I'm looking for the real killer, too, so that my father can get out. I think we have no choice but to tell the sheriff."

Grace's bubble was deflated, at least temporarily. "It is getting complicated. But we can't go back. We can't undo anything we've already done. We've got to keep going until we solve the puzzle, uncover the truth, and the *most important thing of all*," she turned and looked directly at Ethan, completely serious now, "is to get your daddy out of jail. Your father deserves to be free and you deserve to have your dad where you can see him anytime you want to - not just between ten and eleven in the morning." Against her will, Grace felt her eyes begin to fill with tears. In her mind, she could see the little eight year old boy that he used to be, being teased by bullies about his "jailbird" dad. She could see the young man who gave up his plans for law school so that his mother wouldn't be alone while she fought a losing battle with cancer. What was the matter with her, getting all sentimental and weepy? She never did this. Trying to sniffle as quietly as she could, so that Ethan wouldn't notice, she turned her head to look out the passenger side of the truck window. And she realized she was also crying for the little girl that she used to be, being teased by the other kids for being a "bastard" kid. And for the twelve year old child who wouldn't denounce her mother even when it meant facing the humiliation of a whipping. She couldn't stop her shoulders from shaking as the sobs grew stronger.

".....Grace," Ethan said her name for the third time. He was holding out a handful of tissue. She turned slightly and gratefully took the tissue, then went back to staring out the window.

Ethan, for his part, had been praying for Grace ever since he saw her eyes shining with unshed tears. There was some pain buried deep in her heart, he was sure. He wished she would share it with him, let him help her bear it, but he wasn't going to press her. He longed to have more with this woman, be more with this woman, but he believed totally in

God's perfect provision for him, so he chose to simply suffer through the longing, knowing that at the other side God would always be there to catch him. The circumstances of their situation meant that, at least for a short time, they must work closely together to reach a common goal. He speculated that perhaps God wanted him close by so that he could protect Grace, not just from physical harm, but by offering up prayers on her behalf during this time in her life when she chose to separate herself from God.

Ethan drove a little slower to give Grace some extra time to compose herself. They passed the place where Amos' body was found. A minute more and they passed the old churchyard. He decided they would drive on up to the Canfield place first, then stop at the old Lucas house, and swing by the old mine, making the church their final stop. As the truck bounced over and through the potholes in the overgrown trail leading to the Canfield cabin, Grace was able to face forward again. By the time they pulled to a stop, she was almost back to normal. Ethan let her walk around a bit, exploring the cabin and the surrounding area, before he spoke to her. "Great view from up here, isn't it?"

"Fantastic. You can almost understand why they chose to live way up here, away from everything, in such hard conditions, for the sake of being able to sit on their front porch every morning and evening and see that."

"Let's see if the door is locked." Ethan walked up on the porch and tried the door. It swung open. He walked in, followed closely by Grace. The little cabin was disgustingly messy. Vermin had obviously been making their home here for years and Grace was afraid to touch anything. They both stood in the middle of the room and looked around.

"Thelma told me a little about their childhood years here," Grace offered. "About sitting around the fire in the winter, and her granny teaching her to cook and quilt. This may be her granny's rocker." Grace touched the back with the tip of her finger and set it rocking. Ethan was walking over to some shelves nailed to the wall where a few forlorn books lay, half eaten by the cabin's recent inhabitants. One of the books was a Bible. Ethan picked it off the shelf with two fingers and placed it in the fireplace, underneath a huge pile of ashes.

"I don't see anything here that could help us, do you?" he asked. Grace shook her head. They walked back outside, shutting the door behind them, and heading for the truck.

Within ten minutes they were repeating the process at the old Lucas homeplace, only this cabin had had at least a modicum of attention over the years. With four rooms, this house was more than twice as big as the Canfield's, and the rooms were very neat, and fairly clean. The front door had been locked, but they found the backdoor closed only with a simple latch. They tried to figure out which room might have belonged to Floyd, finally deciding it was probably the tiny bedroom to the left of the fireplace. Inside the room, very little was left of the original occupant. There was one tin cigar box, filled with boyhood trinkets, but nothing germane to the case. Nothing else. Disappointed, they left the way they came, through the back door.

Standing a few feet away, with a shotgun cradled in his arms, was Bo Lucas. "What do you think you're doing, going in my house, Preacher? I didn't give you permission to go in there."

"You're right, Bo. I apologize. We should have asked you first," Ethan said in all sincerity.

Grace broke in, "I wanted to see how folks lived up here on the mountain thirty years ago, Bo. It's my fault. We've been to the Canfield place, looked around up there. That cabin wasn't locked, so we went in and looked around. It was really run-down, not like yours. When yours was only closed with a latch on the back door, we went on in, thinking it would be dirty with virtually nothing left inside, like the Canfields. All we did was look around. We haven't taken anything or moved anything, Bo."

"You're a real fast talker, Miss Grace. I can see how you'd be a real good one to make up stories and such. Say you didn't move anything, Preacher?"

Ethan realized he must have been watching them earlier, at the Canfield place. "I did move a damaged Bible. I put it in the fireplace underneath the ashes. That's the only thing I moved."

"Hmmph. Don't know why I should believe you, Preacher. Maybe I need to see what's in your pockets. Maybe I need to check Miss Grace, make sure she didn't steal from me."

Detecting the slur in Bo's words, Ethan knew they needed to defuse the situation and leave as soon as possible. "Come on, Bo, don't talk like that to a lady. I know Miss Sadie taught you better. Miss Sadie is as fine a woman as I know. Grace thinks so, too."

"Absolutely. She's a wonderful lady. I've really enjoyed getting to know her," Grace told him.

"My momma's good. I know that. Y'all better get on out of here now. And don't tell nobody you came up here, either, you hear me?" Bo stumbled a little to one side.

"We won't, Bo," said Grace.

"We're not going to tell anyone," Ethan reiterated.

They jumped into the truck and drove away, each breathing a little easier, the further away they got.

Grace finally spoke. "That was <u>not</u> good."

"Definitely not good," Ethan agreed. "He was watching us earlier at the Canfield cabin. Did you get that part?"

"I did. I don't know where he was hiding, but he saw you move the Bible, didn't he?"

"Yep. We're just now passing the mine road, but that will have to wait. There's no way we're going to the mine, not today. After all that, do you still want to stop at the church? I don't really think he'll try to bother us there. What do you think?"

"I think we'll be okay. We'll be out in the open, right by the road. Not like we were, back in the woods, at his house. I'm okay with it. Let's stop."

She didn't scare easily, he'd give her that. He'd never really been around a lot of women, and the ones he had spent any time with were more like his mother, soft-spoken, on the timid side. He wasn't quite sure how to take Grace sometimes, but he admired her spunk.

Ethan pulled up in the churchyard, to the side of the front steps. "Here's what I suggest. I brought a cooler with some cold drinks, and I've got a sack with some crackers and chips. Let's sit on the steps and cool off a little, while we watch the road and see if Bo comes by, on his way down the mountain. I'll feel a little better if I see him going on past us."

"That works for me. Especially the part about a cold drink." In a companionable silence, Grace, and then Ethan, chose a drink, then dug around in the sack until each of them found a snack they liked. As there were columns supporting each side of the porch, they settled themselves on either side to sip their soft drinks and crunch their chips. Within a couple of minutes, Bo drove slowly by as they both watched.

Fixing her eyes on a point across the vale, where the mountain ridge met the horizon, Grace began talking. "Ethan. Mr. Sawyer told me some things about your childhood. He told me about the boys who teased you about your "jailbird" dad. Didn't that hurt your feelings? Didn't it make you angry?"

"Of course it did. And I couldn't talk to my mother about it. It would only have upset her. But I could talk to my dad about everything. He explained to me why the guys said those things to me. He said most people are afraid of being different. They knew I was different because my dad was in prison. They wanted to make it clear that I was the one who was different, and that they were the ones who were just like everybody else. It hurt when they all seemed to turn on me. It made me angry. But my dad told me, if I could find it in my heart to pray for them, and if I would forgive them, I would feel better. He was right. I did what he said, and I did feel better."

"But how did you keep from feeling that you weren't as good as them? They did have dads at home - you didn't. Didn't you still feel like you had less than any of them?"

Oh, Grace, what has happened in your life to cause you such pain, and to feel so uncertain of your worth? Ethan prayed for the right words before he spoke again. "No, not really. I know you don't go to church, and I'm not trying to persuade you to see things differently." Then he said with a smile. "Well, maybe I am. But there's no other way for me to explain this to you. My status in the world, even when I was a child, didn't have anything to do with where my dad lived. It had to do with my position in relation to God. God considers me his child, as he does all those who love him. He created me, unique from every person who's ever lived, so I know he values me exactly as he created me. God believes that I am worth so much that he allowed his son to give up his life for me, just because God wanted me to have the chance to be with him forever. So, I know who I am. I knew even when I was a child, thanks to my dad nurturing me in the love of God. In God's eyes, my dad being in prison was a non-issue. I guess you could say I adopted God's viewpoint about that."

"I see, I guess. The playing field's even with God, huh? No one's better or worse, in God's eyes, than anyone else?"

"Certainly not because of earthly circumstances. The best way to describe it is to imagine a father with a lot of children. They're all different, but he loves each and every one of them. He brought each of them into the world, he chose to make each one a special individual, and each one of them holds a special place in his heart. You too, Grace. He made you strong, and smart, and endearing, and funny, and beautiful… Maybe just a little bossy…" She swatted at him with her bag of chips. He ducked and went on. "You have a special place in his heart, just as I do. He'd like things to be made right between you and him, when you're ready."

Grace gazed out at the horizon. After a long pause, her attention seemed to change gears. She jumped up, stretched the kinks out of her legs from sitting so long, and smiled at Ethan. "Let's go inside. I think I'm feeling brave enough to climb up in the belfry today. Are you feeling brave enough, Ethan?" she teased.

"That depends on several things," he teased back.

"Such as?"

"Such as whether *you* fall through that rotted ceiling when *you* go up, amazon-girl!"

"I'm much lighter than you. I won't fall through. You, on the other hand, will probably drop straight through to the ground like an anvil."

"We'll see. You'd better watch yourself with all these smart-aleck remarks about my weight. Payback can be tough."

"I'm not scared. Bring it on. I can take it."

After the scare with Bo and the shotgun, and the serious discussion on the porch, it was a relief to let go of all that tension with some light-hearted fun. Thankfully, the floor of the belfry turned out to be very sturdy, which was fortunate, because Grace and Ethan had a contest to see who could get to the top of the two-by-four rungs first, and ring the church bell.

Grace won.

Ethan let her win.

At least that's what he said.

Seventeen

" She will have to sleep with Grandma, She will have to sleep with Grandma, She will have to sleep with Grandma when she comes! Snore, snore!" Singing at the top of their lungs, Ethan and Grace rolled back into Fairmount just a few minutes after five. What a great afternoon, Grace thought to herself. She hadn't let go like that since... Well, she couldn't remember the last time, probably not since her college days. They had subsided into a comfortable silence now as Ethan guided the truck through the tree-lined main street of town, and turned into the side street to the church. Side by side they ambled down the sidewalk and through the office entrance. Mrs. Pons had left Ethan's messages on his desk. While he went through them and returned a few calls, Grace studied the photographs scattered around the room. There was one photo of a pretty young woman with a sweet look about her, most likely taken in the '30's, who was probably Ethan's mother. Next to that a snapshot of a much younger Ethan with his arm around the shoulder of an older man, who had to be his father James, for the resemblance was undeniable. Sadly, Grace noted, you could see on closer inspection, that James wore the usual prisoner's garb, and that the picture was taken somewhere in the prison. Maybe soon she would be able to make them pose outside standing in the grass with the sun shining down on them.

In the next photo, Billy was grinning from ear to ear, holding a fish as big as his forearm, standing beside Ethan, who had their fishing poles, also grinning. In a prominent place on his desk sat a small framed photo of Ethan, probably at about three years old, and his parents, standing in front of the Heaven's Mountain Church, which shone new and clean and white, like a fresh-faced bride.

With the simplicity of a switch being flipped from left to right, Grace realized that her once immovable convictions about the church had begun to tremble a bit. She had never had any doubts about her own innocence or the cruelty of the perpetrators, but for the first time, she had begun to wonder about the depth of bitterness and pain that might be hidden in the hearts of her attackers, that would cause them to lash out at her. She wondered especially about her grandmother, Augusta. Could she honestly not have known that she, Grace, was the daughter of her beloved son, Jesse? And how could she have treated with such contempt Grace's own mother, Nan, whom Jesse loved, and who had borne his child?

Ethan's voice broke into her thoughts. "All done. I was able to clear my schedule for tomorrow, so, if nothing unforeseen occurs, I should be available all day. I wish I could think of something we could be doing to increase our chances of finding some *new* evidence. It doesn't seem very likely that we will though, do you think?"

Grace hesitated just a second. "No. No, the odds are not in our favor. It happened a long time ago, Ethan. I knew when I found the letter and decided to come to Heaven's Mountain that it was a real long shot. Not just for my story, but for the "wrong man" who was in prison. I still want the story, of course, but what I want the most, Ethan, is to get your dad out of prison. If things don't work out, will you be able to deal with that?"

"I can. And so can my dad. Do you still want to talk to him first thing in the morning?" Ethan straightened a few papers on his desk and rose to leave.

"Yes. Meet here at nine, be there by ten?" Grace began to follow him out.

"Sure. I'll even let you drive tomorrow," he joked.

"Oh, well. If you're going to allow me drive, I might just allow you to ride with me, sir!" she retorted. As she pulled the VW keys from her pocket, they slipped from her fingers to the ground. Instinctively, both Ethan and Grace stooped to retrieve them, their foreheads smacked together, and they were both thrown backwards. Laughing and groaning at the same time, they both grabbed their heads; Ethan was leaning over Grace to examine her forehead, holding his own head with one hand, and steadying her by the arm with his other. Still giggling, she lifted her head to look up at him. Without a thought, he bent his head and touched his lips to hers. And there was the connection again, tugging at her heart. Not giggling now, she lifted up on her toes and gently kissed him back. She could hear the logical part of her brain trying to get through to her, reminding her that she should not be getting involved with this man, for both their sakes. Reluctantly, she took a step backward. "I'd better go," she said. She didn't look at him again until she was pulling out of the parking lot. He was still standing where she left him, watching her go.

At the corner of the building, Billy also was watching as Grace drove away. He had come to see if Ethan wanted to go with him to shoot some hoops at the community center, but instead had come upon the scene of their innocent kissing. Immediately, he felt the fury of betrayal. He had imagined Grace would be his girl - they had kissed after the dance, hadn't they? There was only a few years difference in their ages, and he would be in college next fall,

She was just a two-timer, he could see that now. And Ethan, who was always pretending to care about him so much - what kind of friend was he, to move in on his girl like that? They thought they were so smart, but he'd show them. He'd think of something, and then they'd be sorry. Real sorry.

Ethan spent most of the evening praying for Grace, for her safety and protection, for her emotional healing, and for her relationship with God. He was still a little embarrassed that it was Grace who had the wisdom to back away this evening. She was so honest and straightforward, and she stood by her convictions, even when they forced her to deny her own desires. To kiss her had been such a natural action, he had acted before the thought even formed in his mind. And though he wished it were otherwise, moving into a deeper relationship with this amazing woman was not an option. Were it not for the circumstances that required their combined attention at the moment, he would make a conscious decision to avoid spending time with Grace.

But despite the difficulty presented by having to subdue and ignore his natural desires, he had begun to believe that, for this short period of time, God wanted him to stay close to Grace, to protect her, and with his help, to be nothing more than her loyal friend. And so, he would do his best to do just that.

When Grace arrived at the church the next morning, Ethan was already there. With her usual hospitality, Mrs. Pons offered Grace some fresh-brewed coffee while she waited for Ethan, whose door was closed. Grace had duly admired Mrs. Pons' pictures of her grandchildren, and had almost finished her coffee, when Ethan emerged with a cheery, "Good morning!" There was no awkwardness in Ethan's manner, for which Grace was grateful. If he could be easy and relaxed, as if the kiss had never happened, so could she. "Grace, I think we'd both better drive to the prison. Mr. Leach - the man from the ballfield - just called me. His mother is nearing the end. It could be a matter of hours, or another day or so. I've told him he can call me at the prison if they feel I need to come. Is that all right with you?"

"Of course. I wouldn't want you to do otherwise. Are you ready to leave now?"

Since the prison was on the other side of the valley, Grace turned on the radio and sang along to pass the time. That didn't last long, however, as her thoughts turned to the previous evening, which she had spent with Clare, in her private rooms. In between drinking hot chocolate and laughing a lot, they had, supposedly, been working on a gigantic jigsaw puzzle of Elvis Presley, Clare's favorite singer and actor. Of course Clare had insisted that they get in the mood by listening to all of her Elvis records, one after the other.

When she finally returned to her own room about midnight, Grace couldn't stop thinking about things Clare had said to her since she came to Fairmount. Like the fact that the church embraces people no matter what stage of faith they've reached. And Clare's suggestion that she try to forgive the people who had been mean to her. She'd never thought of herself as someone who held a grudge, but maybe that was what she had been doing all these years. Her mother had certainly suffered from humiliation inflicted by Augusta, but there was no bitterness in Nan. In fact, she continued to serve Augusta with kindness even when she no longer had to do so. Her mother had obviously forgiven Augusta. Could she do that, too? Surprisingly, she actually thought she wanted to. She couldn't imagine relating to Augusta as a granddaughter would, or even as a friend might, but the idea was appealing to her for the first time in her life. Ethan's words were haunting her, too. She didn't really see how God could think of her as his own child, but wouldn't that be a totally comforting thing, to be secure in a father's love?

Deep in her thoughts, Grace didn't notice the time until the twenty minute trip was over. Getting into the prison was not as much of an ordeal as she had feared, primarily because of Ethan's presence, she was sure. As he held the door of the chapel open for her, she got her first look at Preacher James, who had his back to her. Having heard so much about him, she was more than a little curious to finally meet the man. From the back she could tell he was of medium height, slim build, with graying hair. But when he turned around, he could have been Ethan, thirty years from now. The same beautiful blue-gray eyes and the same strong face, with a smile that lit up everything around him. The laugh lines only served to emphasize the happiness and peace emanating from within. Even before he spoke, Grace knew they were going to be great friends. Ethan made the introductions, and they all took a seat in one of the chairs placed around a folding table.

"Ethan's told me a little bit about you. It's just wonderful to meet you, Miss Turner," he said sincerely.

"And I'm happy to finally meet you. You have a great number of friends who think very highly of you, Mr. MacEwen."

"Oh, just call me James, if you don't mind."

"Only if you call me Grace."

"It's a deal! How are you today, son?" the preacher turned his attention to Ethan.

"I'm good, Dad. Mrs. Leach is doing very poorly, though. They don't think it will be much longer. They might even call while we're here."

"I'm sorry to hear that, son. In her younger days, that good lady was an absolute delight to be around, just a merry soul all the time. Used to bake chocolate chip cookies for me every so often."

"Yeah, I remember. You used to slip a lot of those cookies to me! The guards will probably want us to stay no more than an hour, so I guess we need to explain to you why we wanted to come see you today. All this started with Grace, so I'll let her tell you what this is all about."

Grace began with finding the letter, and from there, proceeded to relate the highlights of the events that had transpired since. She kept watching James' face for signs of distress or hope or fear, but nothing she said appeared to change the calm, peaceful gaze he gave her.

"That's quite a story, Grace. And intriguing to think that the letter lay there quietly for almost thirty years, then sprang to life a few weeks ago, setting a whole chain of events in motion. God does everything in his own time, as always. Before you say anything else, I want to be sure both of you understand something. I know that you would dearly love to find the real killer so that I can be set free. And I admit, it would be a blessing indeed to walk free again, wherever I wanted, anytime I wanted. But you must believe that it will be all right if I don't. Don't worry or feel guilty if things don't turn out the way you want. I'm content here. God has given me good work to do, and it's made a difference in many lives. Do you both understand what I'm saying?"

"Yes, sir," "Yes, Dad," they replied.

"I appreciate you letting me know what's going on, though, and you can be certain I'll be praying for you."

"Thank you, James," Grace replied. "However, we did have another reason for coming today, besides filling you in about our little investigation. I wonder if you would mind telling me everything you remember about the day Amos was murdered? And I may have some questions, too."

"I'll be glad to do that." James got an impish look on his face, "And I may want to ask you some questions, too!"

Grace chuckled, "Turn about is fair play! You can ask me anything you like, James. Now. Start at the beginning of that day. What you had for breakfast, if you can remember. And then continue from there. If I need clarification, I'll stop you and ask." Grace was poised with her pad and pencil, ready to go.

James told her every detail he could remember of that day in 1940. For the most part, Grace let him speak, uninterrupted. That is, until he got to the part, later in the day, when Deputy Diggs arrived on the scene, and found the knife under the body. "This is the part I have the most trouble with. How did the knife get there, James?"

"I honestly have no idea."

"Was it the same one you took away from Amos during the fight?"

"I believe it was."

"Did you still have it with you when you found Amos? Could it have fallen out of your pocket?"

"No, that's not possible, because after I took it from Amos, everyone was still standing around in the street, so I gathered up Betty and Ethan and we started walking down the sidewalk in town, headed towards home. We had gone about two blocks, probably to the corner of Elm and Gordon Streets, when I tossed it in the garbage can. I didn't want it, and I sure wasn't going to give it back to Amos. So, I threw it away."

"Hmm. Anyone could have picked it up. But if it happened to be Bo or Beamon that retrieved it from the can, that would pretty much tie up our theory in a nice little bow, wouldn't it?" she asked Ethan.

"What theory is that?" James asked.

Ethan explained why they believed that Bo and Beamon were directly involved in the murder, and that Floyd was the writer of the letter. He had just finished when a guard came in and told Ethan he had a phone call. He hurried to answer and was back in a few minutes to say goodbye. Mrs. Leach's family had asked him to come.

"Tell them I'm praying for them, son, and wish I could be there with them," James said.

"I will, Dad. Grace, I'll try to catch up with you, or call you later today, if that's all right?"

"That's fine. Don't worry about me. I'm just going to stay a little longer and ask James a few more questions."

"All right, then. See you later," and Ethan left.

While they were saying goodbye, James had been paying attention to what wasn't being said. Although Ethan and Grace were cordial and polite with each other, there were no special looks shared between them. If anything, they seemed to be rather formal and distant when speaking to each other. Though he was by no means one who pried into the business of others, still he did feel a certain curiosity given the comments made by Ethan a couple of days earlier. He could only surmise that Ethan's concerns about Grace's faith had been justified, which grieved him, not only for Ethan's sake, but for Grace's as well.

Grace turned back to James. "You know more about the circumstances and facts surrounding Amos' murder than Ethan or I. If Floyd wrote the letter, and I believe now that he must have, then, according to the letter, Beamon and someone else was involved in the murder. Since Bo was with Beamon only a short time later, that certainly would implicate him as the accomplice. Do you think that scenario is a possibility?"

James didn't answer her question immediately. "I hate to think of little Floyd Lucas watching that. He was a timid but kind child, just a tiny bit slow, but always hung in there and did his best. He was more or less Sadie's child, while Beamon took over with Bo, from the time he was just seven or eight years old. Many's the time I would be at the church working on various projects, and Floyd would pop in to sit with me for a while. Sometimes we talked. I tried to always make time for him if I could - he seemed to be so hungry for that little bit of attention."

"I wish I still had the letter. You might be able to recognize his handwriting, or his way of talking. But do you think that Beamon could have been the murderer?"

"Do I think that is possible? Yes, it's possible. But do I think we have anything concrete? No. And I absolutely do not want to accuse anyone, not even Beamon, unless we know for certain that he's the one."

128

"James, this is probably a silly question, but, did Beamon or Bo have any blood on them or their clothes?"

James thought a moment. "Not that I remember. They both had their jackets on, though. And I was in my shirtsleeves. I hadn't really thought about it before, but that was a little odd. I was comfortable, not cold at all in my short sleeves. But they left those jackets on the whole time, now that I think about it, and kept them buttoned up, too."

"Very interesting. Just one more question. Deputy Diggs said that he talked to Mrs. O'Dell first, then allowed her to leave. Then, he talked to the Lucases, and asked them to stay. Were they taken to the sheriff's office with you?"

"No, after the Sheriff arrived, and asked them some questions, he let them go, too. They walked back down towards their truck. When we went by a little later, the sheriff yelled out the window and asked them if they needed a lift home. They said no, they thought they had it fixed, so we went on."

"Hmm. Their truck quit, they couldn't fix it, so they got a ride with Mrs. O'Dell. Then, after the body had been found, they suddenly were able to fix their truck? How convenient."

"It certainly sounds odd when you say it that way. I guess nobody even considered them as suspects because the evidence all pointed to me," James mused.

Grace stared at him with wonder. "How can you not be bitter after spending your entire adult life in here, for a murder you didn't commit?'

"Just part of my adult life, Grace. I had ten wonderful years with my wife, Betty, and I'm not dead yet!" James laughed. "Seriously though, it does make me sad to think of the years I missed with Betty and Ethan. I know it was so hard for them. It was very hard for me to trust God to take care of them. But the longer I was in here, and the more I got to know my heavenly father, the more I knew that he wanted only good for me, and for Ethan and Betty. I knew they were safe in his hands, safer than they could ever be in mine alone."

"I still don't see how you could accept being here. How could you trust God after he let this happen to you?" Grace was mystified.

"You're right, he did allow it to happen, not just to me, but to Betty and Ethan, also." James thought for a moment. "Let me see if I can explain it this way. If you were training someone for the Iditerod, you know, the dogsled race, you might allow them to lose their way in a snowstorm. You might let them go without food if theirs fell into the river. You might allow them to experience a great deal of hardship while you were training them, because in the end you want them to learn to deal with all those things in the right way. You didn't cause the snowstorm, though snowstorms are a part of everyone's life in that part of the world. You didn't make the trainee lose their food, though that is the kind of unexpected problem they could encounter on the race. You allowed these things to happen for the ultimate good of your trainee. The events seem harsh and catastrophic when they occur, but the trainer is watching over the trainee, not giving him more than he's capable of handling at each level of training. And the trainee, when he's finally prepared for the race, is grateful to the trainer for the guidance he received." James grinned at Grace. "That may not be an exact analogy, but it's the best I could come up with on such short notice!"

Grace cut her eyes at him as she raised her eyebrows. "No, it kind of makes sense in a weird sort of way. So, you think God is training you for something bigger and better?"

"No, I think he's using the circumstances of my life to make me a bigger and better person." James smiled warmly at her again.

She couldn't help but smile back, shaking her head. How could you disagree with this man, who really seemed to be a bigger and better person than almost anyone she'd ever met. "Well, surely you were mad at God at first?"

"I was mostly bewildered at how I could be accused of murder. And worried about my family. Oh, I loved God, but I had never had to trust him with any problems quite that big before. It took some time. But angry at God? No. I had pretty much gotten that out of my system by the time I was seventeen or eighteen."

"What happened to you at that age?" Grace wanted to know.

"It wasn't what happened then. It started years before that. But, I don't want to take up all our time... Do we need to finish talking about the murder?"

"No, we were finished with that." With Grace's natural curiosity, she was eager for him to continue his story. "Please, continue."

"All right, then." He sat back in his chair and got comfortable. "When I was about five years old, my real daddy died. My momma and me and my little sister lived over in Dahlonega back then. Fortunately for us, my momma's family lived all around us, and between all of them, they saw to it that we were able to live a decent life, no luxuries of course, but we were a happy bunch anyway. I guess I was about ten years old when the whole family went to a big camp meeting in Gainesville. The preacher was a man named Finley O'Ryan. He had us all stirred up, with his hellfire and damnation sermons. Lots of folks were going down the aisle every night. To accept Jesus as their personal Savior, to ask for healing, to confess their sins, to pray for guidance, to rededicate their lives. That's why my momma went down, to rededicate her life.

"Well, Preacher O'Ryan was right taken with my momma. He started favoring her at the suppers, walking with her after the meetings, and before you know it, he had talked her into marrying him. Since he was an itinerant preacher, he didn't actually have a home anywhere, so he moved in with us in Dahlonega and he kept right on traveling and preaching. That first year, things didn't really change much. He was only home for a few days every month or two, so we hardly knew any difference. Then, he broke his leg. He had to come home and stay for several months, and we all got to know him better. Let's just say he did not show the love of Jesus in his home. He was a mean man, just full of hate. It was terribly difficult for my mother. Her family began to suspect things were not as they should be, but before they could get to the heart of it, O'Ryan told us we were moving. To Heaven's Mountain."

"Oh. So, that's how you ended up here." Grace interjected.

"Yes. I was twelve years old when we moved here. O'Ryan seemed a little better for a while after that. I guess he stayed on his best behavior at first. Then, it started again. Never in public, of course. He would accuse my momma of all kinds of things - looking at other men, wasting money, spoiling my sister and me. And he used his belt on me and my sister for every little infraction of the rules. There were lots of rules; some he would just make up when he needed to justify his anger. I would have packed up and left, but I couldn't leave my mother and my little sister, so I stayed.

"Finally, one day he had been yelling at my mother for taking too long when she visited an invalid lady from down the road, and for being late with his supper. He hit her. He took the back of his hand and knocked her down. I had had all I could take, so I charged him and started swinging. He balled up his fist and knocked me out with one punch. When I came to, he had me tied up, and was just waiting for me to wake up so he could beat me. He did a good job of it, too.

"He told us that we had both been inhabited by the devil but that he had driven the devil out, for the time being. He said that we had to confess our sins in church on Sunday. I flatly refused, but he beat me so much more that my momma begged me to give in. I finally told him he could tell the church himself, but that I wouldn't be saying anything. That seemed to satisfy him. Just as he said, on Sunday morning, he made us come to the front of the church."

"Weren't you all bruised and scratched up?" Grace asked.

"He was careful to hit me only where it wouldn't show. My momma's face was a little bruised, but she told everyone she had fallen on a log when she went to the outhouse. Anyway, he told them all how he had recognized Satan's work in us, and how he had called the demons out of us. I didn't mind it for me, but Grace, my mother was the sweetest woman in the world. She never said an unkind word about anyone, and she always tried to show Jesus' love in everything she did. There is no way all the people in that church could have believed O'Ryan. He was the preacher, but he had been there long enough that they knew what kind of man he really was. I would have called him out myself, but I had promised Momma I wouldn't say anything. But Grace, not one person, then or later, ever stood up to defend my momma.

"And that's how I came to be angry at God." James finished.

Grace didn't, couldn't, speak. Here was a man who had experienced harsh treatment at the hands of a so-called Christian, just as she had. He recognized the actions and the attitudes as un-Godly, just as she had. He had even been angry with God and the church, just as she had. But, somehow, he had made his peace with God, and with the church, so much so that he had become an ambassador for God, if you will.

"Grace, I felt strongly that God wanted you to hear that story for some reason. I've never told it to anyone before except Betty and Ethan. O'Ryan died of a heart attack the year I married Betty, and my mother died when Ethan was four, a month before the murder, in fact."

Grace cleared her throat. "So, what happened to your anger?"

"Well, it didn't just disappear. After our "confessions" in front of the church, I did leave home. I told him before I left, though, that I would be close by, and that if he ever hurt my momma again, I would come back in the middle of the night and kill him. I would have, too. Believe it or not, Grace, I was pretty hot-headed back in those days. That same hot-headedness got hold of me in town that morning when I threatened to kill Amos. Only that time, I didn't really mean it. I just wanted to scare him away.

"Anyway, I found a job in Fairmount, making deliveries for the grocery store. I was lucky to get it, what with the depression affecting everything. One of my almost-daily deliveries was to Samantha Sawyer's house. You've probably met her husband, Martin Sawyer."

Grace nodded her head, engrossed again in the story.

"Mr. Martin asked me one day if I could do some odd jobs for him around the house and grounds. They lived in a big, fancy house back then, not over the office as I hear Martin does now. I was thrilled at the chance to earn the extra money, so I could help my mother and little sister. I worked real hard for him, so he would be pleased, and ask me to work for him again. And he did. One full day and several evenings a week, I did whatever needed doing. After several months, he started coming out and talking to me most evenings. I have no idea why he bothered with me, but he did." Even now, James had a look of wonder on his face when he spoke of it. "He told me about philosophers and the accomplishments of great men. And not just what they accomplished for themselves, but about their great contributions to the world. We went on that way for a while. He gave me books to read, and then he'd discuss them with me. Eventually, our talk turned to religion. Religions, I should say, because he guided me on an academic tour of the great religions of the world, including Christianity. Finally, I asked him what he himself believed. Instead of answering, he asked me a question. He said, based on what I knew of all the religions we had just studied, which one did his life best represent? He told me to think about it and give him my answer the next day.

"I went to my little room that night, and I made a list of the principles and qualities each religion emphasized. I considered the founding figure of each major religion, and listed the characteristics of each. When I finished I compared the man I knew to the teachings of each one. And I knew he was a Christian.

"Martin was not a perfect man. I recognized that even then. But he strove to be like Christ to me, and to his family, and to his neighbors. And that was when the realization hit me. O'Ryan professed to be a Christian, and maybe he had accepted Jesus in his heart. But he didn't show Jesus' love. He talked about it in a very impressive way, but he didn't try to be like Jesus. What I realized was, that as good a man as Martin was, and as wonderfully as he exemplified God's love, even he still couldn't reach the perfection of God. And poor O'Ryan never came close. Still, there was no need for me to be angry with God because of O'Ryan's shortcomings. That wasn't what God wanted for him. God had wanted a different life for him, a life filled with peace and joy and lovingkindness.

"The church members should have made him answer to them. Jesus wouldn't have let innocents like my momma and me suffer, and neither should they have. Just like all of us, though, sometimes the church as a body fails to live up to the example of Jesus. But again, I realized, it was the church that made a mistake, not God. We want to see God in our Christian friends and in the church, but when they fail us, as imperfect humans do from time to time, we have the privilege of looking straight to the source of all goodness and wisdom and love. God through Jesus has shown us his perfect love for all time.

"And that's how I got over my anger with God. I began looking to God as my source of strength, rather than at anyone else. He's never let me down."

Grace was holding herself together with some difficulty. This was all hitting too close to home. She could feel her eyes beginning to fill with tears, so she busied herself folding her pad away, and putting her pen in her purse.

The guard came in. "Preacher James, are you about through?"

Grace answered instead, "Yes, we're finished." Rising, she offered her hand to James. "You've been quite wonderful, being so open with me about your life, and especially about that day. Thank you so much. If you think of anything else you think might be important, even if its something small, please call me. I've written the number of the boarding house on this paper for you. Thank you again for so much of your time. It's been a great pleasure, James."

Before she thought too much about it, she gave in to her impulse, and quickly gave James a hard hug. As he overcame his surprise enough to speak, she was already out the door.

Eighteen

Grace had to feel in her purse for her keys; she couldn't see through the tears. Once she managed to get the door open and slide into her seat, she fumbled around trying to find a tissue. Finally, in desperation, she tore a sheet out of her notebook, and blew her nose. For the next ten minutes, she sat in the prison parking lot, hiccupping, blowing her nose, and tearing up all over again. After a while, her emotions had leveled off, and she was able to think again. She determined once again to put this dilemna on the back burner. She was a professional journalist. She needed to concentrate on the task at hand.

She opened her pad of notes and scanned through the information, zeroing in on her scribbling about Beamon and Bo leaving their jackets on. She flipped back to her interview with Mrs. O'Dell. She hadn't mentioned the jackets. The nursing home was right on the way back to town, so Grace decided to swing by and see what else Mrs. O'Dell might remember about Beamon's and Bo's appearance. Besides, she had told the elderly woman that she would try to visit again, and this was the perfect time.

"Good morning, Mrs. O'Dell," Grace called out.

Mrs. O'Dell's head swiveled around, and her eyes opened wide. "Well, I declare, I sure am happy to see you, child. Come sit down awhile. What brings you out here again so quick?"

"I've just been to the prison to visit Preacher James, and thought it would be an excellent time to stop by and say hello. You were right on my way back to town, so it worked out beautifully!"

Mrs. O'Dell reached her wrinkled and twisted hand across to grasp Grace's young one. "And I'm so glad you did, Miss Grace. I have a hard time getting any of these old folks to talk to me! But I don't mean to complain. I have a lot to be thankful for. Did you know my birthday is coming soon?"

"Yes, ma'am. I remember you told me that your family is coming to help you celebrate."

"Yes. I'm blessed to have a family that loves me. Some old folks don't have anybody at all. It's real sad." Mrs. O'Dell drifted into silence.

Waiting a few seconds, Grace said, "Mrs. O'Dell, I was wondering if you remember what Beamon and Bo were wearing when you picked them up that day? The day you found Amos Canfield by the road."

"Oh, my goodness, you're testing my brains, aren't you, girl? I don't know if I've still got that picture in my mind. These days I never know...." Mrs. O'Dell scrunched up her eyes and thought hard. "I can see them up by the body. Standing up there by the preacher, Bo had on his jacket, had some overalls under that. And Beamon, I just don't recollect for sure. He always wore overalls, though, back in those days, before he got rich."

"Was it cold? Were you wearing a jacket?" Grace asked.

"Well, it was the beginning of June, middle of the day. I prob'ly wasn't wearing one, but I don't actually remember it one way or the other." Mrs. O'Dell's bony fingers plucked at her collar. "Wait a minute, what was just going thru my mind? Be patient with me, Miss Grace, it'll come back to me." Eyes shut, her brow was furrowed in thought, then her eyes flew open.

"I got it! I remember when I stopped to pick them up, they had those dogs, the ones that the wild pigs killed, in the back of their truck. Said they had toted those dogs from way back in the woods, and they both had it all over their shirts, the blood from off those dogs. Then they loaded 'em up on my wagon, and they put those jackets on so they wouldn't look so nasty." Mrs. O'Dell was extremely proud of herself for having resolved the jacket question. She waited for Grace to praise her feat of memory.

She only had to wait a few seconds. "Mrs. O'Dell, I don't know how you do it, pulling all those facts out after all this time. You have an exceptional mind! I truly appreciate your help."

"Why, honey, I was glad to help," Mrs. O'Dell said, modestly, of course.

Nineteen

Dark clouds were scudding across the sky when she came out of the nursing home, as the first heavy drops pelted Grace's head and shoulders. With every step she took the intensity of the downpour increased; by the time she reached her car, a drenching rain was coming down. Where did that come from, she wondered. Well, it would probably pass over as quickly as it came. Inside the car, Grace dried off as best she could. Her hair was hopelessly wet. It would have to wait until she got back to the boarding house.

Ah, she thought, it's tapering off a little now. I think I can just drive slowly, and I'll be fine. She started up the VW and slowly made her way across the parking lot to the exit to the highway. Several cars down, a dark blue sedan pulled out also, hanging slightly behind her.

The reprieve of lighter rain was only temporary; the heavy, flooding rain returned with a vengeance. Even with her windshield wipers at the fast speed, Grace could barely make out the lines on the road. She was still going only about fifteen miles per hour when she reached the intersection with the main road to Fairmount. She was inching her way into the crossroads when she was bumped from behind, skidded the rest of the way across the main road, and found herself on the other side of the intersection. The rain was still pouring down, visibility was only twenty

141

or thirty feet, and she was trying desperately to check the view in her mirrors to see if anyone had been hurt in the car behind her. Her attention was diverted from concern for the other car to concern for her own safety when the VW was again nudged on the rear passenger side, hard enough to send the small car sliding across the narrow road into the left lane. Thankfully, there was no traffic to be seen in any direction.

Ethan had been making some notes for Mrs. Leach's funeral, but was having trouble staying focused. Sensing that God wanted to lay something on his heart, he made himself grow still and quiet and attentive. Grace came to his mind, and, as had happened several times over the past few days, he knew she needed his prayers, now, at this moment. He slipped from his chair and knelt by his desk. For the next little while, only the tick of the clock and the murmur of his fervent prayers disturbed the silence in the room.

Grace was able to regain control before the little bug went too far off the shoulder of the road. Wrenching the steering wheel to the right, she punched into second gear, trying to put some distance between herself and the lunatic behind her. She looked in the mirrors again and could see only the slanting vertical lines of the rain close around her. She slowed down a bit, attempting to calm herself.

I'm okay. They're not back there anymore. I didn't hit anybody. I'm not hurt. Oh, God, I'm shaking all over. Grace began to giggle hysterically. I don't know if I'm just freezing wet or if I'm trembling because I'm so scared. The windshield was fogging up, so she opened her window partway, even though the rain was coming in on her. She could tell she was driving uphill now, and she thought she could distinguish a drop-off on the left shoulder. As soon as she could, she would find a place to pull over and stop.

Then, she heard it through the open window. The sound of a motor getting closer, pulling in behind her. They didn't have their headlights on, and with the darkness of the storm and the heavy rain, she could barely make out the shape of a vehicle. They were coming at her again! The little car was pushed sideways again with a jarring bump. What was that idiot doing, bumping her around like this? It was as if she was a mouse, being toyed with by a cat's paw. Another smack on the opposite side almost corrected the VW's position on the road. Grace braced for the next one and, without thinking, began praying out loud.

But the next one never came. Grace looked around. The rain was beginning to slack off a little. She turned to check behind her. Nothing. She faced forward again, leaned back in the seat, and began to sob, trembling, tears coursing down her cheeks. There was no stopping the emotional disintegration now. There was nothing to do but let it run its course.

Gradually, Grace came back to herself. For the second time that day, she called on all her powers of self-control to soothe and calm her thoughts. When she believed she had sufficient control over her faculties, she restarted the car, proceeded up the curvy mountain road until she found a place to turn around, and headed on to Fairmount.

Grace parked the VW in her usual space behind the boarding house, and got out to look at the damage. Surprisingly enough, there wasn't much. Relatively minor dents and scratches, all concentrated in the rear. What a strange attack that had been! Never a full-on crash, just a big car pushing a little car around. She never got a good look at the other car because of the rain, but she thought it was a dark color. Black or blue or... Yes, it could have been dark blue, like Bo's Lincoln. She just wished she had some way to prove it, if it was him.

Grace stepped quietly through the back door of the boarding house, hoping she would not encounter anyone, not even Clare. Thankfully, there was no one about at this hour, though she could hear the soaps blaring away in the living room. Slipping gratefully into her room, she immediately turned on her shower, shed her damp clothes, and stepped under the hot spray.

She couldn't even begin to sort out her day, so she pushed it all from her conscious thoughts and simply savored the heat of the rushing water soaking deeper and deeper below her skin, until finally, finally, she felt warm again. Wrapping a towel around her wet hair, and pulling on her thick robe and some socks, she went to the four poster and crawled underneath the covers. Lying there in a tight little ball, she drifted off to sleep.

Billy had been in an extremely ill mood all day, something to which his friends were not at all accustomed. In contrast to his normally sunny ways, he had snapped and insulted and inflicted pain on everyone with whom he came in contact today. His usual crowd of buddies had eventually given up and left him alone. Instead of improving as the day went on, his disposition had grown even blacker, until, by the time he arrived home from school, his fury had reached a volatile point.

From the window in his office, Beamon watched him as he got out of his car, slammed the door, and stomped into the house by way of the kitchen. He could hear him slamming cabinet doors, and glasses and ice, as he fixed himself something to eat and drink.

Beamon normally paid very little attention to Billy. They lived in the same house, but had little interaction with each other. Still, Billy was generally pleasant and compliant, so to see him angry stirred Beamon's curiosity. When Billy had finished his snack and had started upstairs to his room, Beamon called out for him to come to his office.

Billy came to the door, but no further. "Sir?"

It was plain to Beamon that Billy was in a rebellious mood, and Beamon liked nothing better than to subdue rebellion, make the person swallow their pride and submit themselves to his powerful persona. "Billy, you seem to be a little agitated this evening. Is there something you want to talk about?"

Billy set his jaw. "No, sir."

Beamon was nothing if not patient. "All right. But I think something is bothering you, judging from the way you've been storming around since you got home. You don't have to talk. But if you decide you need to talk to someone, don't forget, your old granddad is here to listen. Maybe I can even help," Beamon added smoothly.

"Yes, sir." Billy continued to stare stonily at him. "Is that all? Can I go?"

"Of course. Just remember what I said." Beamon watched him as he jerked his shoulders around and went upstairs.

Twenty

The room was in shadows when Grace roused from sleep. She cracked her eyes just enough to see that it must be late afternoon. She closed her eyes again, not yet ready to move any other part of her body. Like a slide show being played behind her closed eyes, she saw the incident on the road being played out over and over. To make it stop, she rolled her legs over the edge of the bed, stood up, and stretched.

On the drive home, she had debated going to the Sheriff's office to report her harrowing experience, but had known it would be a useless exercise. Her car was not damaged, she was not hurt, and she had not seen her attacker or his car. She had a strong suspicion that it was Bo, but how could she make that accusation without explaining the entire circumstantial case against Beamon and Bo? For all they knew, she could be a flighty female with an overactive imagination, who made up the whole thing.

She needed to call Ethan and tell him what had happened. Right this minute, though, she just wasn't up to it. She hated to cry in front of anyone, and she knew she couldn't talk about it yet without falling apart. Better to allow herself another hour or two.

"Grace, you in there? I'm putting supper on the table, sweetie." Clare spoke from the other side of the door.

Grace cleared her throat and cracked the door. "Thanks, Clare. I'm feeling a little under the weather, though. I don't think I feel up to coming down tonight. Thanks anyway."

"I'm sorry, Grace. Do you need any medicine or anything? I've got practically a whole pharmacy of over-the-counter stuff down there." Grace shook her head. "No? Okay. Well, if you change your mind, you know where to find me. I'm going to fix you a plate and put it in the oven, so if you get hungry later, just come on down to the kitchen, and get whatever you want. And I'm going to come check on you before I go to bed, if that's okay." Grace nodded her head in agreement, and giving Clare a little wave, closed the door.

Now what? She tried lying back down on the bed, but she was wide awake now. She sat on the side of the bed with her head in her hands. Through her fingers, she could see the nightstand, with an open shelf holding a Bible. No, she didn't want to think about that tonight either. She felt ashamed that, when she thought she was in trouble today, she had called out to God for help. If you did believe in God, you shouldn't just call out for him when your life got a little rough. Nobody wanted a friend like that, not even God, probably.

She needed to dry her hair. That's what she would do. And then she would roll it. Glad to have something to do, Grace busied herself with the dryer and then, when the electric curlers were ready, she rolled her hair. When they had cooled, she took her hair down and filled another thirty minutes experimenting with different hairstyles. She was afraid if she ceased all activity, her thoughts would steamroll her, flattening her completely, taking away her capacity to control herself or anything else. Eventually, she ran out of hairstyling ideas. She decided to get dressed and go downstairs. Maybe some television would distract her for a while.

Finding that she was, in fact, extremely hungry, having skipped lunch and then supper, she went first to the kitchen where she found the promised plate of food, still nice and warm in the oven. Clare had already finished the clean-up, and had apparently retired to her rooms for the rest of the evening. Grace fixed herself something to drink, and sat down at the kitchen table. A feeling of thankfulness filled her, for the simple privilege of eating a good meal, for being safe inside the house, for having the freedom to come and go as she pleased, unlike James and Mrs. O'Dell. Before tears could overtake her once more, she forced herself to pick up her fork and eat. With the first bite, her very real hunger was incentive enough to continue eating.

After finishing the plate of food and indulging in a serving of this evening's leftover dessert, Grace was washing up her dishes at the sink, when she heard the phone ring in the living room. A few minutes later, one of the boarders stuck his head in the kitchen doorway. "Oh, there you are, Grace. Telephone!" Duty done, he turned and went back to the living room.

With no chance to refuse or make excuses, Grace reluctantly went to answer the phone. "Hello?"

"Hello, Grace. This is Ethan. I apologize for not calling you this afternoon. Mrs. Leach passed away, and I needed to spend some time with the family, and work with them on the funeral arrangements. Did everything go all right with my Dad? And did you work on anything else this afternoon?" Ethan waited on her reply. "Grace? Are you still there?"

"Ahem. Yes. I'm still here. I, uh, everything was …fine …" Grace was unable to go on, the words just couldn't get past the huge lump in her throat.

"Grace, what's wrong? Can you tell me?"

"It's, uh…I'm okay," she managed to squeak the words out in a higher than normal voice.

"I will be there in less than five minutes. If you can, go out on the porch and wait on me. I'm coming right now."

"Uh, okay."

When she hung up, Grace went straight across the room to the front door, hoping no one had noticed her being upset. Within three minutes, Ethan's truck turned the corner and stopped in front of the boarding house. He jumped out quickly and came to kneel at Grace's side as she sat in the rocker.

"Would you like to sit out here, or do you want to go for a ride?" he asked gently.

She felt the need to move, to try to escape, to avoid the frightening pictures and persistent questions smoldering in her mind. "Let's go for a drive," she said in a fairly normal voice.

Ethan guided them through the quiet streets of town and onto the Heaven's Mountain Road. Because of the storms that afternoon, the air was still heavy and damp. However, the temperature was unseasonably warm, so it felt wonderful to roll the windows down and let the air rush in on them. Grace was grateful that Ethan wasn't talking or asking her any questions, but she realized the reprieve would be short-lived. Even with Ethan driving slowly, it seemed to Grace that they reached the churchyard within a few minutes, though it was actually closer to twenty.

Ethan pulled the truck around so that it was beside the church, facing the road. Still, they sat without speaking. Finally, Ethan broke the silence. "Grace, please tell me what's wrong. Whatever it is, I will try to help if I can."

Grace felt some of the day's terror begin to drain away. This man was so filled with peace that it almost seemed to radiate from him, and, if you were close enough, as she was tonight, to penetrate flesh and bone to fill the heart of the recipient. Grace began, "Today, after I left the prison, I stopped to see Mrs. O'Dell, to ask her about Beamon and Bo's appearance that day. I'll tell you about that later. When I left the nursing home, it started to rain, hard. As I was about to make the turn onto the main road, my car was shoved from behind. It knocked me across the intersection. I tried to see who it was – I wanted to make sure no one had been hurt – because I thought at first it was just an accident, with the rain coming down so hard. But then, they bumped me again. So, I tried to start moving, maybe outrun them. They pushed me again, and almost pushed me off the left shoulder of the road, which was very steep. Then one more time after that, they hit me. After that, the rain began to slack off a little. I suppose they were afraid of being seen, because they disappeared before the visibility improved."

The anguish was evident in Ethan's voice, "I should have stayed with you today." He reached for her hand and held it as he said again, "I'm so sorry."

"No, no," she protested. "You can't be with me all the time. And besides, I'm fine. No damage to me or my car. Not much, anyway."

"But there's damage to your feelings. That would have scared anyone. I can't imagine how you felt, by yourself, not being able to see anything because of the rain. Did you make a report at the Sheriff's office?"

Grace explained why she had not done so. "Ethan, it doesn't seem logical that a perfect stranger would have done that. I hate to say it, but it seems far more likely that Bo might have done it, because of all the questions we've been asking. What do you think? Do you think he's capable of something like this?"

"I don't know. I guess if he could be involved in murdering someone, he wouldn't have any qualms about running you off the road."

Grace exhaled slowly. "I feel better. I think talking about it helped to clear my mind."

"I'm glad. But, Grace, we can't let this happen again. I don't want you put in another dangerous position, alone and far away from any help. I'd be blaming myself if you were hurt because no one was there to help you. Will you promise me you won't set out on your own for any reason?"

"That's a promise I have no trouble making! Yesterday, you might have gotten an argument from me, Miss Independent, but not today."

"Good. You were going to tell me about Mrs. O'Dell?"

Grace told him about the blood on the shirts. "If the Lucases did kill Amos, and got blood on their clothes, then it would make sense to create their own alibi for the blood, wouldn't it? Plus, your dad said they left their jackets on all afternoon, which was corroborated by Mrs. O'Dell. At the beginning of June, on a sunny afternoon, most people would not leave their jackets on. Oh, and James said he was in shirtsleeves. Mrs. O'Dell couldn't remember what she was wearing that day."

"We could probably check the actual temperature for that day."

"Good idea. Not that it really counts for anything, but if it was hot, it makes it very strange that they kept their jackets on."

"So, what else did you and Dad talk about?"

"After you left, not too much more about the case. He told me some stories from his childhood, though."

"Which ones?" Ethan said eagerly.

"He told me about his step-father, and moving to Heaven's Mountain. And about working for Mr. Sawyer." Grace didn't really want to get more specific.

"He must really like you, Grace. He doesn't share those stories with just anybody."

"Really? I liked your father very much, Ethan. You didn't exaggerate about how special he is."

"I know. He is, isn't he?"

"What made you decide to go into the ministry, Ethan? Hadn't you started law school before that?" Grace ventured to ask.

"I did finish a year of law school, then my mother was diagnosed with cancer so I came home for a few years so I could be with her."

"That was really good of you, you know. No, don't shake your head like it was nothing. It was a big deal, as a law school student, to give it all up, and live at home again to take care of your mother. I hope I would do the same thing if faced with a similar situation."

"You would, because you love your mother, too. You asked me why I chose the ministry. When I came back to Fairmount, I spent more time with my dad than I ever had before. And you've seen for yourself what an enthusiasm he has for everything, but especially for God. He guided me as I sought for myself a deeper intimacy with God. Then, when I was ready to hear it, God let me know what path he wanted me to take. It wasn't a hardship at all to give up the law, so don't make me out to be a martyr!" Ethan chuckled.

"No, you don't seem too unhappy about it," Grace responded. "You know, I was very disappointed to find out you were a preacher, because my experiences along that line have been pretty poor. But, having gotten to know you and your father a little bit has made me begin to question my perception of the church."

Ethan's heart seemed to skip a beat. Though he had tried diligently to maintain their relationship as friends only, the fact remained that the desire of his heart for Grace had never wavered. He didn't want to anticipate the moves of his heavenly Father, but he couldn't keep from feeling that a seed of hope had been planted inside him. Even now, however, he accepted that, should Grace never make a decision for God, he could and would walk away, believing that God always had his best interest at heart.

Ethan said, "Sounds as if you've been doing some thinking about this."

"I have. Clare and I have talked about some things the last few days. She said I should consider the idea of forgiving the people in the church who hurt me. The idea is actually beginning to appeal to me, I think."

"Imagine it this way. When we forgive, it frees us from the burden of carrying that hurt around inside us, as if we had a cocklebur stuck in our heart, and we plucked it out and threw it away."

"A cocklebur, huh? You know, you and your dad certainly have some interesting examples when you're trying to explain something to me. Today I heard his Iditerod analogy. Are you familiar with it?" Grace teased.

Ethan's laughter rang out. "No, I don't believe I've heard that one!"

"It was actually pretty good. Get him to tell you sometime," she giggled, then grew quiet. Should she go on? Did she really want to explore these questions? Was she ready to knock down the last barrier between herself and the church with which she had so long been angry? In the last few days, she had seen for herself that even hardships and imprisonment could not quench the peace and love emanating from these Christians. She knew she wanted that for herself, and if it meant admitting that she had allowed herself to become unduly hard and close-minded about the church, then so be it. Grace feared the consequences of dishonesty with herself far more than the sting of facing the truth. The truth was worth any price. She decided she was ready to risk it.

"Seriously now, I want to ask you some things, Ethan. If God exists and if he is this great all-powerful, all-knowing, completely loving God, why didn't he just create us as better human beings to start with? Why deal with all the trouble we manage to stir up as we live our lives? Can you answer that, Mr. Preacher-man?"

"Very funny! Ahem. First of all, I don't presume to know the mind of God, so I'm only speculating on this, you understand?" Grace nodded, and Ethan continued. "My thinking is that by allowing us to make our own choices, which, unfortunately, includes making a lot of mistakes, God has the pleasure of knowing that, when we do make a decision to live for him or follow his leading, that we ourselves actually chose that path. It wasn't programmed into us, we didn't make that decision because it was forced on us. We choose him because we want to choose him. We come to him freely. Maybe, and as I said I'm only guessing here, maybe, God likes knowing that not only did he choose us, but that we also choose him."

"What about - when you see that you want God in your life - are you supposed to already feel that you love him?"

"Boy, Grace, you're really giving me a pastoral workout, aren't you?" Ethan laughed and shook his head. "Let's see now. That word 'love'. We usually think of it as an emotional feeling we have, and that can be one definition, certainly. But if you don't feel the emotion of love when you make a decision, that doesn't mean your decision is not real. Maybe, for you, the emotion will come after you've spent some time getting to know Jesus. More importantly, 'love' refers to a commitment of the heart, a decision to stand by the other person, to do what's right for them, to put the other person's interests ahead of your own. That's love in action, a decision of the will to love. When we finally see with clarity the incredible love God showed for us, that mind-blowing knowledge motivates our decision to turn our lives over to him. That is the commitment that we make, to return his love with our love. Not our emotional love, but our love in action."

"I see. Sort of like when you marry someone. It's not the emotion you feel that's the most important. It's the commitment you make to stand by them for a lifetime."

"Exactly." Ethan waited to see if Grace had more to say.

She did, but hesitated. Perhaps she should think about this on her own for a day or two. She probably should read that Bible in her room, and try to pray, if she remembered how. Still, the journalist in her wanted more information, information that Ethan could easily convey. Grace formulated her request in a very formal way. "This next question I'm going to ask is to improve my understanding of the process of becoming a

Christian. If someone were considering making a decision, what would you say to them about why they should do so, how the process works, and what they could expect afterwards?"

Ethan was elated at the interest Grace was evidencing. However, before he opened his mouth, he said a heartfelt, though instantaneous, prayer both for wisdom and for provision of a shield to allow no personal desires of his to intrude in his words, looks, or actions that might jeopardize Grace's understanding. That done, he proceeded to explain to her God's plan of salvation, completed by Jesus. For each question she asked, he patiently told her every detail she wanted. Time was no master, and when Grace had exhausted her mental list, they found that it was well past midnight.

"Thank you, Ethan, for not pressing me. I've got to ponder on all this for a while." She tried to stifle a yawn, then a laugh, as he followed with a yawn of his own. "Right now, you need to take me home so I can get some sleep. What is it they say to the dogs in the Iditerod? Oh, yes. Mush!"

Twenty-One

The bright sunlight coming through the window finally roused Grace from her sound sleep. To prolong the moment, she rolled over and pulled the pillow over her head. She didn't even want to look at the clock. Missing breakfast went without saying. It was way past eight-thirty, she was certain. She remembered now why she was so sleepy. It was because she stayed up so late. After Ethan brought her home, she had spent another two hours or more reading the passages he had suggested. It had felt both strange and familiar to be reading scriptures. She had thought she would never do so again.

She was still undecided; the only thing she had decided was not to rush her decision. A few more days or hours, or weeks for that matter, would not make any difference in the long run. She wanted to be absolutely certain before she did anything she might later regret.

And now, it really was time to drag herself out of bed. A quick shower did a lot to get her juices flowing. When she was dressed to meet the day in a casual pants outfit, she went downstairs in search of a cup of coffee. Clare was busy in the kitchen, and thankfully, still had a pot going.

"Well, good morning, sunshine! Do you feel better? I saw where you had eaten the supper I left you. I came to check on you, but they told me you had left with Ethan, so I knew you must have felt a little better. I guess you're out and about again today. Looks like we're going to have another beautiful day."

All Grace could do was nod her head, smile, and occasionally raise her eyebrows. Breaking in and actually replying was not an option, at least not until Clare came up for air, which she eventually did.

"Thank you, Clare, for leaving the plate for me. And yes, I feel much better today. Mmm, good coffee. You make the best! I'm off to meet Ethan at the church. I think he has a funeral at two o'clock today, so we may not be able to accomplish very much."

"Now, I'm confused. What does Ethan have to do with your research?"

"Well, I guess you could say I've more or less narrowed my research down to Amos Canfield's murder. You know, the man Ethan's dad was convicted of murdering."

"Oh, my goodness! Thelma's brother, the one the Lucases found? Well, shut my mouth! I guess I missed that little tidbit of gossip somehow! It happened so long ago, I suppose it doesn't come up very often, and you know I try to avoid gossip." Clare winked at Grace. "I love to talk, but I do know the difference between talking and gossiping.'

"You know what? I actually believe you, Clare," Grace laughed. "I'd better get going, especially since I've already slept half the day away! I'll probably see you tonight at supper. 'Bye." And Grace was out the back door.

On the short drive to the church, Grace analyzed the difference between the way she had felt yesterday morning and the way she felt today. Yesterday, though she wanted to see Ethan, she had dreaded having to suppress her natural inclinations to smile and laugh and be genuinely friendly towards him; their different beliefs required that she avoid entanglement with him. Today, there was a possibility that the difference could soon be eliminated, and consequently, her heart felt light and buoyant. Though there was still a need to be somewhat reserved, she could at least do so with a modicum of hope. She could bear it with a happier outlook.

Mrs. Pons was not in the office today. Ethan saw Grace come in, however, and asked her to step in his office. "Good morning. Did you sleep a little late this morning, too?" Ethan said, laughing. "I'm afraid I'm going to be tied up this morning also, Grace, in addition to the funeral this afternoon. It will be four-thirty or five before I can even think about breaking free."

"That's okay. Please, the Leach family is your priority. Don't waste one second thinking otherwise or worrying about me. I'll try to find something constructive, and *safe*, to do today."

"Please, make it safe, otherwise I will worry, after what happened yesterday. If nothing happens, I should be free again tomorrow."

"Great! That's good for me. Now, I can tell you're really busy. This is probably something you would have finished last night if you hadn't very gallantly come to my rescue! Am I right? So, I'm going to go and leave you to your work. If you have time tonight, you can call and see if I uncovered anything earth-shattering today with my superb investigative skills."

"I'll do better than that. How about if I stop by around six and take you out to dinner?"

"Even better! See you at six." With a little wave, Grace left him with his work.

After tidying up Sadie's room, Thelma had begun her customary round through the bedrooms, stripping sheets, making beds, picking up dirty clothes and hanging up clean ones. As usual, she saved the worst for last. Billy's room normally took twice as long as anyone else's. It wasn't that he was so terribly messy, he just seemed to have so much more going on in his bedroom than any other member of the family. Sports gear, homework and school projects, model cars in various stages of completion, cards and games, late night snack dishes that never made it back down to the kitchen – and this was in addition to the normal clothes, towels, and shoes that more often than not rested in very odd places throughout the room. At least straightening up this room was never boring, Thelma often thought to herself.

Today was no different. She began on the other side of the room and gradually worked her way back to the door. She had almost finished, and had picked up Billy's jacket to hang it up in the closet when a piece of paper fell out of the pocket. Thinking it was more of the usual trash she found stuffed in his pockets, she unfolded it to be sure, before she tossed it in the waste basket. She stopped the movement of her hand in midair as she noticed something vaguely familiar about the paper. Why did she think she had seen this before? She drew it closer so that she could better examine it. It seemed to be a letter, obviously old, much faded, and very difficult to read. As she ran her eyes across the letter and reached the closing signature, she gasped. Dropping the dirty clothes she held in her other arm, she first looked toward the door, to be sure no one was watching. There was normally no one about at this time of day, but Beamon could appear at odd times and places with no warning. She did not want to have to deal with him right now.

Thelma was not a well educated woman, but she was nobody's fool. She immediately realized what she was holding in her hand. She knew it had to do with the murder of her brother and that that meant it was somehow connected to Miss Grace, who seemed to be searching for something having to do with the murder. What to do? She decided to proceed as if nothing of any importance had taken place this morning. She refolded the letter, and using one of the safety pins she always kept on her apron, she pinned her pocket safely closed so that it could not fall out. Then, she picked up the dirty clothes she'd dropped, and finished cleaning up Billy's room.

After loading some clothes in the washer and tidying up the kitchen, she was finally free to visit Sadie's room again. Sadie was in her sitting room, working on a hooked rug, when Thelma came in and sat down close beside her. She didn't want to upset her friend, but she knew that Sadie was capable of handling a great deal more than most people realized.

"Miss Sadie, would you mind if I got out those letters Floyd wrote you when he was in the war?"

"Why, no, I don't mind, dear. They're in my treasure box, right up there, and I believe I have a ribbon tied around them." She waited while

Thelma took down the box, then came back to sit beside Sadie again. "Now, what is this all about, Thelma?"

Thelma had opened the box and removed the letters, but now she paused to take Sadie's hand in hers. "Ma'am, I think I've found another letter from Floyd. I want to take a look at the ones you've got first, to see if I'm right."

"My goodness, how can that be? Wherever did you find it?"

Thelma did not answer. She had opened one of the letters and was noting all of the similarities. She laid Sadie's letter out flat on the low table in front of them. Then she removed the letter from her pocket. Carefully unfolding the old paper, she gently smoothed it out, and laid it beside the other one on the table. Only the contents of the letters were different. The letters were written on the same fine stationery paper, white with a border of blue flowers on a delicate green vine. The handwriting appeared to be identical also, as well as the way the letter and the paragraphs were arranged. The two women sat in silence for several minutes, looking at and comparing the letters.

"I found this letter in the pocket of Billy's jacket, when I was cleaning up his room this morning."

"Well, upon my word! Where do you think Billy got this?"

"I don't know, ma'am. But if I had to guess, I would say it had something to do with Miss Grace. Can you read this first line in the letter?"

"Not very well, dear. What does it say?"

"It says something about "wrong man in prison". And the letter is addressed to the Sheriff at Heaven's Mountain."

"But why would Floyd write to the sheriff?"

Thelma picked up the letter and tried to read all the way through, skipping over the illegible parts. As she put together a few of the phrases, her heart dropped. "Miss Sadie, I'm not certain about this, because this letter is real hard to read. Maybe we should take this letter to the sheriff and let him figure it out, and then do whatever he thinks needs to be done."

"Thelma, dear, do not dissemble with me. If my eyesight was not so poor, I would be reading that letter for myself. Now, tell me what it says. I've borne a great deal of heartbreak in my life; I think I can stand just one tiny bit more." She smiled gently at her old friend.

"Yes, ma'am. There's a couple of places in this letter where it says 'my daddy'. We're pretty sure Floyd wrote this letter, so his daddy would be Mr. Beamon. From the few phrases I can read – and Miss Sadie, there's a lot of it I can't read – it sounds like Floyd saw his daddy and somebody else kill my brother."

Twenty-Two

That morning, Grace spent a pleasant hour or so talking to Joe Wilson's uncle. As promised, he remembered every detail of the murder story. Without revealing any of her own theories, Grace was able to coax from him many corroborating facts that had not been published in the paper or the court records. He had known James as a young man, and confided to Grace that he had never been able to believe that the young preacher could have killed anyone, not even aggravating Amos.

After lunch, Grace chose to take a hiatus from her legwork. Instead, she sat down at the desk in her bedroom and began organizing her notes into some semblance of order.

Sadie and Thelma had discussed at length what course of action they should take, if any. Neither of them had any illusions about what kind of man Beamon was. They believed it was only a matter of time before he would somehow ferret the fact of the letter's existence out of Billy, and therefore only a short time beyond that before he would be asking questions of them. By the middle of the afternoon, they had decided that Thelma should make a trip to the drugstore in Fairmount. While there, she would call the boarding house and try to arrange the return of the letter to Grace. If that failed, she would take the letter to Joe Wilson at the Fairmount Chronicle. He had a Xerox machine there. She would get several copies made, leave the original with him, and take a copy to the Sheriff. As soon as she could, she changed out of her housedress and set off on her errands.

Billy skipped practice with the track team that afternoon; he lied to the coach and said he felt sick to his stomach. In fact, his stomach was starting to churn by the time he got home, and he barely made it to his bathroom before throwing up. He felt hot and feverish. All this turmoil and rage was beginning to take a toll on his normally placid existence. He was tired of putting up with everybody, and he just wanted everything to be fixed.

He was on his way to the kitchen to get something cold to drink, when Beamon met him in the hall. "After you get yourself a soda, come on in my office, Billy."

A few minutes later, Billy was esconced on the leather sofa, waiting for his grandfather to speak. 'Billy, you look as if you don't feel well."

"I'm all right," he grunted.

"I still feel that something might be bothering you. Want to tell me about it, son?"

Billy's brain felt hot and tired; he wanted someone else to carry out his vengeance. He was just too tired to do it himself, but he didn't really think his grandfather would be terribly interested in his thwarted love. Then, he remembered the conversation between Beamon and his father. Billy realized he did have something his grandfather might be interested in. When his grandfather was finished dealing with Grace, Billy felt sure his own desire for revenge would be adequately fulfilled also.

Billy came to life a little. "I've got something you might want to see, Grampaw. I'll be right back."

A few minutes later, he was back and appeared even more agitated. "I had found a letter, Grampaw. I think it used to belong to Miss Grace. Anyway, I had it in my jacket pocket, but now I can't find it. I guess it fell out at school yesterday."

Beamon was extremely pleased that this piece of information had made its way to him, but was careful to show no indication of his pleasure. "Tell me about this letter. Then you can go back to your room and search again. You may have overlooked it. Now, what did the letter say?"

"Well, it was addressed to the sheriff. It was real old. The wrong man was in prison. Something about a knife. And the church, I think. Throwing something and hiding the knife. I'm sorry, I can't remember any more, Grampaw."

It was worse than he thought. Grace Turner was probably aware by now of how Amos Canfield died. Drastic measures would have to be taken. "Where did you get the letter, Billy? I won't be angry, but I need to know exactly where you found it."

"You're not gonna be mad at me, right, Grampaw?"

"Absolutely not, I'm delighted that you found the letter. There will be no punishment, no matter how you obtained the letter."

"Well, I sort of took it from Miss Grace's room a couple of days ago."

Well, well, well. Like father, like son. Who would have thought little Billy could pull off such a feat? "Bravo, Billy. You went and took what you wanted. We all must do that at one time or another in our lives. Did you take anything besides the letter? No? Did you see other papers she had? Could you tell what she was working on?"

"Sir, it mostly looked like it was all about that man's murder. I didn't really sit and read any of it."

"Why did you choose to take just the letter and nothing else?"

"It .. looked familiar. Like I recognized it. It had blue flowers on it. So, I took it."

"All right. Now, Billy, I know something's been bothering you. Does it have anything to do with why you went in Miss Turner's room?"

Billy's anger finally erupted. "She's a two-timer! I wanted to make her hurt like she hurt me. I heard you tell Pa to keep an eye on her, so I thought I'd really get something on her if I went through her stuff. So I did," he said belligerently.

"I would have done the same thing, Billy. Now, go on back to your room and look for that letter. Come and tell me whether or not you find it. If you don't locate it, I want you to drive back to school before they lock up today and look for it there."

Billy had never been included in anything his grandfather did, nor been spoken to as an equal. It was a heady feeling, and he scurried to do exactly as his grandfather asked.

After a perfunctory knock on her door, Beamon entered Sadie's suite. It had been at least a year since he had been in these rooms. Neither the rooms nor his wife held any significance for him, so he kept an accounting of them only insofar as he considered them possessions of value. Sitting near the window to take advantage of the afternoon sun, she was writing letters in her spidery, delicate hand. "Good afternoon, Beamon," she said without looking up.

"Sadie. Where is Thelma?"

Sadie detected in his voice more than a casual question. She and Thelma had been right to remove the letter from the house as quickly as possible, she thought. She prayed that she would be able to present a calm, unconcerned demeanor so that he would not suspect anything. Grace's safety could well depend on her and Thelma.

Glancing up only for a moment, Sadie replied, "I'm sorry, dear, did you need her for something? I just sent her to the drugstore to get my prescription refilled. And then I believe she was going to run by the grocery to pick up a few things. She should be back, oh, by five o'clock, I would think. Can I do something for you, dear?"

"No, thank you. I'll just wait til she returns. Sorry to bother you."

"Not at all, dear." Sadie held her breath as he walked toward the door. Hopefully, he was convinced by her casual attitude, but she waited until she heard the door close to exhale.

Accustomed to being on the move all day every day, Grace had had enough of her desk work by four o'clock. She decided she deserved a treat after her afternoon's diligence, and the memory of a scoop of chocolate ice cream in a sugar cone came to mind. Perfect. It was a nice little walk to the diner across town; her appetite would be enormous by then. She threw a sweater across her shoulders, locked her door, and skipped down the stairs.

Billy kicked at a rock in the school parking lot. He hadn't found the letter. The one chance he had to prove himself to his Grampaw, and he had failed. As he drove back home, he became even more anxious about pleasing Beamon. It was more than not wanting to incur his wrath. He earnestly desired to gain his approval about something, about anything.

At the time Billy turned in the driveway, Beamon was just answering a call from Bo. "She's where? Eating ice cream. Stupid girl. Bo, answer this question for me. After we did Amos, what did you do with that knife? No, not the one the Preacher threw in the garbage. The one you used on Amos. … Up in the tree? Did you ever get it down? So, it's still there? You guess? Well, never mind about that now. Forget about following the girl. Come home. I need you here tonight."

Through the window, Beamon watched as Billy climbed the steps. He evidently didn't find the letter, from his dejected appearance. No matter. He would be that much easier to persuade when it came time to reel in the girl.

"I'm sorry, Grampaw. I looked everywhere. Maybe the janitor already swept it up and threw it away," Billy offered.

"It doesn't matter. We don't really need it. I'm just glad you told me about it, Billy. That means a lot to me."

Basking in the words of praise, Billy wouldn't have considered refusing whatever his Grampaw might ask of him next. "Billy, we're going to get back at Miss Grace Turner for you. She'll have a really good scare, and then she won't ever treat you like that again. How does that sound to you?"

"Yeah, Grampaw. Thanks. We'll show her a thing or two, won't we? What are we going to do?"

"Well, first we've got to trick her into thinking we have something she wants. How good an actor are you, Billy?"

Twenty-Three

Thelma was not having much success at completing her assigned tasks, except for picking up the prescription, of course. She tried several times to call Grace, but was told each time that she was out, and no one knew for how long. Then, she went to the Fairmount Chronicle, but they had closed early. Thelma was faced with a dilemna. What to do with the letter. She finally decided that she trusted Mr. Joe Wilson to do the right thing. She had already placed the letter in another envelope, so she wrote a brief note to Mr. Wilson asking him to be the caretaker of the letter, and slipped it under the door. Then, worried about what Sadie might have had to face, Thelma hurried straight home.

"All right, Billy, have you got it all straight?"

"Yes, sir."

"Good boy. Okay, dial up Miss Turner, and let's get this show on the road." Beamon rubbed his hands together in anticipation.

Grace was just walking through the front door when the phone rang. "Mees Grace, you have menee phone call to-day." One of the Philippine sisters handed Grace the receiver.

"Hello, this is Grace."

"Hi, Grace. This is Billy. Grace, I have to tell you something. You dropped something out of your bag the other day, and I kept it."

"A letter, Billy?" Grace knew he was lying, but hoped by playing along she could get the letter back, unharmed.

"Yes, ma'am. I'm really sorry about it. But anyway, I read the letter and I guess you're looking for that knife that was thrown away, the one that they used to kill Amos with."

"Ye-es," Grace said cautiously.

"Well, I know where the knife is, Grace. I can take you to it, if you want. But we have to hurry. Somebody knows you're looking for it, and they'll move it pretty soon, maybe even tonight. So you've got to come now. Right this very minute."

"Billy, I can't come this very minute. I'm not going to. I don't even know where you're taking me. No, I don't like the way that sounds. It's too dangerous. I'll just take my chances on losing the knife."

Beamon was writing a note to Billy, telling him what to say, when Bo came sauntering through the office door. "But, Grace, if you don't have the knife, how will Preacher James ever get out of jail?"

Bo listened with amazement to the words coming out of his son's mouth. If not for his father glaring him down, he would have snatched the phone from Billy's hand the moment he walked in.

On the other end of the line, Grace was considering Billy's words. She knew Ethan would be mightily upset with her for doing something so terribly foolish, but the possibility of actually having the evidence to free James tilted the scales toward meeting Billy wherever he said.

"I can't believe I'm saying this, but okay. Where do you want me to meet you?"

"Do you know where the road to the mine is, off the old Heaven's Mountain Road?"

"Yes, I remember."

"Meet me there. Leave right now. Just grab your purse and come."

"Okay, I'm on my way." After hanging up, Grace quickly dialed the number for the church office. No one answered, but she left Ethan a message telling him where she was going, and that she hoped to be back in time for their dinner date. As she grabbed her purse and ran for the door, Grace told the Philippine sisters, who happened to be the only ones in the house at the time, "If anybody wants to know where I am, tell them I went to the mine."

"The mine. The mine."

"That's right. The mine."

Open-mouthed in amazement, Billy watched as his father rampaged through the office. He had never before seen him so agitated. Bo seemed ready to jump out of his skin as he stopped short in front of Beamon. "You leave my boy alone. He has no part in this, you hear me?" Bo's voice rose several levels as Beamon gave him no response. "You ruined my life – you're not going to ruin his! Leave – him – alone!"

Beamon calmly said, "There's not going to be a problem. Everything will work out fine. I've got it all taken care of. Just do as I say, both of you, and there will be no problem."

Billy's attitude was swiftly changing from vengeful, rebellious teen-ager to timid, scared child. He sat as far back as he could in the big wing-back chair, eying his father and his grandfather with trepidation. What had he done? He just wanted to teach Grace a lesson, make her hurt as he did. Now he was afraid that something bad was going to happen – to Grace, and maybe even to him.

"Thelma! Oh, I'm so glad you're back. I think they're up to no good, but I couldn't get close enough to hear them. I did try, dear!" Sadie's words tumbled out the moment she saw her companion coming up the back steps.

"I'm sure you did. I had to leave the letter under the door at the newspaper building. Miss Grace wasn't at home. What do you think is going on, Sadie? Where are the men?"

"I don't know where they went. They left about five minutes ago. Beamon and Bo – and they took Billy with them, too. Why would they take Billy, Thelma?"

"Mmnn. I don't know about that. I don't like it, Miss Sadie. Billy shouldn't be with them; you know that, too."

"They left in the jeep, all three of them. Does that mean anything?"

"Beats me. Were they in the office? Let's go look around, see if we can tell what they were doing. One of us can keep a look-out, while the other one rummages around."

"I'll stand watch, dear. I'm so flustered, I wouldn't know a clue if it bit me on the finger!"

The closer Grace got to the mine, the more uncertain she was that she should be going alone, in the dark, to meet Billy. Twice she pulled over on the shoulder of the road to have a discussion with herself. "This is completely illogical. Billy probably has no idea what he's talking about. Wherever the knife is, it will still be there tomorrow, when Ethan can go with me. But what if Beamon or Bo is about to retrieve the knife and put it somewhere else, somewhere we'll never find it. The knife is important. It could still have traces of Amos' blood on it. We need that knife. James needs that knife. Nothing is going to happen to me. What could possibly happen? This is silly. I'm going to meet Billy, get the knife, and take it straight to the sheriff's office." Having thus convinced herself, Grace once more pulled her little bug back on the road, and continued up the mountain.

At the insistence of the Leach family, Ethan had spent an hour or so after the funeral at the family's home. Though they urged him to stay and eat dinner with them, he was able to graciously decline and now, was debating whether he should swing by the church office to check his messages or go straight home to get ready for his dinner date with Grace. He did a quick "systems check", and decided his body needed a few minutes of down time before going to pick up Grace.

He had changed into slacks and a knit shirt, fed the dog, and was lying across the bed to rest his eyes for a few minutes. All in all, it had been a good day. This had been one of those uplifting funerals where, in the midst of the grieving, there was celebration - of God's goodness and of the hope shared by the family of faith. A good day so far, and even more to look forward to this evening. "Thank you, Father. You are so good to me. I can't count your blessings; they're like the stars at night.

Thank you, thank you." Ethan relaxed into the pillow and breathed deeply. Then, like a little trickle of water, building slowly, growing into a rushing stream, the urgency of Grace's need made itself known to him. He uttered her name to God, asking without words for a physical and spiritual shield around the young woman.

Twenty-Four

The tiny automobile hit another huge pothole and rebounded a foot into the air, causing Grace's head to hit the headliner of the car. Thankfully, she was literally at the end of the road. Straight ahead, in the beam of her headlights, Grace could see the trappings of the old edifice. In front of the mine's entrance was an old, battered jeep, with Billy waving beside it. She drove just past his feet and rolled down her window.

With no pleasantries, no smile, she held out her hand and said, "Give me the knife now, Billy." He was obviously nervous, and couldn't seem to make himself look straight at her.

"It's in the mine. I can't get it by myself. You'll have to help me." Billy's eyes kept sliding over to the left, toward the mine.

Something was definitely not right here. No way was she getting out of her car and going into that pitch black tunnel. She was just about to say as much to Billy when her passenger door was snatched open. Before she could grab hold of her keys in the ignition, her own door was opened and she was being dragged out of the car by Bo. She could see Beamon reaching inside, getting the car keys and her purse. Knowing she was doomed if they got her into the mine, Grace began kicking, scratching and yelling for help. The last thing she remembered seeing was Bo's beefy fist coming toward her face.

Ethan had continued to pray even as he prepared to go pick Grace up for dinner. As he passed near the church, he felt a need to stop in and check his messages. He was somewhat used to following the gentle leadings of the Spirit when they came, and he had plenty of time, so without any hesitation, he turned down the street and into the church parking lot.

Floating in and out of consciousness, Grace could hear men's voices raised in anger. Occasionally she heard her own name mentioned, but she couldn't focus her mind enough to understand what was being discussed. She was lying in a very uncomfortable position, she knew that much. She just didn't have the energy to get her muscles to cooperate in realigning her body. Finally, after several minutes of bearing the discomfort, she mustered her faculties and began concentrating on one limb at the time, slowly sliding around until she had achieved a better arrangement. The movement brought home to her the unhappy fact that her hands and feet were bound.

Up to this point, her eyes had remained closed. Now, she cracked one eyelid, and tried to get her bearings. The men were still some little distance away from her, their anger having diminished to a quieter level, but she recognized the voices now, which brought clearly back to her memory the events leading up to her present calamity. There was very little light, wherever she was, barely enough to see her own hands tied in front of her. The men were barely distinguishable, standing fifty or sixty feet away from her near the far wall of what must be a huge natural cave, probably tied into the mine tunnels somehow.

Though her head was aching terribly, Grace had enough wits about her to realize that her best course of action for the moment was to lie still, work on unobtrusively loosening her bonds, and, most important, listen to the men talk. Maybe she could find out what their plans were before they realized she was no longer unconscious.

Beamon was speaking, "There's no other possible choice. Do you want to spend the rest of your life in prison? I'm not going to. And what about your son and your mother? Where will they live when our home and all our money is taken away?"

"But, why would we lose the house, or the money? And as for going to jail, I don't know if I care anymore. Living with this all my life has been like living in hell."

"Oh, you have no idea of what hell will be like 'til you hit that prison, boy. You ought to be willing to do anything to keep from going there. And losing everything? You remember how we got this mine don't you? Everything else we've got came from the gold from down in this hole. After they make a claim against us for the entire fortune from the mining, there won't be anything left. We'll be scraping the bottom of the barrel for the legal fees we'll have to pay to defend you, worthless as you are."

"Hey, I'm not the only one responsible for Amos, in case you've forgotten. And that I.O.U. wasn't paid to me, either." Bo was getting agitated again. "Everything you touch turns nasty and mean and filthy. You're not getting Billy. No matter what happens, Billy is out of it. I'll kill you, old man, without a shred of guilt, if you make a move to pull him in."

"That's fine, Bo. We don't need Billy. As long as you do what needs to be done, Billy can go, right now, as far as I'm concerned. The only thing is, can you guarantee his silence? Bo?"

"Yeah, he'll keep quiet. But whether you get his cooperation or mine depends on what you have in mind. I'm not doing the girl. Not gonna do it again." Bo began walking in a tight circle, muttering under his breath, "Not gonna do it. Not gonna do it this time."

"You won't have to do anything except keep her knocked out. We're going to leave here, and you're going to put on those gloves and drive her and her car to the gorge just the other side of the old Canfield place. You send her over the edge, and that's the end of our problem. You keep to the woods, all the way home. It's almost all downhill, shouldn't take you more than two or three hours. By the time they get around to seriously looking for her, you'll be home, asleep."

"Don't you think they're going to come looking for us, seeing as how she came up here to the mine tonight?"

"Maybe at first, at least until they read the letters Billy wrote to Grace."

"What are you talking about? What letters?"

"Letters I found in his room, saying how much he loved her. So, you see, he called her to meet him here at the mine, she came, they had a fight, and she left. Billy came home, which we can all vouch for. What happened after that has nothing to do with you, me, or Billy."

Bo was quiet, considering Beamon's plan. "I just don't know." He walked away from Beamon, towards where Grace lay unmoving on the floor. Only he veered slightly to the right and ended up at her back. Grace kept her eyes shut and tried to regulate her breathing so that it was slow and smooth. Behind her, she heard Bo scuffling in the dirt a bit. He must have knelt down because his voice was coming from closer to the ground now. In a low voice, he spoke, "Billy. I know you're not asleep. Sit up and talk to me." She heard movement.

"What do you want?" Billy replied.

Bo's voice was no more than a whisper now. "Listen to me carefully, son. I know I haven't been much of a father to you. But I'm about to tell you some things you need to know. I did some real bad things when I was young, and haven't done much with the rest of my life since then. Your grandpa wants me to hurt Miss Grace, but I just can't do it. I'm not going to do it. So, son, no matter what happens in the next few minutes, I want you to get yourself and Miss Grace out of here. Alive. Can I count on you to do that?"

"Yes, sir." Billy's voice shook slightly when he answered.

"Good. Now, I'm going to pretend to your Grandpa that I'm going along with him. See if you can untie Grace, but you can't let him see you working on it. I'll try to keep him turned the other way. Okay? You ready?"

"Yes, daddy."

"Good. I love you, son. I'm sorry I haven't told you that more often. I love you and I'm proud of you." With that, Bo got up and headed back across the cave.

Twenty-Five

Thelma didn't recognize the phone number she found on a crumpled piece of paper in the office waste basket, but she was dialing it now. The only other thing written on the paper was "knife", which did not sound particularly good.

"Boarding house," came the voice over the phone.

The boarding house? So that's who they called. "Uh, yes, is – uh – Miss Grace Turner there?"

"No, no. She ees not here," one of the sisters said.

"Can you tell me where she went? It's very important that I speak to her," Thelma insisted.

"Jus' a minute, plees." Thelma could hear two female voices chattering.

"Mees Grace has gone to 'hers'," she stated.

Thelma had her repeat her answer several times, but could never figure it out. She finally thanked the sister and hung up. Sadie had come back to the office and Thelma repeated the conversation, hoping she might be able to translate better than Thelma had.

"Let me call her this time, dear. Perhaps she will say it in a different way."

Sadie went through the entire question and answer process again, with identical results, until she asked, "Just what exactly did Grace say to you, dear?"

The sister patiently replied, "She say, 'if anyone ask you, tell them I go to mine.' She go to hers, just like I tell you before."

"Oh. Oh, so you did, dear. Thank you so much. You have helped us immensely." A little giggle slipped out as Sadie hung up the phone. "Thelma, she's gone to the mine. I'll explain it later. Do you think that's where Beamon and the boys went? To the mine?"

"Probably so. They always do use that old jeep when they go the back road to the mine. Miss Sadie, I'll leave this up to you, because that's your husband and your son and your grandson. If it was up to me, I'd call the sheriff. But whatever you decide is what we'll do." Thelma waited for Sadie's answer.

"You're absolutely right, Thelma. We cannot leave that poor girl defenseless. Call the sheriff."

While Thelma was dialing the number, she asked, "Miss Sadie, I hate to ask this, but do you think that Mr. Beamon might have this sheriff in his pocket the way he did the one before him?"

"I don't really know. I suppose we'll just have to take the chance."

After explaining their concerns to the dispatcher, Thelma replaced the receiver, and told Sadie, "They got sent out to another call just a few minutes ago. Right before I called. They're working a wreck on the other side of Fairmount, but he said they'd get someone up here as soon as they could."

"Thelma, dear, I'm going to the mine. I have a feeling that if I'm there, nothing will happen to Grace or Billy. But, I don't think you should go with me…"

Thelma interrupted her, "Of course, I'm going with you. The very idea that I'd let you go to that old mine by yourself!" Thelma grumbled and continued mumbling as she left the room. "You'd better get your coat. It'll be cold inside the mountain."

Before Bo had gotten halfway back across the cavern, Beamon passed him, heading straight for Grace and Billy. "There's been a change of plans, Bo. Apparently, you've forgotten how every little whisper carries in these caves. Whatever little rescue attempt you were planning, you can forget it." Beamon now stood over Billy, who had stopped trying to scoot closer to Grace when he saw his grandfather heading his way. Beamon now had a gun pointed at Billy's head. "Now, first of all, we won't be untying Miss Turner. Indeed, the new plan is to tie Billy's hands so that he won't be so tempted to help her. Bo, as you can see, I am in control of this situation. Oh, and if you're looking for the gun that was in your jacket pocket, don't trouble yourself. I've already taken care of that for you. So, unless you want to see your son's brains spattered all over the ground, you will do everything I tell you to do, starting with tying Billy's hands. And I want them tied tight."

Bo hesitated more than a few seconds. His father's gun was only about three feet away from Billy's head. He knew Beamon could and would pull the trigger before he could try to wrest the gun from him. For the present, he would have to do as Beamon said, bide his time and wait for an opportunity to jump him. That decision made, he took the rope Beamon threw at him, and secured Billy's wrists.

"What now?" Bo asked.

Sadie and Thelma had parked some distance behind the jeep, and were slowly and carefully making their way across the rocky terrain in the dark. They had come alongside the vehicle, and Sadie was using it to keep her balance. On her other side, Thelma, turning her head to speak, failed to notice a rut washed out by the rain; her foot slid on some loose gravel and twisted sideways into the ditch. Her legs buckled beneath her and she cried out in pain.

"Oh, dadgum it, I think I sprained my ankle!"

"Oh, dear, let me help you. Do you think you can stand on it?"

"Maybe. If I can get up, I might could. I don't know if you're strong enough to hold any of my weight, Miss Sadie."

"Pish, posh. I'm a lot stronger than I look. I've told you that for years, Thelma, dear. Just let me get a good stance, and then you must turn on your side, use your good leg to push up. That's it; not too fast. There we go. Now, if you lean on me a little, can you make it back to the car?"

"Yes, ma'am. I'm sorry I've messed everything up, Miss Sadie."

"Nonsense. You've been my constant help for years, dear. Even if by some rare chance, you did make a mess, I would forgive you instantly." She squeezed Thelma's hand. "You know you are my dearest friend, don't you?"

Thelma's eyes were teary, from the pain, and now from the compliments. "I feel the same way, ma'am."

While Thelma leaned on the hood of the car, Sadie opened the driver's side door for her. Coming back around, she guided Thelma until she was able to sit down. "I'm going to go in now. Do you think you can drive back down to the highway, maybe leave your headlights on, and tell the sheriff's deputy where to find us when he gets here?"

"Yes'm. But I don't like the idea of you going in there by yourself."

"The hard part is getting safely to the entrance. The ground is really quite smooth once you get inside. I went in there quite a lot while the mine was in operation. I'll really be fine, dear. Now, please, go on down to the highway for me, all right? I have a feeling the sheriff's deputy's help is going to be needed, and soon."

Twenty-Six

"$\mathcal{N}$ow, we're going to take a nice long walk. Bo, you remember the big ravine, the one we had to bridge to get to the last part of the vein? That's where we're going. Miss Turner, as it turns out, has terrible balance. In fact, I'm afraid she's going to lose her footing and fall right in to that bottomless gully." The blood lust in Beamon's eyes was sickening to Bo. He had watched and listened to his father long enough to know that Beamon, assuming he had heard all of Bo's conversation with Billy, would never let Bo's disloyalty go unpunished. Or Billy's either, for that matter. He would be willing to bet that all three of them would end up dead at the bottom of the abyss, victims of the fall, and probably of gunshot wounds also.

After a lifetime of following Beamon's perverted orders, something snapped in Bo. He wanted better for his boy. A different life. A good life, with good people around him. People like Miss Grace Turner.

Beamon continued, "Bo, you're going to carry the girl." He waved his gun toward Grace. "Pick her up. Billy, stand up. Let's get going."

At the opening to the cavern, Sadie stood motionless in the shadows, listening and watching. Bo made no move toward Grace. Billy was standing now, waiting to see what his father was going to do.

"Did you hear what I said, boy? Pick up the girl!" Beamon was shouting now. Still Bo did not move. Beamon's voice became even more shrill and out of control. "Do you think you can disobey me? You're nothing without me. You would have nothing if not for me. You're just a stupid, worthless piece of trash! Now, pick up that girl. Do you hear me?"

"I hear you, but I'm not gonna do it! I'm getting my son, and this lady, and we're gonna walk out of here. I know what you're planning to do when we get to that ravine, and I'm not gonna let that happen. Not this time."

"I'll shoot all three of you. Don't think I won't. I'll drag you one by one and drop you over the edge like the sacks of dung you are." Beamon walked over to Billy and held the barrel of the gun against his grandson's forehead. "You pick up the girl now, or I'll put a bullet through his head."

Bo had no intention of allowing Beamon to carry out his scheme, but for the moment, he wanted that gun pointed somewhere other than Billy's head. He bent down and picked Grace up, noticing that she was not out cold as she had appeared to be, but stared straight into his eyes, obviously aware of every single thing that had been said. He tried not to let his surprise show, especially as Grace was continuing to make her body totally limp. As he had hoped, Beamon lowered the gun from Billy, and now had it pointed at Bo, motioning with the barrel towards the opening on the opposite side of the cave. Bo took a few steps, then pretended to stumble. He went to his knees, tossed Grace a little roughly to the ground, then sprang back up to face his father. Billy was to the side, out of the line of fire, and Grace was on the ground behind Bo, still pretending to be unconscious.

"This is where it ends, Pa. We're not going down there to die. Now, you can shoot, maybe once, before I'm on top of you. But, if you don't shoot me right in the heart the first time, I'm taking that gun away from you, and if you make me, I'll shoot you. Either way, alive, wounded, or dead, you're going out of this mine, and you're going to have to pay, just like I am, for the wrongs you've done. It's your choice which way you go out of here."

By the light of the lantern, Beamon's eyes were gleaming with a crazed, feral shine. His eyeballs were trembling and jumping in their sockets, whether from pure rage or from evil unfulfilled. Even in the cold chamber, his face was dripping with sweat. Through clenched teeth, he forced each word out in a voice like sandpaper. "You're – all – dead! Dead! Dead!" He straightened his gun arm so that the gun was aimed at Bo's chest, less than ten feet away. His finger was already on the trigger when he saw Bo looking in horror just to the side of Beamon. Bo stretched out his arms, moving toward Beamon, his mouth forming the word "No-o-o!". From the corner of his eye, Beamon saw a blur of movement coming from behind and as he started pulling the trigger, he saw someone grab the barrel, pulling it away from Bo and toward themselves. The gunshot echoed all around them, over and over in the cavernous chamber, followed by a gentle rumbling, the mountain's restrained answer to the reverberation of the gunshot.

Beamon stared down at Bo who was kneeling beside a crumpled form, a woman. An old woman with white hair. He realized, with a detached sort of interest, that it was his wife. What was she doing here? Just another complication to deal with, he thought, as he raised the gun again.

Billy recognized his grandmother and fell down beside her, weeping. Before Beamon could prepare himself, Bo launched himself from the floor with an anguished roar. The two large men grappled with each other for the gun, twisting and turning, landing mostly glancing blows, until Beamon, using the gun as a bludgeon, caught Bo full force on the side of the head. Stumbling backward, Bo released his hold on Beamon, who, as soon as he was free, raised the gun and shot Bo in the stomach.

Bo staggered back with the force of the shot. Grabbing his abdomen, he doubled over. Beamon stood over him, watching with no emotion at all as his only surviving son struggled to live.

Meanwhile, in the shadows, Grace had been frantically working to untie the knots in the rope binding her ankles. With her wrists bound also, it seemed to be an impossible task. She couldn't get a decent grasp on the right loop to loosen it. Frustrated, she was in tears when she felt a pair of hands taking over the job for her. Billy! Working quietly but quickly he was able to remove the ropes from her legs. He moved to start on her wrists, but stopped momentarily when she took his hands in hers and mouthed the words, "Thank you". His only response was a slight nod of the head. She saw that he still had the ropes around his wrist, so she pushed his hands aside from her bonds, and began untying his first.

Satisfied that Bo no longer represented a threat, Beamon turned his attention back to the young people. Sniffing in disdain, he noted their pathetic attempts to untie each other. Little good it would do them, he thought, against the bullets he planned to plant in their heads. Thinking of the most efficient way to proceed, he figured he should probably shoot Billy first, since he was now completely free of the ropes that had bound his wrists.

Billy had seen Beamon turn back towards them, and had put himself between Beamon and Grace, moving away from her a few feet. When Beamon came to stand above Billy, Grace began to edge around, sliding into the shadows against the wall, as Billy cried and pleaded, "Grampaw, don't. Please, don't. I thought you cared about us. Why are you doing this, Grampaw?"

In a calm and reasonable voice, Beamon replied, "I don't have any choice, Billy. This was all your father's fault. Anyway, quit blubbering and take it like a man." With that, Beamon raised the gun to fire. As he pulled the trigger, his arm was knocked askew as Grace rammed into him with the full force of her body, making him fall to the ground. Knowing she did not stand a chance in a frontal fight, she rolled back into the shadows. Billy had also seen the wisdom of being less in the light, and had found the shadows on the other side. After this last shot, there were even more rumbles all around them, coming from every direction now, it seemed. From a distance, a different kind of roar could be heard, starting low and now growing louder.

As Beamon regained his feet, he headed towards Grace. He could see enough of her shape to know exactly where she was. He was in such a fit of temper now that he scarcely paid attention to all the warning signs of the mine. He fired at Grace, once, twice, but his eyesight had changed, and his marksmanship was not what it once was. He missed completely both times. The air around them was growing dusty, and the floor seemed to be trembling now. Even Beamon was beginning to take notice. He walked straight towards Grace, though she was attempting to keep moving along the wall, hoping to allow no decrease in the distance between them, but he did seem to be closing in. The roar was growing more insistent, getting closer and closer. Beamon raised his gun once more, and this time Grace had a sinking feeling that he might not miss. She was looking directly into his eyes through the swirls of dust between them, and could see that he was enjoying her fear. She knew his slight smile meant that he was about to shoot her. She closed her eyes and braced herself. The shot came. She heard the sound of it, hitting the wall above her head. She looked across the chamber, and there was Bo, holding both of Beamon's arms aloft. Beamon used his foot to knock one of Bo's legs out from under him. They fell to the ground, locked in each other's grip, the stronger but wounded, versus the more experienced and mean. Grace was running towards them, hoping to do – she didn't know what – when another deadly shot rang out, this one muffled by the bodies above and below the weapon,

The growling in the ground and above their heads had reached an ear-shattering level, and the dust had all but obscured the meager light provided by the lantern. Grace coughed and rubbed her eyes. Just a few more feet and she should be at the spot where the two men lay. She could barely hear Billy calling to her.

"Grace? Where are you? Are you okay? Grace!"

"Right here, Billy. Over here. I'm all right," Grace answered. "Billy, come toward my voice." Shifting her attention, she saw, at her feet, Beamon lying on top of Bo's body, neither of them moving. Bending down, she grasped Beamon by the shoulders and tried to push him off of Bo. The older man was dead weight. Billy appeared on the other side and began pulling as she pushed. Together they shoved Beamon to the floor. Bo was still not moving, not breathing. As Billy clutched his father's head in his hands, Bo took in a ragged breath, and his eyes fluttered open then back shut.

"Dad! Please don't die!" Billy whimpered.

"..Not going anywhere, sport," his father whispered.

"Grace! Billy! Anybody! Is anybody there?" Grace thought she had never heard such a sweet sound in her life as the voice of Ethan calling through the dark and dust, over the continued rumbling in the mine. On the other side of the cavern, from the direction of the doorway, the beam of his flashlight was barely visible. She stood and waited anxiously to see him materialize from the clouds of swirling dust. When she could finally make him out, she immediately ran to him. Fearing that she would completely fall apart now that he was here for her to lean on, she forced herself to give him a status report.

"Beamon and Bo have both been shot. And Ethan, Sadie was shot, too. I think she's probably dead. Bo is breathing, but just barely. Beamon may still be alive, but I don't know. We need to check him, and Sadie, too. The gunshots - the shots must be causing reverberations in the tunnels and caves. The rumbling started right after the shots, and it's gotten worse with each one."

By this time, they were kneeling over Beamon. There seemed to be no sign of life, no pulse, no breathing, no response of any kind. When they got to Sadie, it was obvious that she, too, was gone. Gently, Grace straightened the gentlewoman's limbs and arranged her clothing as decently as possible. She pushed the hair back from Sadie's face and used her fingers to style it in a becoming way. Then, bending down, she closed the eyes that had sparkled with such inner peace and placed a kiss on the paper thin skin.

Ethan said, "The sheriff's office has already dispatched someone, Thelma told me, but because they were busy on the other side of the county, it may take them a few more minutes to get here. Let's go see about Bo now."

Billy was still kneeling beside Bo, though it was clear he was not comfortable with the blood and visible wounds his father had sustained. He seemed happy to yield his place up to Ethan.

Sensing his distress, Ethan suggested that Billy wait outside the mine entrance for the law enforcement officers to arrive, and ask them to call an ambulance for his father, and the coroner for his grandparents. Billy appeared grateful to have something to do that required no special skills, and went straightaway to accomplish his assigned duties.

No sooner had he left the chamber than an explosion rocked the entire mine. Pieces of rock and debris were falling throughout the cavern. Ethan stretched his body over Bo's in an attempt to keep the dust and debris from contaminating the wound. Then, from over next to the entrance, the entire ceiling began falling in, huge rocks and support beams, one after the other, piling up on the floor.

"Ethan, what should we do?" Grace yelled.

"Is there any other way out of here?" he yelled back.

"I didn't see one."

Then, Grace felt a tugging at her sleeve. Looking down, she saw Bo's mouth moving. Leaning close, she heard him say, "Over there, where the walls make a corner. The walls don't really meet. Go through there." He pointed to the far corner of the room. He tugged at her again. She heard him say, "Go without me. I'm dying. You can make it if you leave me."

After telling Ethan what Bo said, Grace told him, "We're not leaving you. We'll be as careful as we can, but it's probably going to be painful for you. I'm sorry."

"If we help you stand, do you think you can work with us to walk towards that corner?" Ethan asked.

Bo whispered, "I'll try."

With Ethan and Grace supporting Bo on each side, they managed to pull him to his feet. A rock the size of her fist hit Grace in the head, momentarily dazing her, but Ethan managed to hold Bo up on his own, until she was able to resume their journey. One of the beams hit Ethan a glancing blow, also, cutting a gash in his forearm and causing him to drop his flashlight, but he somehow retrieved it and they were able to cross the rest of the room being hit by only smaller debris. The dust was actually more of a problem, as it was now so thick their noses and throats were completely coated and breathing was not just difficult, it was becoming almost impossible.

Finally, they reached the false corner, and entered the narrow tunnel, turning sideways as they went through so they could continue to hold Bo.

Outside, Billy heard the explosion, tried to go back in, but was completely blocked by stones and beams across the entryway. When he went back outside, he heard Thelma calling his name. Going to her, he collapsed into her arms, exhausted from the emotional roller coaster of the last few days. When he had cried himself out, he was able finally to give Thelma the heartbreaking news about Sadie. Holding each other then in truly shared agony, they remained that way until Billy saw the headlights of the sheriff's car come into view. Jumping out, he explained the need for an ambulance and the coroner, as well as the new complications presented by the mine caving in. The officer radioed in for help, and they all settled down to wait for reinforcements.

Once through the connecting tunnel, Ethan, Grace and Bo were standing in what appeared to be a natural tunnel, augmented by man with support beams, shelving and wiring. The dust diminished drastically, which was a huge relief. Bo directed them, telling them which way to travel down the tunnel, and where to turn off into another tunnel.

Due to the extra care required to ease Bo along, they were traveling at an extremely slow rate. A half an hour after leaving the large chamber, they were resting, sitting with their backs against the wall of the tunnel. It didn't seem as if they had traveled very far at all. After catching her breath, Grace did a quick check on Bo. Though his clothing was wet with blood, the bleeding had slowed. Using Bo's knife, she cut off the lower part of his once-white T-shirt, and, using that and a red bandana she found in his jacket pocket, she made a pressure bandage to cover the wound. While she was working on him, Ethan prayed aloud, thanking God for their safety, asking for healing for Bo, and for God's mercy on Sadie and Beamon. It occurred to Ethan that Bo might not be conscious for the entire journey out of the caves, so he asked Bo, who was already not entirely lucid, about where the tunnels led and how they could make their way to the outside. In general, it seemed that the alternate entrance to the mine was at a slightly higher elevation and to the east of the main entrance. The tunnels, according to Bo, would lead down and around the side of the mountain, before turning deeper into the mountain and rising about fifty feet. Bo was starting to lose consciousness again, but said something about a bridge. Ethan tried to make mental notes of all he said, in case it became necessary to find their way out without Bo's help.

"Please tell me you have fresh batteries in that flashlight," Grace said.

"I have fresh batteries in the flashlight," Ethan teased.

"No, really. Do you?"

"I really do. After your incident on the highway yesterday, I replaced all my flashlight batteries, checked my emergency kits, the whole nine yards."

"Wow. You're a genius. Or maybe you're obsessively neurotic. I really don't care which at this point." Grace leaned her head on Ethan's shoulder. It felt wonderful. And even better when he put his arm around her shoulder and pulled her closer. Her practical mind took charge for a moment though, as she instructed him, "Turn off the flashlight while we're just sitting here. We might need every minute of power later."

"You're right," Ethan agreed, and switched the light off, leaving the three of them in pitch black darkness.

Twenty-Seven

than eased his shoulder out from under Grace's head and lowered her to his folded jacket. He figured they had been resting about twenty minutes. Switching on the flashlight, he checked his watch. Only eight thirty. Sliding across to where Bo lay, he checked to be sure that the bleeding had not started again. His hands were gently pushed aside by Grace, as she adjusted the make-shift bandage and checked his pulse and respirations.

"You look like you know what you're doing," he said.

"I took some basic EMT courses at college. Actually, I worked a couple of summers with the ambulance service, too." She looked up with a little smug smile.

"Oh. I gotcha. When we were at the athletic field for field day, you knew exactly what you were doing with that broken leg, didn't you?"

"Mmm-hmmm. I took care of my uncle for about a year, too. He died of cancer a few months ago," she murmured, intent on her work. "Hold the light over this way. It's okay. You didn't know me very well then."

"Thanks for being so gracious about my acting like an idiot."

"Oh, were you acting like an idiot? I didn't notice," she teased, while rebuttoning Bo's clothing. "Well, I'm afraid that's all we can do for him.

He should be in a hospital, not a cold, damp cave. We need to keep a close watch on him to be sure he doesn't start bleeding. It's a through and through wound, though, I think, and I don't see any signs of internal bleeding, so I think it's worth the risk to try to keep moving toward a way out of here."

"I hope I can remember the directions he gave me. It doesn't look like we'll be able to ask him again, does it? I think if we keep on staying to the left, until the floor starts rising, then sort of bear to the right, maybe we'll happen upon the second entrance. I'm hoping that Billy's explained the situation to the law enforcement folks. Maybe someone will think to come in from the other side and start searching for us. That's assuming they know about that entrance. Bo made it sound as if the other mine opening might have been a secret."

"Do you think we're going to able to manage Bo's weight between us?"

"If he rouses up and helps a little, we can make it. If not, I can carry him a short distance, but not for more than ten or fifteen minutes at the time."

"Resting in between, that will be pretty slow going. But, looking on the bright side, we'll have lots of time to get to know each other better." Even in the dim light, Ethan could see the genuine warmth in her smile.

"I'd like that," he said with sincerity.

It took several minutes, but they were finally able to get some response from Bo. He indicated his willingness to walk, so they carefully assisted him in rising to his feet. Ever so slowly, they resumed following the beam of the flashlight as it illuminated only the tunnel floor a few feet ahead of them.

So began the routine of that long night. They would travel several hundred feet, then rest for fifteen or twenty minutes. Then repeat the process, over and over. During their stops, Ethan and Grace took turns sharing stories from their childhoods. By four o'clock in the morning, they had covered most of the highlights up through their high school years, and talking had become less pleasurable. They were all getting sleepy and tired. By unanimous consent, they agreed that getting a few hours sleep would be more beneficial in the long run than trying to continue in their exhausted state.

They found a fairly level spot in the tunnel and made Bo as comfortable as they could. Grace was thankful she had grabbed a heavy sweater before leaving the boarding house. Ethan had also come somewhat prepared with a lined windbreaker, so they settled down a couple of feet from each other. Even with her arms covered, after the group stopped moving, the cold of the cave seemed to bore into Grace's bones, and within a minute or two, she couldn't control the chattering of her teeth. Ethan, who was only slightly warmer himself, heard her shivering. "I hear your teeth chattering," he said softly. "Grace?"

"Wh-what?"

"Because of the circumstances, maybe we should make the most efficient use of our bodies' heat and lie close together. I can promise you that nothing will happen other than two friends trying to stay warm."

"Oh, th-thank goodness! Oh, I meant, thank goodness you're going to help me get warm, not thank goodness n-nothing will happen." Grace was so cold from lying on the cold ground, and shivering so much, that she didn't wait for Ethan to move towards her. As she spoke, she was already sliding up right next to Ethan, and was curling into the warmth of his shoulder.

Though it was still a far cry from her usual comfy bed, Grace was so tired that, once the cold became moderately bearable, she was out like a light.

"What time is it?" Grace asked as she rubbed her arms and legs which were aching from the night spent on the cold ground.

Feeling around for the flashlight, Ethan finally put his hand on it and then checked his watch. "Not quite nine o'clock."

"I would love to sleep some more, but my body can't take lying here one more minute." Crawling over to Bo, she motioned to Ethan. "Come over here and give me some light while I check him. Bo? Can you hear me? Bo. Wake up now." Grace noted that he was beginning to move a little, then Bo opened his eyes slightly. "Good morning. How are you feeling, Bo?"

"Like a truck ran over me," he mumbled. "I'm thirsty."

"Bo, we're in the tunnels in the mine, remember? I'm afraid we don't have any water," Ethan reminded him.

"Oh, yeah. How far have we come?"

Ethan answered, "My guess would be almost half a mile. Of course, I could be wrong."

"Have we passed the place where there's a huge rock sticking out on the left side of the tunnel?"

"Uh, yes, we did," Grace grumbled. "My head made contact with that rock right before we stopped to sleep."

"Then, we've got about that much farther to go before we get to the other outside doorway."

Grace wanted to groan aloud, but didn't want to come across as the complaining female. Instead, she tried to be encouraging, saying, "That's not too bad. We can handle that. About seven or eight more hours and we'll be on our way home. Bo, do you feel like you can get up and walk? Your bullet wounds don't look any worse than last night to me."

"You guys can leave me if you want. I'm just slowing you down."

Ethan said, "No way. We're not going without you. If you don't think you can walk, we'll just wait here with you until someone finds us."

"Okay, okay. I'll try. Just help me up."

"Just a second, Bo. I think we need to take a minute to pray." Ethan grabbed each of their hands. "Father, thank you for your mercy in sparing our lives. Please, especially strengthen Bo today for the difficult task ahead. Be with us and guide us safely to our destination. Thank you, Father. In the name of Jesus, we ask these things of you. Amen." With that, the three of them got to their feet, and started down the dark tunnel once again.

The day continued much as the night had, but with far less conversation. With Ethan and Grace bearing some of his weight, Bo was able to keep up with the physical pace, but after an hour or so, he began to alternate between talking out of his head, and refusing to speak at all.

Grace and Ethan were silent, feeling a need to conserve all of their energy for the physical task of assisting Bo. The hours of going without water were taking a toll on all of them. Though she tried not to dwell on the way she was feeling, Grace found her attention concentrated time after time on her dry mouth. She had the thought that someday she might look back on this ordeal and actually laugh. She decided that she would remind herself at that time that some things were never funny and should not be laughed at. She noticed that Ethan's energy appeared to be flagging just a bit, too. His attitude never wavered, however. He occasionally spoke to her or Bo, words of encouragement or praise, and was unfailingly patient when they needed to stop, or when they became frustrated and irritated. If she had to be stuck all day in a maze of tunnels with no food, no water, and a wounded man to carry, she was glad she was stuck with someone like Ethan.

Her thoughts were drawn back to the present. She realized something was different; something in their surroundings was changing. They were starting to ascend, just slightly. "Did you...?" "Are we....?" They both began talking at once. "Yes!" The excitement was apparent in Ethan's voice. "We're going uphill, just like Bo said. I don't know how far, but not nearly as far as we've come already!"

Having walked at a very slight decline up to this point, they noticed a tremendous increase in difficulty in placing one foot in front of the other now that they were traveling at a three or four percent incline. Grace was puffing after ten minutes, and Ethan was breathing heavily. Bo's almost limp body was becoming more and more of a burden. They found themselves stopping after every five minutes of walking, and still needing a ten minute rest. After more than an hour, Ethan commented, "I could be wrong, but I think it's leveling off just a little. Can you keep going another minute, you think?" Grace couldn't spare the breath to speak, but did manage to nod her head once. By the end of that minute, Grace could feel the difference, too.

They no longer sat down to rest. It was simply too hard to get Bo back up anymore. So, leaning against the wall of the cave, they rested a few minutes, then resumed, feeling some hope that they might be nearing the end. The flashlight showed a curve and a narrowing just ahead. As had become their practice, they turned their little entourage to the side, and Ethan led the way sideways through the narrowed walkway. Supporting Bo from the other side, and following into the tight opening, Grace had penetrated about two or three feet when she heard Ethan say, "Stop, stop. Let me see what's ahead. I'm leaning Bo against the wall. Hold on to him, Grace." And then, there was nothing but pure darkness, and the feel of Bo's arm and shoulder with her arms wrapped around him. Oh, the strain of her muscles, so tired, and having to give still more to keep Bo upright. What if something happened to Ethan? What would she do? She had come too far to find the way back. And there was no way she could possibly handle Bo by herself, even for a few feet. Panic was gaining a foothold in Grace. Against her will, her breath was coming faster and faster. Hating for him to know she was frantic, but desperate to know that he was still there, she had to call out, "Ethan! Are you there?"

"I'm right here," she heard him answer, from just the other side of Bo. Relieved, she tried to calm herself, and barely registered his next few words. "It's the bridge that Bo talked about, just ahead. There's a drop-off of a couple of feet, when the tunnel widens back out, six or seven steps beyond where I'm standing now. So, go slowly and watch out for the drop. That puts us in a small room, about ten or twelve feet across. There are three other openings into the room. The one to the right leads to the bridge. Come on, let's get into the room. We'll rest there a while, then cross the bridge."

Twenty-Eight

*E*d had been waiting to hear from Grace all day. Now, he was getting worried. It wasn't like her to simply forget to call. He could have called Nan, and gotten the phone number for the boarding house, but he knew it would only make her worry, and probably unnecessarily. Making up his mind, he called information and got the number for the Fairmount Chronicle.

"Hello? This is Ed Broadman with the Jackstone Gazette. Is the editor in today?"

"Yes, Mr. Broadman. This is Joe Wilson. I'm the editor and the owner. Sir, I'm sure glad you called. The sheriff and the boarding house owner have been trying for the last few hours to put their hands on a phone number to call Miss Turner's family. We've got a situation going on here, and unfortunately, Miss Turner is involved."

Ed's heart sank. "Oh, our precious girl! She was supposed to be careful! What – What's happening over there?"

"Now, let me set your mind at ease, first. We believe that Miss Turner is fine. She and several others were in the old gold mine up on Heaven's Mountain, when there was a cave-in. We think that Miss Turner and a young man, the preacher at the church here in town, are trapped, but alive, beyond the cave-in. There may be another injured man with them, too. We've got men and equipment up there, doing everything possible to clear away the rubble so we can get to them. The sheriff could probably tell you more about how much longer they think it might be, that sort of thing. I'd like to give you his number, let you call him and talk to him. Does Grace have some relatives in Jackstone?"

"Yes, sir. I certainly hate to have to tell them about this. Especially since I encouraged her to follow that story. But, I will call the sheriff, as you suggested, and give him their number, then I'll head over to the Turners' home to do what I can to ease their minds."

Leaving Bo for a moment, Ethan and Grace went to take a look at the bridge. Even to Grace's untrained eye, it looked quite questionable. The timbers looked dry and rotten, and there were a few places where the odd board here and there had already fallen away. Other than the bridge, there was definitely no way to get to where the tunnel continued on the other side of the chasm, which dropped away into nothing below them. It looked as if the mountain had been sliced straight through at this point. Pointing the flashlight up or down, there seemed to be no ceiling or floor to the abyss.

Grace had to be honest about her misgivings. "I don't know about this, Ethan. Even if it was strong enough to hold each one of us individually, do you really think it would hold all three of us?"

"I truly don't know. It worries me, too. The bridge is only about seven or eight feet across. I could just about jump that far, for what good that would do us. Anyway, how about this? I'll test the boards as much as I possibly can, before I step onto the bridge. Then, I'll go across, going slowly, testing each board before I put my full weight on it. If it holds me, I'll return to this side, then you can go across, by yourself. Then, I'll come with Bo."

"Mmmnn, I don't like it. There's so much difference in the weight of one man versus two men. And if you have Bo in your arms, how can you catch hold of anything to save yourself if the wood gives way?"

"Actually, I agree with you, but if we don't cross, and nobody searches from this direction, we may not get out of here."

"Okay. Test it out a little, and let's see how it goes."

The bridge had only one hand rail, on the left side. The right was wide open. The floor of the bridge was about two and a half feet wide, formed by two-by-fours spanning the width of the bridge, and apparently secured by nails, as well as rope wound around and over each plank. The base to which the two-by-fours was nailed consisted of two four-by-four beams which had been inserted into holes dug out on either side in the ravine walls. It was these beams that Ethan had the most faith in, and which he believed would most likely hold, even when he and Bo had to cross together.

Leaving his weight firmly planted on safe ground, Ethan began sticking one leg out over the bridge and putting as much weight as he could on it. Experiencing no problems, he told Grace, "I think this side is pretty good. The far side is more rotted out, so that's where we'll have to be most careful."

Taking a deep breath, Ethan said, "I'm ready. Here, you take the flashlight." He took hold of the rail and started to place his foot on the bridge.

"Wait! Don't you think you ought to say a prayer first, Ethan?"

Ethan stopped and chuckled, "Believe me, I have been praying! But let's pray together right now. Lord, please protect us as we cross this bridge. Let your angels guard all around us and allow us to reach the other side unharmed. Show us the way, Father, to get home to our families. Thank you. Amen." He had been holding Grace's hand tightly. Now he let it go and turned to face the bridge.

"Here we go." Ethan slowly and carefully stepped onto the first plank. He tested each board before he shifted his weight completely. When he got close to the other side, one board cracked and gave way a little, so he moved to the next one. Otherwise, his passage was uneventful. After pausing on the other side for a few seconds, he turned and made his way in the same manner back across to Grace.

The two of them went back to the small room where they had left Bo, and brought him to the bridge. Then, it was Grace's turn to cross. She had never been particularly afraid of heights, but she would freely admit she was feeling anxious about this little escapade. She made herself take hold of the rail. She put her right foot gingerly out on the first board, and eased her weight on to it. So far, so good. Firmly grasping the rail with both hands now, she turned towards it, and began to traverse the bridge, as in a simple dance. Right foot to the right, left foot over to meet it, over and over until she reached the other side without incident.

Grace had unknowingly been holding her breath. Now she let it all out in a rush. Feeling weak in the knees, she took a few wobbly steps away from the edge, and sat down on the ground. For some reason, she envisioned Ethan and Bo falling through holes in the floor of the bridge and clinging to the beams.

She stood up and started removing her belt. "Ethan, take off your belt and Bo's. Hook them together, tightly. Run one end through two of Bo's belt loops. I'm coming back across to connect the end to my belt. I know it's not much, but it might be enough to give you a few seconds to pull yourself up." Grace was even now going back across. Ethan quickly did as she asked. Thankfully, Bo was aware they were moving again, and was trying to help. Ethan had him stand close to the edge, leaning against the cave wall to keep his balance. He ran the buckle through Bo's belt loops and tightened it, then passed the end to Grace, who went as far as she could toward the far side. When Ethan was ready, he got a good grip around Bo's waist, put Bo's arm around his shoulder and instructed him to hold on to the rail with his other hand.

Things went smoothly for the first few steps. Grace was able to get back on solid ground, then, she took her end of the belt rope and wrapped it around the end of the handrail. As the men came towards her, she kept the belt tightened around the rail. Then, right about the halfway mark, Bo became agitated and started pulling Ethan back in the other direction. He was mumbling about the bridge, and had let go of the rail. As strong as Ethan was, it was all he could do to overpower Bo and force him to move towards Grace. He was so involved in keeping Bo steady that he forgot about the weak board. Ethan was about three feet away from her when his foot went completely through and was dangling in the air.

Grace laid the flashlight on the ground and held out her hand to Ethan. Between holding on to Bo with one hand and the rail with the other, he couldn't reach for Grace's outstretched hand. But Bo surprised them both. He seemed to realize that Ethan needed his help; he used his own strength to assist Ethan in regaining his footing. Ethan stepped past the hole and had almost closed the gap between himself and Grace. Bo's first foot had made it past the break, but his other foot slid from its secure plank into the opening, going in up to the hip. Instinctively, Bo had tightened his hold on Ethan, and pulled him off balance when he dropped. The extra force exerted on the surrounding boards caused them to splinter and break also. Now one of Ethan's feet had gone through again. Fortunately, he had retained his grip on the rail and on Bo, but, even so, couldn't get enough leverage to pull him up. Grace could just barely reach Ethan's shirt with her free hand, with the other she still held the belt, which had slid back in Bo's direction when he fell.

"Ethan, can you get up?"

Ethan didn't answer. All his concentration was focused on getting his foot on something solid again. Trying to not lose any more ground with the rest of his body, or with Bo, he worked his foot back and forth until he got it free from the crack, and set that foot nearer to Grace.

"Grace, you can let go of me now. Just get hold of that belt with both hands and give it a slow sustained pull when I tell you to. Nice and easy, okay? Bo, listen to me, man. We're going to wrap our arms together. I need you to use my arm to pull up on, while you raise your leg up out of the hole, all right? When I say go, Bo, you give it all you've got. Ready, Grace? One, two, three, go!"

Grace began pulling, Bo was straining, and the cords on Ethan's neck were bulging as they each gave all they had left to get Bo to safety. For a second, it seemed as if it simply would not be enough. Then, Bo's body began rising upward, and within a few more seconds, his leg was free. Ethan reached down and guided Bo's leg free of the break. The next few steps brought them safely to Grace, who moved out of their way so they could move on into the tunnel. For a long time, none of them could say anything. It was Bo who broke the silence.

"Why did we come this way?" he asked.

Ethan said, "We came over the bridge to get to the other mine entrance, like you said."

Bo sighed. "No, I tried to tell you *not* to go over the bridge. This is a dead end. There's no way out from this side. I'm sorry. My mind hasn't been right all day. I might have told you to go across the bridge. I just don't know what I said." Bo was clearly upset about his mistake and began sobbing.

"Bo, it's all right. We understand that you were shot, you've lost a lot of blood, and you've been through an ordeal last night and today. Don't blame yourself. We're not blaming you," Grace said kindly. "Here, you'd better let me take a look at you after all that pushing and pulling." Bo was bleeding again, but not heavily. Grace redid the pressure bandage, and that seemed to stop the flow.

She had just gone back to sit with her back against the wall when they heard a cracking sound, followed by splintering and popping. Grabbing up the flashlight, Ethan shone it at the bridge. The whole middle section had completely collapsed, and the outside beam was cracked and sagging in the center.

"What time is it, Ethan? I'm just wondering whether it's my supper or my evening snack I'm missing right now."

"Very funny. It's your supper. It's six o'clock. And I still owe you a dinner, you know."

"I have absolutely not forgotten that. And I do intend to collect on it."

Ethan's voice changed to a more serious tone. "You realize, of course, that we could have been on that bridge when it fell apart."

"Yes. We were supremely lucky," Grace said.

"Luck had nothing to do with it," he answered.

Twenty-Nine

When Ed drove in to the Turner's driveway, he saw Nan and Grace's grandmother hurrying across the yard from the Brittain house. By the speed with which they were moving, he knew that they had heard the news about Grace already. He met them at the back door to the little house.

"Ed, come on in," Nan said breathlessly. "What have you heard about Grace?"

"Probably not any more than you," he replied. "The sheriff says they're digging as fast as they can, trying to get to them. Grace is a smart girl, with a good head on her shoulders. I guarantee you she's using it, too."

By this time, they were all three sitting at the kitchen table. Granny Annie, in her raspy, no-nonsense voice, let her thoughts be known. "The best thing we can do for our girl is pray. And that's exactly what we're going to do right now." She turned loose with a heart-felt prayer, not minding at all that a few tears flowed along with the words. When she was finished, Ed added his hearty "amen" right along with Nan's.

"What can I do to help?" Ed wanted to know. "Would you like me to drive you ladies over to Heaven's Mountain? We could be there in about six hours, give or take."

Nan was just about to answer when the back door opened and Augusta walked in. She must have been listening to their conversation, for she came straight to the point. "We can take my car. The Lincoln has plenty of room for all of us, and room to bring Grace and her luggage back, too. If Mr. Broadman would be so good as to drive us, we could leave just as soon as everyone is ready."

Nan and Granny Annie were momentarily stunned – and speechless. Nan was able to speak first. "That would be just wonderful, Augusta. It's very generous and thoughtful of you. Thank you so much. Why don't I call the sheriff back and tell him we'll be on our way in a couple of hours?"

The weary, dehydrated trio had settled themselves into a thirty foot round room which Ethan had found just twenty feet or so further down the tunnel beyond the bridge. There, they all realized, they would have to wait out their fate, whatever that might be. There was no way in or out of this room other than through the tunnel, and no way to get back across the bridge.

Other than the few hours sleep they had gotten early that morning, this was the first prolonged rest they had allowed themselves. Each of them allowed themselves a little space to stretch out. And, it appeared, a little space in which to think, also. In the dark, in the total silence, there was nothing to keep the truth at bay. The possibility of a slow, agonizing death had a way of setting straight the priorities of one's life, the things done that should have been omitted, the things undone that should have been accomplished, the regrets, the failures. It made one wish for a second chance - a few moments, a few days, time to say what needed to be said, to ask for forgiveness, to live at least briefly with the joy that life deserved to be lived.

Bo's continued fidgeting and tossing around broke into Grace's reverie. "Bo, are you all right? Do you need me to re-do your bandage?"

Bo stopped moving. They heard him sob out, "No, it's not that."

Grace got the flashlight and moved over next to him. "What is it? Are you in pain? Let me see."

He pushed her hands away. "No, I'm not hurting too bad." He took a deep, shaky breath and let it out slowly. "In case I die in here, I want you both to know the truth about what happened to Amos. You can turn the flashlight off. Might be easier for me to talk that way."

Ethan moved over close to Grace, turned off the flashlight and took her hand in his, squeezing it hard. Grace returned the squeeze and turned all her attention to Bo. For the moment, her energy and alertness returned to her full force, as she determined to remember every bit of Bo's statement.

"I may as well start early in the day. We had been hunting with the dogs, just like I said, Miss Grace, real early. About daybreak, we went to our still, 'cause we had some work to do, some orders to fill that day. Only we didn't have enough jars, so Paw sent me to town to buy a case. I went to the general store, just a block off the square in town, got the jars, and loaded 'em on the truck. I went back in, to get a soda, I think, and we heard a commotion, a man yelling. I stood in the doorway and I could see Preacher James out on the square in front of the drugstore. He grabbed Amos' arm away from Ethan (back then he was just a little boy), then the preacher wrestled the knife away from him. He yelled at him some more, then he got his wife and kid and walked down the square in my direction. They turned onto Oglethorpe and came right past me, standing in the doorway. I watched 'em go on past, and I saw Preacher James throw something in the trashcan. So, I went to see what it was. It was a pretty good knife, so I got it.

"I went on back up the mountain, showed Paw the knife, and he stuck it in his pocket. About eleven, eleven-thirty, Amos came through the woods from his house and bought the last jar of shine we had. But he wanted a pile of it, he said. He told us he had just found that vein of gold his grandpappy had searched for all his life, and he said it was a big one. He said he stumbled and fell in a hole and there it was! We were all excited then, jumping around and singing. Paw told him to go on home and put on his best clothes. Paw said we'd finish pouring up this batch of shine, and we'd meet him behind the church in the cemetery in about an hour, and bring all the shine with us. Then, we'd all go out on the town to celebrate.

"Well, Amos went home and we poured up the shine but we didn't load any of it. Then we went on up to the church. We pulled around to the back and waited on Amos. He showed up, already pretty drunk. Paw told Amos to write a I.O.U. to Paw for a gambling debt, for all his property. Amos wouldn't do it. Paw got out his knife, but Amos still wouldn't write it. Paw told me to beat him. So I did. Paw gave me his knife and told me to stick it in him. So I did. Then Amos said to give him the paper. He would write the I.O.U. He wrote it and signed it and gave it to Paw. Then Paw told me to use the knife some more until he was dead." Bo's voice was quivering again. "I did it. I did what he told me to. I killed him."

Ethan and Grace did not say anything. Bo composed himself and went on. "We loaded Amos up in the back of the truck and covered him up with some croker sacks. Paw told me to follow him in Amos' truck. We went back to the still. Paw called the dogs and then - he killed our dogs. Took his knife and gut-cut them. Then he threw the dogs on top of Amos' body. We went back to the paved road. And I guess you know the rest. We dumped Amos out on the road and left his truck there. Paw said we had to leave the body out where it could be found fast. Said we needed to look like innocent bystanders. So, we went back down the mountain a-ways, and we pretended like our truck quit. We covered up the blood on our shirts with our jackets. Then Mrs. O'Dell picked us up, and when we got back up there where Amos was, there was Preacher James leaning over him. Paw just figured that was too perfect, framing the preacher for murder by putting Amos' knife right there underneath him. And it worked."

Thirty

For a long time, they all sat quietly in the blackness, contemplating the chain of events that had affected so many lives for the last thirty-odd years.

Still lucid, Bo broke the silence. "What in the world got you started, asking questions about Amos?" he asked Grace.

She explained how she had found Floyd's letter in her father's possessions.

"So little Floyd told on us, after all these years. How about that. My little brother, who was scared of his own shadow. Did my daddy know?"

Ethan answered, "We're not sure. Somehow Billy got the letter out of Grace's room. He may have shown it to your father."

"You know, I think I remember Floyd mentioning a boy from Georgia who was in his unit. Best I recollect, they were pretty good friends. Was that your daddy, Miss Grace?"

"I believe it must have been," she mused.

"Bo, what happened to the knife, the one you stabbed Amos with?" Ethan asked.

"I... well, stupid of me....I threw it as hard as I could. Probably 'cause I hated what I did so much. It got stuck up in the trees somewhere. I went back a few days later, but I couldn't ever find it."

"That's because Floyd went and got it down after you and your father left," Grace told him. "He said so in the letter. He also said he hid it somewhere. Hey, your father must have known about the letter. Otherwise how would he have known I wanted to find the knife?"

"Do you think my daddy and my momma are both dead?" Bo asked.

"Yes, Bo. We checked them both before the explosion. I'm really sorry," Ethan said.

Bo sobbed, "Did you see what my momma did?"

"We saw it. She must have loved you very much." Grace replied.

"I didn't deserve it."

"She evidently thought you did," said Ethan.

After a quiet, but tense, night of driving, Ed, Nan and Augusta arrived in Fairmount at about four o'clock in the morning. A brief search of downtown brought them to the sheriff's office, and Ed went in to discover the current status of the search for Grace. Striding back to the car, he got in and turned around in the driver's seat to talk.

"They haven't gotten to them yet and they don't expect to clear enough debris to get through until late tomorrow afternoon. I got directions to the mine up on Heaven's Mountain, but it's not going to be light for at least another couple of hours. Do you want to go anyway? The sheriff took the liberty of making reservations for us at the same boarding house as Grace."

They didn't answer, so he continued, "I'll do whatever you ladies desire, but my recommendation would be to go to the boarding house now, sleep for several hours, then head up to the mine sometime before lunch. I can go back in and tell them we'll be at the boarding house, and they can call us if anything happens before that."

Nan and Augusta looked at each other, and Augusta made a gesture to Nan that it was her decision. Nan told Ed, "Let's go to the boarding house. There's nothing we can do at the mine right now. It makes more sense to be rested so we can take care of Grace when she's freed."

After all the physical and emotional stress he had endured, Bo fell into an exhausted sleep. Grace and Ethan had found a spot on the floor that had a slight incline, so they attempted to get comfortable enough to sleep themselves.

For a long while, neither spoke, though they were both fairly certain that the other was not asleep. Then, in a very soft whisper, so as not to wake him if he was asleep, Grace breathed, "Ethan."

"Yes," he whispered back.

"Can we have another 'religious' talk?"

"Of course. What's on your mind?"

"After we talked the other night - whatever night that was – I'm losing track of time in here… Anyway, afterwards, I decided I would not rush myself, because, for one thing, I didn't want to make a mistake, and for another, I assumed that there was no limit to the amount of time I could take to decide." Grace paused. "I was almost out of time several times last night. And every time, I was calling on God to help me. I know what I want to do. I've known for several days, but I just didn't want to have to admit that I was wrong. I didn't want to have to say to God that I needed him. I like being strong and independent, but I realize now that I don't really have control over anything, not even myself."

Grace continued, "You know what Bo was saying about Sadie, throwing herself in front of him, taking the bullet meant for him? That's what Jesus did for us, isn't it? He takes the bullet for us, if we want him to. And we don't deserve it, either."

"But he loves us anyway," said Ethan.

"Exactly," said Grace. "I was sort of hung up on the concept of loving God with all your heart, mind and soul, committing to serve him, all those ideas that sound like you're giving yourself into slavery. But, everything comes from him to begin with, so anything we give back, including ourselves, we don't really have control over anyway. And besides that, he's taking the bullet for me. How can you not love someone who's willing to die so that you can live?"

"How can you not?" he repeated.

"I'm ready. If I leave anything out that I need to say, just tell me." Grace took a deep breath and began. "Lord, I know that I am a sinner, human and imperfect and willful and disobedient. I ask for your forgiveness. I truly want to change and live in a new way, your way. I believe that Jesus died for me and paid for my sins on the cross. I want you to live in me, and I commit myself here and now to live for you."

Ethan squeezed her hand. "That was perfect, and beautiful."

"Good. Would you say a prayer for me now, Ethan?"

Ethan laughed out loud. "Grace, ever since you came to town, that's all I've been doing!" He sat up and helped her to do so. Sitting cross-legged in front of each other, they held hands and said their first prayer together as believers.

In spite of the lack of water, food, and rest, the joy of the moment gave them renewed energy to enjoy each other's company. For the first time since they met, there were truly no impediments to nurturing their relationship. It was exciting and satisfying to finally allow their natural attraction to each other to be expressed and the delight was evident in their voices, and in the touch of their hands, and in the occasional sight of each other. When the flashlight was on, of course.

Eventually, the exhilaration of those hours gave way to a contented tiredness, and they fell asleep for the night snuggled close together.

Thirty-One

"*P*reacher James?"

"Yes?"

"This is Clare Morgan. I own the boarding house in Fairmount. I don't mean to intrude on your privacy, but has anyone been keeping you up to date on what's been happening at the old gold mine?"

"Not as much as I'd like, ma'am. The warden and the guards let me know yesterday that Ethan and Grace were trapped in the mine, and that both Beamon and Sadie Lucas were dead. But that's about all I've heard. Do you have any more news?"

"Not that much, but I know you must be worried sick about Ethan, and you're sort of isolated from the news… Anyway, they're working on clearing out all the beams and rocks that crashed down during the explosions. They were hoping to break through after lunch today, but the blockage goes a lot further back than they had anticipated, so it looks like it may be sometime tomorrow before they can get to the tunnels. I wish I had something better to tell you."

"I'd rather know the truth than not know at all. You were very kind to think of calling me, Miss Morgan. When you see Ethan, would you tell him I've been praying for him and for Grace, and that I love him very much. I'm sure he'll get out here to see me as soon as he can."

"I'm sure he will, too. I'll keep calling you a couple of times a day, James, if that's all right, to let you know how things are going. And would you like to take this number in case you have a question? The number for the boarding house is 555-7322. There's pretty much always someone there."

Waking up was not a pleasant thing when your arms and legs were aching from lying on the cold ground, and your stomach was hurting from being so empty. The persistent blackness alone was enough to frustrate and enrage the most patient of persons. And the need for water! How Grace longed for the feel of the cool, soothing liquid filling her mouth and flowing down her parched throat.

Trying to occupy her thoughts with something other than her unmet needs, she gently removed herself from Ethan's arm, turned on the flashlight and went to check on Bo. At first she thought that he was simply sleeping, but her attempts to rouse him failed. His bandages, though they certainly needed to be replaced, showed no fresh blood, and his wounds did not appear to be severely infected, in spite of the fact that they had not yet been properly cleaned. She had to guess that his body had simply been through so much that he had simply shut down for a while. There was really nothing more that she could do for him beyond what had already been done.

Feeling rather weak and lethargic herself, she went back to where Ethan lay, and eased back into her former position. She must have drifted back to sleep, because the next thing she was aware of was Ethan lightly shaking her shoulder.

"Grace, do you hear anything?"

Both of them were totally quiet, listening. "No, I don't. Did you hear something?"

"I'm not sure. I thought I did. Maybe I'm starting to hallucinate sounds! I'm sorry I woke you. You can go back to sleep."

"That's all right. I'm not really sleepy anymore. What did it sound like?"

"It was so faint, I couldn't even tell you."

They lay there in silence for a minute or more. And then Grace heard it, too. Very, very faint and muffled, but definitely a sound they had not heard before inside the tunnels. To keep from making any noise, she pinched Ethan's arm, hard. The sound did not disappear, and in fact, seemed to ebb and flow in volume. It actually seemed a little familiar to her. Feeling more confident that it would not vanish if she broke their silence, she whispered to Ethan, "What is it? It's something I've heard before, I think."

"Me, too. But it's so indistinct, I can't place it."

They listened again, then Ethan jumped. "It's the church bell! At Heaven's Mountain Church! That's got to be it. Is that it?"

"Yes! I think you're right! But why can we hear it?"

"We need to figure out where it's coming from. Let's try to pinpoint the source."

"Give me the flashlight. I'm going back down the tunnel."

Grace got the light and moved several steps into the tunnel, then a few more, then several more. She came back into the room and told Ethan, "It's definitely not coming through the tunnel. It's got to be somewhere in here."

"Okay, hand me the light. I'm going to check all the walls. You walk around and listen, try to narrow it down that way." Minute after minute passed as they each moved around the room. Grace was praying that the bell would keep ringing until they found something. Finally she thought she detected a very slight difference in volume if she stood in one particular spot. Ethan had now eliminated the entire surface of the wall up to about ten feet. When he got even with Grace and raised the beam a little higher, there in the wall they saw a cylinder of shadows. Moving around with the narrow shaft of light, Ethan could tell that the small tunnel, perhaps three feet in diameter at the most, went back into the wall at least several feet, though he could see no further than that. Then the bell ceased to ring.

"What do you think it is?" she asked.

"I think," he said, "it's an opportunity."

"What do you mean?"

"I mean, I think God could be opening a door for us. We need to do our part and check it out."

"How? That's at least ten feet off the ground."

Ethan thought for a minute. "The bridge."

"The bridge?"

"Yes. Maybe we can pull enough boards off the bridge to make some kind of ladder or stand to get me up there."

"What are we waiting for?"

After considerable trouble and effort, Ethan, with Grace's help, was able to scavenge two loads of planks and boards which they carried back to the chamber. Together they fashioned a combination ramp/stand whose sturdiness was questionable at best.

"Before you attempt to climb that monstrosity we just created, we need to discuss everything that needs to be discussed before you put your head in that tiny tunnel. Once you get up in there, there will be no turning around to tell me something."

"And we don't know how far I'll have to go. There's always the possibility that it will get so constricted that I won't be able to go forward any further. In that case, I'll just back myself out, which will probably be a lot harder than going forward."

"You'll need to take the flashlight."

"No, you need to keep it."

"Not as much as you need to take it. I know what's in this room. You have no idea what you'll run into. You have to take it, Ethan. You know I'm right about this."

Ethan reluctantly agreed.

"And another thing," Grace said, "If you break through to the outside, don't waste time coming back to tell me. Just go find somebody who knows where that entrance is. Then, you can tell them how to get in here to get me and Bo. Just be sure to tell them to bring some water with them, *please*."

"I will. All right, let's see if I can even get up there. Steady that platform while I walk up the ramp." Their rickety structure was quaking as Ethan put his weight on it; Grace had to use all her strength to hold it together. Fortunately, it only took Ethan a few seconds to get up the ramp, and on to the platform. Then, while he used his grip on the edge of the tunnel to pull himself up, Grace wedged more short boards against the wall to give him a fake stair to step up on. Eventually he succeeded in clambering into the passageway, with just his lower legs still sticking out. He shone the beam of light back at Grace. He prayed loudly enough for her to hear. "Please, Father, watch over Grace; let her be totally at peace here in the dark with you. And give me strength and wisdom to find the way out. Amen. I'll be back as soon as I can, Grace."

"Be careful, Ethan." Grace felt a tug at her heart, stretching out to Ethan as he moved further and further away.

Grace was used to the dark after a day and a half in the mine. But the notion that she could not turn on a light was a little unnerving. She would just have to keep her mind on other things. She could think about the story, what she would use as the opening sentence, how she wanted to approach the telling of it. But for some reason, even after all of Bo's revelations, she couldn't focus on it. Her mind kept wandering. Wandering to home, her mother and her grandmother. Her grandmothers, she should say.

She had never really spent much time thinking about Augusta or what her life was like, either at present or as a young woman. Now, as the question entered her mind, she used her reporter's logic, and the facts that she was aware of, to try to reconstruct the framework of Augusta's existence. Grace knew that Augusta grew up in a neighboring county, but she couldn't remember a single visit by any members of Augusta's family to the Brittain home. That could mean either that she had no family, or that she did not maintain contact with her family. Now that she thought about it, Grace also couldn't recall Augusta having many friends come to visit her through the years. Augusta was a regular church-goer, of course, and she was involved in a few community activities, usually the ones that the very rich supported with their time or money.

Augusta's husband had died while still a young man. That meant that she had to raise Jesse alone. Of course, the estate went into trust for Jesse until he came of age, but she would have been the one managing the trust for him, which meant taking responsibility for the farming operation, the investments and the estate household. Uncle Zach said he moved back home after Jesse died. That was logical, since he would have been next in line to inherit after Jesse's premature death, and because there were no other known heirs.

So, at that point in time, Augusta would have lost her husband, her only child, and most of what had previously been her day-to-day duties. What would she have done with herself then, with a life so devoid of relationships and responsibilities?

She grieved and brooded. Maybe she felt lonely or depressed. Maybe she was angry at God and the world for taking the ones she loved away from her. Maybe the bitterness and hurt were so strong in her that it kept at bay those who might have befriended her.

Maybe, maybe, maybe. It was all supposition, certainly, but it opened Grace's eyes to the difficulty of the situation Augusta found herself in after losing her family.

Even if Augusta chose not to allow the bonding of grandmother to granddaughter, Grace promised herself that she would try very hard to develop a friendship with her. She would start today, right now, by forgiving her grandmother for all the accumulated wrongs she had borne since childhood. She understood that that meant that she would hold those things against Augusta no more, regardless of Augusta's response to Grace's new attitude.

While she was sitting in this cold, dark place, with nothing to do and no place to go, it was the perfect time to hash all of this out with God. So, for the next hour, Grace poured out her heart to him. She told him every hurt she could remember, and asked him to wipe the slate clean. She asked him to remove the bitterness she felt towards her grandmother, and replace it with the same kind of love God showed to her.

When there was nothing left to say and Grace's eyes were dry once more, she recalled what Clare and Ethan both had said to her about how the release of that burden from her own heart would make her feel. "You were right," she said aloud with wonder. "It's gone. That heaviness in my heart is gone. Oh, Augusta, Grandmother, you are not going to know who this person is when you see me, because no matter what you might say or do, I'm not loading myself up with that anger again."

"Billy, Billy, stay back!" Bo was mumbling and writhing in his sleep. Groping around in the dark until she could feel him, Grace did what she could to check him over. When she put her hand on his forehead, it was burning hot. Wishing she could do more, she made sure his head was raised a bit by using one of the slimmer planks that were left over and padding it with her socks. Ethan had left his jacket with her, so she used it to cover Bo's upper body for the chills that would probably soon follow. Staying nearby, she sat and leaned against the wall, wishing that the time could pass faster. She was so thirsty. Hungry, too, of course, but the thirst was overwhelming. She could tell that her strength was far less than yesterday. And sometimes, she had trouble focusing her attention. Woozy, she felt slightly woozy. Wasn't that a funny word? Woozy? wOOOooo—zeee. Woo....

Thirty-Two

Pulling forward inch by inch, Ethan had been crawling and clawing his way through the tunnel for several hours. As dehydrated as he must be, he wondered how he could still be perspiring. Several times so far he had come to places that were so narrow, he had to dig them out some before he would risk trying to get through. He was very much aware that, were he to get wedged into such a place, he would have no way to gain any leverage to shove himself back out. And the chances of being rescued would be almost nonexistent. Were it not for the fact that he could definitely sense a steadily intensifying freshness in the air, he might have been tempted to return to Grace's side. Not to mention the fact that, even if he wanted to, he doubted that he could crawl backwards through the most constricted of the passages.

This was not an experience he ever wanted to repeat. His nails were all broken and jagged, he had hit his head too many times to count, and his pants legs had to be in shreds by now. He had never been claustrophobic, but he would most definitely have sympathy from now on with those who were. He looked at his watch. Four o'clock. He had left Grace around eleven-thirty. He was tired, and he was thirsty. All he wanted was to lay his head down and rest for a while. And he would have, were it not for remembering that Grace, and Bo, too, were sitting in total darkness, counting on him, waiting on him to find the way out.

So, he kept going, inch by slow inch. He had been reciting scriptures passages to remind himself of God's constant presence, but had stopped when he could no longer make his dry mouth and tongue work properly. He had tried thinking them to himself, but kept losing track of where he was. Now, he was saying them with his mouth closed, sort of in a hum, the sound without the articulation. That seemed to be working better.

Oh, no, he thought. Not another one. The light from the flashlight showed another tightening of the tunnel about ten feet ahead. That would slow him down yet again, as he would have to spend time digging to widen it enough for him to get through.

He reached the spot and examined the edges in order to locate the softest places to dig. He raised himself to the right so he could look through the small hole and see what was ahead. Shining the light as far as it would go, he saw with a sinking heart that the tunnel appeared to dead end about twenty feet beyond where he lay. Now, he did lay his head down and close his eyes, not to sleep or rest, but to throw himself on the mercy of his God.

"Father, I'm at a loss here. I don't know what to do. I'm really tired, physically and emotionally, and I'm discouraged. I don't understand how you're working in this, but I'm telling you now that I'm trusting you. I put myself in your hands. Lord, show me what to do now. I need you. Help me, please."

Wiping the tears from his eyes, he slowly raised up on his elbows. He had turned off the flashlight after he saw the closing off up ahead, so the tunnel was dark again. But somehow not as dark as it should have been. He pulled himself up to look down the passage again. There, at the very end, were tiny pinpricks of light. Sunlight! There was sunlight out there! And he was close, so close. Not much longer, not much further! Using the flashlight as well as his hands, Ethan began digging with all his might, throwing the dirt anywhere, back on himself, up ahead, in his mouth, anywhere! He decided the dirt in the mouth wasn't the best idea, so he closed his mouth and began to hum, one hymn right after the other.

Twenty minutes later he had slithered through the enlarged hole and crawled to where the pinpricks of light could still be seen. He hated to think of what might have happened had he arrived at that spot at night. There would have been no dots of light. He might have given up then and there. "Thank you, Father. You are so good. Thank you, thank you." He continued those heartfelt thanks as he pushed away the dirt and roots and thick vines that covered the tunnel's opening, until at last he was free.

She wondered what time it was. She tried to concentrate and figure it out. They had heard the church bell at about nine o'clock in the morning. It took them at least two or three hours to build the stand. Ethan had been gone for hours. But how many hours? It was really hard to tell; time passed in such a weird way in the dark, with no one to talk to.

What should she think about now? Ethan. Yes, she wanted to think about Ethan now. Beautiful Ethan. Kind Ethan. Strong Ethan. She didn't know if he felt that strange and wonderful connection in the same way she did. She would have to ask him about that. She did know without a doubt that there was something very special going on as far as she was concerned, something that could grow, if they nurtured it. And she wanted it to grow. Ethan was the kind of man she had always dreamed of. She would never, ever have thought that she would be attracted to a preacher, of course, but she found that it didn't matter at all anymore. It was just part of who Ethan was. His joyful way of living was part of what had captivated her in the first place.

Losing herself in pleasant, but totally disjointed, daydreams of herself and Ethan, Grace fell asleep sitting up.

"I know you spoke to the sheriff an hour or two ago, but I would like you to speak with him again. Please, Mr. Broadman. Nan will feel better if she has the latest information," Augusta regally requested. With a little shrug, Nan gave Ed a helpless smile, as if to say, "You may as well not fight it, just do whatever she says."

In the waning light, Ed walked over to the operation center the sheriff had set up and began talking to him. Nan stood at Augusta's side, put her arm around the older woman's waist, and hugged. "You'll never know how much I appreciate all you're doing for us, and for Grace," she said.

"Nonsense. We've practically lived together and been friends all our lives, Nan." Turning to look her straight in the face, she said, "I could do no less for you, my dear friend." Before she could face forward again, Nan detected the tears forming in Augusta's eyes. Which of course brought tears to her own eyes, again. Reaching in her pocket, she took out a pack of tissues, removing one for herself, and one which she handed to Augusta.

Ed had gotten his update from the sheriff and was on his way back to the ladies, when they all stopped what they were doing to watch the commotion beyond the dense jumble of law enforcement vehicles. A truck was coming down the dirt road from the highway, the driver was waving, and some people were running alongside as the truck got closer and closer. Pulling to a stop as close in as possible, the driver jumped out, and bystanders rushed to help the passenger disembark, and support him as they all approached the sheriff. When the sheriff turned and saw who it was, he hurried over to them. Motioning to the EMT's to come, they all began moving in the direction of the ambulance.

Ed told Nan, "I'll go see what's going on." But by then, the news was spreading to the outskirts of the crowd. "Ethan." "It's Preacher Ethan."

"But where's Grace?" Nan whimpered, and would have sunk to her knees if not for Ed and Augusta catching her on either side. "Oh, God, why isn't Grace with him?"

Thirty-Three

Tap, tap, tap. Tap, tap, tap. The faint sounds were floating around the edge of her subconscious, inaudible until that moment when they pierced through, and were processed by her brain as a sound for which she should awaken, in order to listen more closely. Probing her way into a wakeful state, she finally reached a level of reason and realized where she was and what she was hearing. Eyes flying open and fully awake now, she knew that someone must be trying to reach her and Bo. Trembling with excitement, she groped for the wall and felt her way around the chamber to the tunnel. They had to be coming that way. She would go to meet them. Running her hands along the side of the passage, she quickly traversed its length. In her rush to let them know her location, she completely forgot about the ravine and the bridge which they had scavenged, leaving not much more than the support beams on this end. About the time her hand felt the wall disappear, her right foot stepped off into nothing. She instinctively turned to the left and thrust her upper body back on to the tunnel floor. She tried to grasp anything with her hands but there was nothing but smooth, packed dirt, and her hands were simply sliding further and further down. Her left knee was barely hanging on to the edge, but was slipping, slowly. Her right leg was dangling.

She couldn't die this way. Not after all they had already been through. Whimpering and gasping, she tried to hold on. Help would be here soon, if she could just hold on. Unbidden, she heard words she had memorized as a child going through her head, words she hadn't heard in years...... "My grace is sufficient for you... My strength is made perfect in weakness... I will bear you up on eagle's wings... Be strong in the Lord... My help comes from the Lord... I can do all things through Christ, who strengthens me..."

As the words continued in her head, Grace felt a calmness and a peace come over her. She could feel the words welling up within her now, and she had to say them out loud. "From everlasting to everlasting, you are God... Where shall I go from your presence? ... the darkness doesn't hide from you, the night shines like the day; the darkness and the light are both alike to you... Yea, though I walk through the valley of the shadow of death, I will fear no evil, for you are with me... Thank you, Jesus, for coming into my life. Please always be with me the way you are right now. Don't ever let me forget this moment."

As Grace grew quiet, she realized that she was standing on the support beam of the bridge. She didn't remember her left foot touching down on it, but here she was, only a step below the tunnel floor. Carefully, she raised her right knee up over the edge, and having that one firmly placed, she brought the other knee up. Then she crawled several feet away from the edge.

She couldn't even think. There was nothing in her mind but pure thankfulness. There just wasn't room for anything else. Tears were rolling down her cheeks, but she was crying for joy, not from fear.

After a few minutes, she was able to think again about her original purpose in coming to the opening. She could still hear the tapping sound, only louder now. Whoever was there must still be behind a door, or a wall, or something, trying to get in. On the off chance that they could hear her, she yelled as loud as she could, then waited for a reply. Just as she thought. No response.

Then the noise seemed to change, to a banging, and a crashing. Shortly after, Grace thought she heard voices. She yelled again, and waited. This time the noise came to a standstill and a voice called out, "Grace? Grace, can you hear me?"

It was Ethan.

Thirty-Four

Sweet. Fresh. Grace couldn't pull the clean mountain air down into her lungs fast enough. And the light! Oh, the blessed light. Even though the sun had already set and it was twilight, it was so wonderful to see more than a small circle of your surroundings at a time. Grace was filled with new wonder and appreciation for the pleasure such simple things could bring.

As soon as the rescue team could stretch a new - and sturdy - bridge across the chasm, Ethan had come to her immediately, and, before he even hugged her, had handed her a bottle of water. She felt no shame either, in grabbing hold of it and drinking her fill before leaning into him in exhausted relief. The emergency team had gone on to treat Bo with some basic care, and then loaded him onto a stretcher for transport. Now, she and Ethan were traveling with one group in a jeep, and the others were following in a pickup truck with Bo and the medical team in the back. They were riding on a rough, overgrown road, which wound around the side of the mountain and ended at the clearing near the main mine entrance.

"What happened, Ethan? Did that tunnel lead to the outside?" Grace asked.

"It did, eventually. I crawled about five hours before I got to the end. Then I got my bearings from the view of the surrounding mountains and I headed for the new Heaven's Mountain Road. A kind stranger figured out who I must be," Ethan chuckled, "Probably by the way I looked! He stopped and gave me a ride. Brought me to the main entrance where all the law enforcement and emergency folks are set up."

"But you came back in through the other entrance, the one Bo was talking about, right?" Ethan nodded. "Well, who told you where it was?"

"Er, that'd be me, ma'am," the old-timer chimed in from the front.

Grace recognized the voice immediately. "Diggy?"

He turned around and grinned at her. "Yes, ma'am, that's me! They had me working at the jail tonight, but when Preacher Ethan said there was another way in, they called up old Diggy pretty quick-like. And it's a good thing they did, too. Not too many of us left who remember the old days when the Lucases used that entrance to sell their moonshine out of. I had plumb forgot about it myself."

"Diggy, you're an angel. Thank you," Grace said sincerely.

When they reached the clearing, Grace was amazed at the number of vehicles crowded into that small area. There seemed to be barely room enough to walk between them, but somehow the jeep snaked its way right to the hub of activity. The first ambulance team was already moving Bo from the truck into the back of the ambulance and was getting ready to transport him, when he apparently got very upset over something and refused to leave. One of the sheriff's deputies was hailed; he spoke to Bo a moment, then went in search of the sheriff. In the meantime, Billy had just arrived and made his way over to where his father lay in the ambulance. Billy hovered over his father, and the two were holding hands when the sheriff came to stand outside the door. Giving his father a brief hug, Billy indicated he would follow the ambulance when it left for the hospital. The sheriff then climbed up into the ambulance and they spent several minutes talking.

All this Grace watched as the second ambulance team asked her questions and checked her vital signs. After receiving the "all clear", she was finally able to stand in her mother's embrace and rock back and forth, back and forth, repeating, "I love you, mom, I love you. I love you."

"What am I going to do with you, young lady? You had us all scared to death! Granny sends her love. She says to tell you she's baking all kinds of goodies to fatten you up when you get home." Nan let her go long enough to reach out and include Augusta into their circle, taking the older woman's hand and drawing her closer. "Grace, Augusta insisted that we come in the Lincoln so we could all be more comfortable. Ed drove us. I think he's somewhere over there talking to that other newspaperman."

Throwing caution to the wind, Grace threw her arms around Augusta and gave her an emphatic hug. "Thank you so much, Augusta. I love you, too." Though her grandmother did not actually return her embrace, Grace could feel that her tense, rigid body seemed to relax and bend a bit in response to Grace's spontaneous overture. It was a good beginning, she thought.

"Ace, did you not learn anything I've been trying to teach you?"

"Ed, you big, old cuddly bear. I'm so glad you're here. Thanks for driving my mom and Augusta. That was so good of you."

"Well, I couldn't very well turn them loose up here in the mountains, now could I? Why, there's no telling what they might get into if left to their own devices. Hey now, Ace, aren't you about ready to go to Miss Clare's and fill your empty stomach with some good hot food, and then take a nice, hot shower and crawl into your clean, soft bed?"

"My mouth is watering. Let me see if Ethan wants to come, too."

Ed spotted Ethan talking to the Sheriff and pointed him out to Grace. "You want me to go ask him? You can sit in the car with the ladies."

"I'll do that. Oh, and Ed! Ask them about getting the VW home. Beamon had my keys. I didn't bring an extra set with me."

"You got it."

There was enough food on the table to feed a small army, and Grace needed no urging to eat her share of it. The little bit she had eaten before taking a shower and changing clothes had only whetted her appetite. It felt so good to be in a warm house, with comfortable, clean clothes, and a full tummy. Grace could have purred, she was feeling so contented.

Ethan had gone home to bathe and change first also, but had then come to the boarding house to enjoy the hearty meal Clare had prepared, as well as to meet Grace's family and her boss. By the end of the meal, he and Grace both were on the verge of falling asleep sitting up.

Clare finally said, "Grace, if your head sinks any lower, your face is going to be in my sweet potato pie. Both of you kids are dead on your feet. You need to get some good rest, now. Preacher Ethan, I don't trust you to drive. Come on. Say good-bye to everybody. Tell Grace you'll talk to her tomorrow, and I'm going to follow you home. Nan, I'm sure you can handle Grace. Let's go, Preacher."

Ethan didn't have the energy to contradict her. "Good night, everybody. It was a pleasure to meet you all. Grace, I'll see you tomorrow." Ethan casually leaned over Grace's head, and kissed her on the top of the head before walking, more or less like a zombie, out the back door.

Nan, Augusta, and Ed all exchanged knowing looks, but none of them ventured to say anything. Nan just gathered Grace up, and took her upstairs, there to tuck her safely into her own bed.

Thirty-Five

race lay in the bed, coming awake slowly, luxuriating in the comfort of a soft pillow and warm covers. As was her habit, she stretched her body this way and that before opening her eyes and glancing at the clock. Eight o'clock! She didn't want to miss breakfast. After going without food for two full days, the thought of missing a meal was too much to bear. Tossing the covers away, she hurried to brush her teeth and wash her face. Then, grabbing her robe, she was out the door and down the stairs within five minutes of waking.

Everyone was still gathered around the dining room table talking, but when Grace made her appearance, there were cheers all around by boarders and family alike. Grace sheepishly smiled and thanked them, gave her mom a hug, and began fixing her plate.

"Honey, you could have slept as long as you liked this morning. I would have saved your breakfast for you," Clare declared.

"I didn't want to take that chance!" said Grace, laughing at herself.

"How're you feeling, Gracie?" Ed asked.

Grace brought her heaping plate to the table and sat down. "Much better! Maybe not quite back to my usual self yet, but close." She ate several bites of pancakes and sausage. "Mm, this is so good. I don't think I'll ever take food for granted again."

One by one the boarders left the table to go about their daily business, and Clare rose to begin clearing away. However, as she assured Grace, "I'm not taking any of the food yet. You eat all you want, honey, and I'll get those dishes in a little while." Grace smiled her thanks, and continued chewing.

When she was comfortably full, Grace got a second cup of coffee, and enjoyed the company of Ed, Nan and Augusta as they caught up on everything that had happened. They were anxious to hear the details of the events that occurred in the mine, as well as the resolution of the questions raised by Floyd's letter.

Ed finally intervened. "You know, the sheriff wants you to come down first thing this morning and give a statement. If you want, we could load up and go home right after that."

Grace looked around the table at their expectant faces. Her mother, she could tell, wanted nothing more than to get her daughter safely home. She didn't want to disappoint them, but she needed just a little more time to tie up all the loose ends. "Ed, I know you probably need to get back to the paper. Could I make a suggestion? Maybe you and Augusta could go on home today; you could leave right away if you want. And I know my mother is not ready to let me out of her sight, so, if she wouldn't mind staying one more night, she and I can drive my car home tomorrow morning. That is, if I still have any car keys?"

"Ah, you sure do. They were in Beamon's pocket. The sheriff gave them to me last night." Reaching into his pants pocket, Ed pulled out the keys and handed them to Grace.

"That's a relief!" she said. "What do you think, Mom? Would that be all right with you?"

"I don't mind a bit. Augusta?"

"I am agreeable to that. Now that we know Grace is safe, I will be perfectly content to ride home with Mr. Broadman."

"I seem to have missed a lot, being at the sheriff's convention the first part of this week," the sheriff sighed. "Makes me wonder if I can afford to ever leave town again."

"Look on the bright side, Sheriff. An innocent man is being set free, and a guilty man put behind bars, and it all happened on your watch," Grace said encouragingly.

"Still, you handled this entire "story" thing in a way that endangered you and many other people. I have two people dead, and I'm not convinced it couldn't have been prevented. You should have come to me with that letter the minute you hit town."

"In hindsight, I tend to agree with you. But sheriff, look at this from my point of view. Bringing you the letter would have accomplished nothing. It would have been a long shot at an attempt to clear a convicted murderer. You would have had no reason to give it more than cursory attention. Without the digging I did, which, if you're honest about it, your office would never have done under the circumstances, there would have been no known evidence to connect the Lucases to the murder. As for the deaths of Beamon and Sadie, I truly regret that Beamon became so crazed that he started shooting people, but he is the one to blame for their deaths, not anyone else."

"All right, all right. We'll close that part of this discussion. But I hope you'll think twice before you discount the assistance of law enforcement again. You might even find that you like having us on your side upfront." The sheriff opened up a file on his desk and read for a few minutes while Grace waited quietly. "I see you've given us a complete statement concerning the events at the mine. It coincides with what Billy said. So, I see no problem there. Bo also has corroborated everything the two of you said."

"How is Bo doing?"

"Surprisingly well, considering the gunshot and the two days without water, food or medical treatment. He said you did some crucial first aid right away. Probably made a big difference in his recovery, Miss Turner. I understand the doctor has said he can probably be released in three or four days." The intercom on the desk buzzed. "Yes?"

"Sheriff, Preacher MacEwen is here."

"You can send him in, Martha."

The sheriff stood and shook hands with Ethan when he came in. "Preacher. You're looking a lot better than you were last night."

"I feel considerably better, too." Ethan sat down and gave Grace a warm look. "Good morning, Grace. Sheriff, I just finished giving my statement to the deputy. He said you wanted to talk to me."

"Yes, as you can see, I've asked Miss Turner to be here, also, since she has been instrumental in this case in greasing the wheels of justice, so to speak. I think you both know that Bo Lucas gave a full confession to the murder of Amos Lucas. He'll eventually spend some time in prison, it'll just take a while to go through the process to get him there. As for your father, Ethan, I've talked to the Governor's office this morning. Told them about the situation we've got here. They said it sounds like there should be no problem in arranging for his release. There is always a short processing delay, usually about two weeks, they said. I thought you might like to tell your father yourself, Ethan."

Ethan couldn't speak; he was trying to swallow the huge lump in his throat, as well as fight back the tears welling up in his eyes. Grace reached across to cover his hand with hers. In a choked voice he said, "Thank you, Sheriff. I appreciate that. I'll tell him today. Grace, would you like to go with me?"

"There's no way you could keep me away."

Thirty-Six

The prison normally discouraged any type of visitation immediately after lunch, so Ethan and Grace made plans to meet at the church around two-thirty and ride together to visit James. In the meantime, Grace went back to the boarding house to start packing for the trip home the next day.

Clare and Nan were in the kitchen getting ready to serve lunch when Grace arrived. Watching them talk and carry on as if they had always known each other made her smile. Already they had swapped a couple of dozen recipes, and Nan was moving around Clare's kitchen as if she owned the place. Looks like they've discovered they're kindred spirits, Grace thought with satisfaction. Ed and Augusta were long since gone, and there were only a few other boarders there for lunch.

One by one the others ate and left, but Grace, Nan and Clare spent a leisurely hour sitting around the table, conversing about everything imaginable. Eventually the talk came around to Grace's love life. Despite her protests, Clare and Nan were speculating about the looks passed between Grace and a certain eligible bachelor.

"You know, Nan, I've never seen that young man so taken with anyone before. He's been our minister for about two years now, and he's always very careful to steer clear of any unmarried girls, or their mamas for that matter, who might be looking to snag a good-looking catch such as he is."

"He's certainly a fine-looking fellow," Nan agreed. "Gorgeous blue eyes. And, oh, my goodness, he must lift weights!"

"Momma! I can't believe you. You two are just awful, ganging up on me like this. Clare, you are definitely a bad influence on my mother!" Grace complained good-naturedly. She decided that two could play at this game. "Now, for one of you women, if you wanted to discuss a slightly older, but extremely handsome guy, just wait until James MacEwen gets out of jail, ladies. Then, this town will see some flirting and finagling over the most eligible man in that category." Then, conspiratorially, she continued, "He looks a lot like Ethan, only older. His hair has turned almost white, but he's got the same eyes as Ethan, and the same jaw-line, the same smile."

Clare scoffed. "I don't care how pretty he is! Why would I want to tie myself down? I have more fun than a body should be allowed to have as it is. No, no, I've had my one true love – and he was a precious man, let me tell you - but that isn't likely to come again. Your mother, on the other hand, might be in the market. She sure seems to be a sweet home-body type…," Clare teased.

"Oh, no! You're not going to match me up with anybody. I'm very happy just as I am. Of course, I would be even happier if I had some grandchildren to love…," she said, looking pointedly at Grace.

"Mom, don't you think you ought to let me get married first?" Grace laughed. "Besides, I still have places I'd like to go career-wise. I've got this great story to finish writing, and who knows what doors that may open?"

"I know, I know. I'm only teasing you, sweetheart! I want you to follow your dreams, always. Most of the women who came before you didn't have that choice. It's a blessing to be able to use your talents."

Grace looked at her watch. "I have some things I need to do before Ethan picks me up. But I've got time to help you clean up…"

Clare broke in, "Fiddlesticks! If you're going to impress that hand-some, available preacher, you need to get upstairs and get busy with your hair and make-up and clothes!"

"And don't forget the perfume. I do want grandkids before I'm too old to enjoy them." Nan reminded her.

"I give up. You both are crazy! Are you sure I'm your offspring, Mom?" Grace left the room rolling her eyes and shaking her head.

Ethan and Grace had deliberated over what would be the best way to give his father the news about Bo's confession. Ethan wanted Grace to have the pleasure of informing him, while Grace felt Ethan should be allowed to tell his own father something so important. In the end, they agreed that Grace would describe the events in the mine, except for Bo's confession. Ethan would tell him about Bo, as well as what the sheriff had said about his probable imminent release. Grace was excited and happy, but Ethan, who was usually rather calm and steady, was acting just like a child at Christmas. He couldn't keep still, he kept talking nervously, and he kept hugging Grace. When they were finally ushered into the little prison chapel, James had not yet been brought in.

"I still find it very hard to imagine what this must have been like for him. Being incarcerated would be bad enough if you were guilty, but to lose your freedom when you're not even guilty must have been so devastating," Grace said.

"At first, maybe. But you saw my dad. He's truly content wherever he is, happy with whatever God wants him to do. He's an exceptional person."

"A bigger and better person," Grace murmured, recalling her last conversation with James.

Just then, James came through the door smiling. "Hallelujah! I'm so glad to see you both safe and sound. Come over here and let me hug you both." James gave each of them a hearty hug, "Clare called last night and asked the guard to come and tell me when you were found. I guess she told you that."

Grace nodded. "I vaguely remember her telling us. Last night is a little fuzzy.."

Ethan broke in, "We were dehydrated and hungry, but otherwise all right. Dad, did Clare give you any of the details? Or has the scuttlebutt around this place reached your ears?"

"I guess not. Something in particular I should know about?"

"It's a long story, but one worth hearing. It's sort of Grace's story, so she's going to do the telling. Grace?"

"Why don't we all sit down and get comfortable?" Grace led them across the room to the small table and chairs. Ethan could tell that his father's curiosity was peaked, but that he had decided to allow the young folks to do this their way.

Grace began with the phone call from Billy, and had reached the part where she could hear the tapping through the tunnel by Ethan and the emergency crew. As she went on, Ethan was surprised to hear of her near-fatal episode when she almost slipped into the ravine. She had to stop talking when he grabbed her to him and wouldn't let go. She heard him saying, "Thank you, God, thank you. Why didn't you tell me this before?"

With her face pressed flat against his shirt, she could hardly breathe, much less answer him. In a muffled voice, she answered, "I just hadn't had a chance! The subject hadn't come up. Ethan, you can let me go now!" she laughed.

While Grace was extricating herself from his ardent embrace, James was grinning on the inside, while managing to maintain simply a pleasant smile on the outside. Whatever the problem had been – and he suspected it was the matter of Grace's salvation – it had obviously been resolved, completely and to everyone's satisfaction. He himself was overjoyed. Grace had an open, honest way about her that he admired, as well as a playful exuberance that was a good counterbalance to his son's serious nature. They made a good pair. Where they went from here was up to them and to God, but he had to admit, he liked the way they looked together.

Grace had now laughingly patted her hair back into place and was ready to continue. When she told them about hearing the scriptures, then finding her feet safely on the beam, they were as much in awe of the mercy of God as she was. When she had finished her part of the story, she looked at Ethan, relinquishing the floor to him.

"Dad, while we were trapped in the mine with Bo, he told us…" Ethan had to choke back the tears, and clear his throat. "Bo told us that he murdered Amos. He was following Beamon's directions. He told us all the details, which don't really matter right now. But when we reached the outside, Dad, the first thing Bo did was confess to the sheriff. Bo had to be taken to the hospital for the gunshot wound, and he'll be there probably a few more days, but when he gets out, he's planning on turning himself in. The sheriff said there'll be a good bit of paperwork involved, and it'll take a couple of weeks, but real soon, Dad, you're getting out." Ethan was smiling through the tears rolling down his face. James' expression was simply stunned. One could almost hear all the little wheels turning inside his head, as he attempted to make all the pieces fit together and grasp the full meaning of what his son was saying. Finally, a smile broke through, as well as a few tears, and he began nodding his head in understanding. He couldn't speak. Grace and Ethan appreciated how overwhelming this moment must be for him, as he contemplated the vast prospect of freedoms, both large and small, which he would regain in a relatively short time.

A little flicker of concern passed across his face. "What will I do when I'm released? I'm not a young man anymore."

Ethan felt a swell of love for this man who, though he poured himself out in joyful obedience to God day in and day out, still was only human, and needed encouragement just as all souls do from time to time. "Dad, God found something for you to do when you came to this place. I'm sure he will have something for you to do when you leave it."

Grace added, "You may want to take a few weeks, maybe even a few months, to just enjoy things you haven't been able to do for a long time. You might want to travel a bit. Catch up with old friends. Work in your yard?"

"Hmm. I don't actually have a yard anymore. I don't have any material possessions, come to think of it. Not that that worries me."

"It shouldn't, Dad. You'll live with me, as long as you want to. That idea thoroughly delights me. I missed you growing up," he admitted. "Having you actually living in the same house with me is something I've looked forward to my whole life."

"Then that's what I'll do, at least for a good long while. Who knows? You may eventually need a little more room for a wife and a family, somewhere down the road."

"Let's just concentrate on the next few weeks, Dad!"

Thirty-Seven

That evening, Ethan felt revived enough to lead the evening service. He thanked the lay preacher and the congregation for carrying on the business of the church not only that morning, but during the days of his absence. He knew his flock, and knew that they had been praying for him and the others the whole time. He was very aware that this was Grace's first corporate worship experience since committing her life to Jesus, and he prayed that it would be a good beginning. She was sitting with Clare and her mother halfway back on Ethan's left; the expression on her face let him know that her heart was filled with thankfulness and joy, for her eyes were shining back at him in agreement, as he spoke of the mercies shown to them by God over the last few days.

At his request, Grace waited after the service so that Ethan could drive her home. They sat on the porch and talked for a little while.

"You will keep in touch with me about James' release, won't you?" she asked.

"I promise I will. I'd really like for you to come for a few days when he's released. Would you mind?"

"Are you kidding? I'd love to. I'm going to work on my story in the meantime. But Ethan, I want to ask you something, and I want you to be honest with me. Do you think it will be detrimental to your father in any way, for me to tell his story? Because if it is, I won't write it. Your father is much more important to me than the story."

"No, Grace, you've got to write the story. Nobody knows the whole truth about it like you do. I think Dad would be pleased for you to tell the story. We both know you'll do it with respect and dignity. Someone will write the story, it's such a good juicy one. We want it to be you."

"All right, then. I'll tell Floyd's story. I'm sure he never thought it would take this long to 'set the record straight'."

A small car had pulled up to the boarding house. Watching with interest, Grace saw Joe Wilson get out.

"You're a hard lady to track down, Grace! I couldn't get to you before you left the mine last night. And you must have been on the move all day today."

"Hi, Joe. I have been gallivanting just about all day. What brings you out tonight?"

"I've got something that belongs to you. Thelma slid this under my door Thursday evening, with a note to make some copies, give one to the sheriff, and to return this original to you. So, that's what I'm doing now." Joe handed her a familiar ragged envelope. "The letter. Floyd's letter. Wow. Who would have thought that old letter would have produced such a maelstrom of change in our little community."

"It's been surreal," Grace agreed.

"I heard that your father will most likely be released real soon, Ethan. I'm very happy for him and for you."

"Thanks, Joe. I'll pass that along."

"Grace, I wondered if you – and you, too, Ethan – would be willing to give me an interview about the events in the mine and your rescue? You know, it's such a huge story for our little town, I'll have to report on it in a big way. I'd rather have it straight from your mouths, if you're willing. Of course, I understand if there are any parts you'd prefer to keep private."

"I'll be happy to do that, Joe. You've been such a help to me since I've been in Fairmount, how could I possibly refuse? I'm supposed to go home to Jackstone in the morning, though."

"How about right now? If you're not too tired, that is."

Grace and Ethan exchanged looks. They had hoped to share a quiet hour or two, and now saw it shrinking to a much shorter visit. However, it needed to be done; Grace truly felt she owed the same professional courtesy to Joe which he had very generously shown to her, so she responded, "Sure. Let's go inside to the kitchen table, and I'll make us some coffee."

By the time Joe had gotten all he needed, it was almost eleven o'clock. Against her will, Grace could feel her eyelids drooping. She could almost feel the energy draining out the soles of her feet. It had been another one of those long, emotion-packed days, of which she had had many lately. A quick look in Ethan's direction confirmed that he was in the same shape she was.

"Ethan, why don't you go on home?" Grace sighed. "I can tell you're exhausted, and I'm bushed, too. Come on, I'll walk you out."

Reluctantly, he got to his feet and stretched. "It kind of catches up to you all over again, doesn't it? Okay. Let's go." Putting his arm around her shoulder, Ethan leaned against Grace, and she against him as they strolled back to the porch.

They stood facing each other, holding hands. Ethan spoke, "I hope I can keep myself awake and coherent long enough to say what I want to say to you, Grace. I admire you and I want to take our relationship further. I hope you feel the same way."

"Yes, you know I do. That first day, on the square, right after we met, you turned and looked at me. Something happened between us in that moment. I don't know if you felt it, but I did. We haven't really had a chance to get to know each other in a normal way – we've been dealing first with a difference in beliefs, and then with solving a murder. I'd like for us to spend some 'normal' time together, and see where that leads."

"We will. I'm leaving now, but I'll be back in the morning to see you off. And I'd really like to kiss you goodnight, but only if you promise not to hold it against me if it's a little slow and relaxed and sleepy."

"Don't worry so much. Come here," Grace murmured. She curved her hand around his neck and pulled him down to her. It was slow and gentle, but nonetheless sweet and exciting. When they began swaying a little too far to one side, Grace reluctantly pushed him away.

"Are you awake enough to drive?" Grace asked.

Ethan shook himself all over. "I'm good. I'll roll down the windows, and I'll sing as loud as I can, all the way home."

"And what are you going to sing?" she wanted to know.

"I'm going to sing 'our song'," he said as he went down the steps.

"I didn't know we had a song. What is it?"

"She'll Be Comin' Around the Mountain, of course!" he laughed, and waved goodbye. She could hear him singing all the way down the street.

Thirty-Eight

"It's about time you graced us with your presence," Ed growled in an angry voice. He might have pulled it off had it not been for his huge grin spanning from ear to ear. Grace ignored his growling and patted his shoulder.

"When are you going to learn that I'm never fooled by your 'disgruntled boss' act?" she asked.

"Shucks, I thought I had my facial expression down pat this time. Anyway, how's the story coming along? Want me to edit it for you?"

"I would if there was a story ready for you to edit. Don't be so impatient. Monday we spent all day driving home, and yesterday I did nothing but lay in the bed, sleep and eat. I'm back to my usual brilliant self today though, so after I straighten out all the messes you've made while I was gone, I might actually have a little time left over to work on the story. Depends on how bad the messes are." Grace wiggled her eyebrows up and down with a knowing smile.

Ed laughed out loud. "I sure have missed you, Ace! Ducky and I did the best we could, now, so don't be upset with him – or me!" he protested. They spent the next few hours hunched over the layout table as they worked to put the paper together.

It felt so comfortable and satisfying to have her hands in the ink again. It was almost engrossing enough to keep her mind occupied. Almost. Every so often, she would find herself staring down at the columns and seeing nothing but the image of Ethan smiling at her, or Ethan singing, or Ethan pulling her closer. With a jerk, she would snap herself back to the task at hand.

What was the matter with her? She had had boyfriends before. Nothing too serious, of course, but it had never affected her ability to concentrate and do her work. Good grief, she thought. I'll be seeing him again in just two or three weeks. You would think I could compartmentalize the romance in my life and keep it in its place. I need to be focusing on work right now, and that is exactly what I'm going to do.

Then, despite the stern talking-to she gave herself, within thirty minutes her thoughts were drifting again. Giving up, she did the best she could to corral her wayward daydreaming and finish the job before her.

Finally, she and Ed were done. Ducky made an appearance in the meantime, so Grace did not feel quite so guilty admitting that perhaps she was not quite up to her normal routine yet. "Ed, if you don't mind, I think I'm going home and rest. Maybe work a little in my office. I know, I know, I'm a baby kitty, not a lioness. I admit it, I'm bushed. I'll see you tomorrow, okay?"

Grace had fashioned a neat, modern office space for herself in one of the six bedrooms in the big house. Her house. It was still hard to get her mind wrapped around that idea. After Uncle Zachary's death, she had moved a few personal items into this little-used room, primarily because her mother's cottage was so small and she needed more room in which to work. But on further analysis, she had come to the conclusion that moving into the big house was an idea that had merit, even if it meant sharing the house with Augusta.

They had always been cramped for space in the small cottage. Someday she would be moving out anyway, so a lateral move such as this might ease them all into, if not a separation, at least a more adult relationship. Grace realized that she was unintentionally guilty of allowing her mother and granny to take on many personal tasks for which she ought to be taking full responsibility herself. But it was the showdown between Grace and the two of them over the Heaven's Mountain trip had been the final straw. And so, right before she left for Heaven's Mountain, she had spent half a day transferring the majority of her clothes and belongings over to the estate house into the bedroom that adjoined her office. The other half of that day was spent helping her mother transform Grace's old room into a sewing and sitting room for Nan. In spite of her sadness to see Grace leave the home she had known since birth, Nan had known it would be a good thing for Grace, and, she had to admit, the sewing room was going to be a joy for her and Grace's granny.

Ensconced in her office, Grace settled into the soft plushy armchair with her feet on the ottoman, and spread her notes out on her lap, including those she had jotted down a few minutes at the time while the events of the past week were still fresh on her mind. With the best of intentions, she began outlining her piece. Ten minutes later she noted that, once again, thoughts of Ethan had taken over.

Reluctantly, she realized that she needed to examine the depth of her feelings for this man who had entered her life less than two weeks ago. She knew the attraction was there, an attraction that could easily become an infatuation. But of course she wanted more than that. She wanted a love that would last forever, a life with someone who would share her dreams, a commitment to someone she respected and admired. Was it possible that she could have all of that with Ethan? Was it even possible after just two weeks to know enough about the man himself?

She thought about the time they had spent together. Though they had known each other such a short time, they had actually spent a lot of that time together. Through dangerous moments, and silly times, over days of deprivation, and hours of serious spiritual discussions, she felt that they had reached an intimacy that months of normal dating would not have produced.

But did she love Ethan? She wasn't sure. She could imagine giving herself in marriage to him. And having babies with him and watching them grow up. What a wonderful father he would be, with his gentle words of encouragement and love. He would certainly impart to his children his joy in living each day, and his awe of the greatness of God. And she could picture the two of them many years from now, when their children were grown, still enjoying their life together, whatever it might hold. Surrounding the circle of their life would be an awareness of God's hands holding them, guiding them and blessing them.

She yearned for that life, as she ached for Ethan. Did this ache mean that she was in love, for the first time in her life? Did love mean that you put the other person's well-being before your own? Did it mean that you were ready to be committed and loyal to someone until parted by death? Did it mean that you desired your love and wanted to be with him? She knew the answer to all those questions was "yes".

She loved him, she thought in amazement. She loved everything about him. How could she have fallen in love, and not even realized it? It was so clear to her now. And to think that she would have let this man walk right on out of her life, after touching it only briefly, if she had not been so blessed by all the people, circumstances and events that had been placed in her path in Heaven's Mountain. Ultimately, it came down to the fact that if Floyd had not written the letter and given it to her father, among whose belongings it lay waiting until just this moment in her life and Ethan's, they might never even have met. Mysterious ways. Boy, was that an understatement!

She wondered if Ethan was meant to love her in return. The last time they talked, he definitely gave the impression that he wanted to continue their relationship, and even take it to a deeper level. When she realized that she was fretting over it, she stopped herself. Whether they ended up making a life together or not, she willed herself to leave that up to God. Maybe she shouldn't even be feeling this way about Ethan yet, she thought. Maybe she should bury her love, suppress these emotions, until it was evident that Ethan felt the same way.

She searched her heart and saw no wrong in the love she felt, regardless of Ethan's reaction, so she determined that she would allow herself the happiness of loving. Since she had committed her life to God, she had sensed that they would now be striving toward the same direction in their lives. And she wanted to travel that road with Ethan.

Excited now at the discovery she had made, she was eager to talk to Ethan. However, they had agreed that he would call her tonight at eight o'clock, so she resisted the urge to call him at this very moment. Nevertheless she couldn't sit still and decided to run down the hill to visit her mother. Exhilarated by the thrill of this wonderful new knowledge of first love, she was almost skipping through the house, down the wide front hall, when she heard Augusta call her from the sunroom on the back of the house.

Since their return from Heaven's Mountain, a fragile air of reconciliation had existed between Grace and Augusta. Though still quite formal towards her, Grace could sense in Augusta a degree of kindness and warmth that had never been there before. Without actually saying so, she seemed to have accepted Grace as her granddaughter. And Grace was anxious to have that relationship grow into what it could be. She suspected that Augusta had much to share if she would only let someone get close enough to her.

Grace stepped into the bright sunlight pouring through the sunroom windows. "Yes, Augusta? Did you need me?" Grace asked pleasantly.

Augusta actually gave a small smile in return. "I don't really need anything. I thought you might like to sit in here with me for a few minutes and watch the birds bathing in the birdbath." She pointed through the window facing the garden in the rear of the house.

"Oh, look at them!" Grace was immediately enthralled. There were half a dozen birds sitting around the edge of the concrete basin; at any given moment, several of them would flutter their wings and splash water all around.

"I usually sit out here at this time of day, while I'm reading my Bible, so I can enjoy the birds. Some of them are regulars, but there's a visitor or two every day. If it's not too cold or too hot, sometimes I'll go to the gazebo and sit out there instead."

"The gardens are really beautiful this year, Augusta. I like the little changes you made here and there. I don't know that I could ever create such lovely spaces as you, but maybe you could teach me some of the basics. If you have time, that is."

"I have nothing but time, dear. And I would very much enjoy spending some time showing you the little I know."

They fell silent for a few minutes, commenting occasionally when a particularly rowdy bird would show off. Augusta broke the silence. "The thought occurred to me that you might not have seen many pictures of Jesse, your father. Would you like to look at my photo albums?"

Grace was astounded and touched. Trying not to appear too ridiculously eager, she managed to say simply, "I'd love to, Augusta. Are they in here?"

"They're in my sitting room. Would you like to go look at them now?"

"Yes, I would."

Grace had never dreamed she would spend such a pleasant hour with Augusta as the one that followed. The pictures seemed to take Augusta back to a happier time, one that was reflected in the way she spoke, and the way she acted. She even laughed several times as she told Grace of some scrape or antic that Jesse had pulled. The most surprising thing was when Augusta offered several of the pictures to Grace to keep.

As Grace held out her hand to receive the pictures, she noticed the age spots and the bony knots in the joints of her grandmother's refined hands, and she remembered Mrs. O'Dell's old, callused hands, and her statement about some old folks not having anybody to care about them. Though the two older ladies' lives had been very different, they shared a common loneliness, Grace thought. But she, Grace, could make a difference in this woman's life. She could offer Augusta a new sense of family, by loving her and caring for her. The groundwork was already laid, and Grace felt great hope that this new relationship would be built upon love and respect and forgiveness.

Thirty-Nine

"Grace, is that you?"

"Yes! I'm so glad to hear your voice, Ethan."

"It's wonderful to hear yours, too. Are you starting to feel normal again?"

"Even better than that!" Especially when I think about you, she thought. "How about you?"

"I'm feeling great. How is the writing coming along?"

"Oh, a little on the slow side. I think I was just too tired and washed out for a day or two there. But I'm ready to attack it in earnest tomorrow. What's the latest on your Dad's release?"

"One week from today."

"Wow. That's even sooner than we anticipated. Do you think James is prepared, emotionally I mean, for the huge change he's going to experience?"

"Well, I guess as much as he can be. I truly believe he will handle it well, but he knows, just as we do, that there's going to be an adjustment period. By the way, he's told me several times to be sure to thank you again."

"Tell him no thanks are needed. Do you have a room ready for him?"

"Hoo, boy! Grace, you simply would not believe how the women of the church have come in and moved furniture, or rather, made me move furniture. Then, there were all the color schemes, and different styles, and lighting choices! I finally had to tell them to just choose everything themselves, just so I could get a little peace, and get some work done. It's been a real learning experience!"

Grace giggled. "I can imagine. Took off like a horse with the bit in his mouth, huh?"

Ethan laughed. "I'd say that's a pretty accurate description. Are you still planning to come for Dad's release?"

"Absolutely. Would you call Clare and tell her I'll be there in the late afternoon, Monday?"

"Sure, I'll call her. Grace, I'm so glad you're coming, and not just for the story. I really want you to be there with me, to welcome my dad home."

"I want to be there, Ethan. You know how I feel about your father. I would not miss this, story or no."

"...I've missed you, Grace," Ethan said. "I know it's just been a few days, but I'm glad it's only another week before you'll be back."

"I feel the same way."

"Will you call me when you get to Clare's?"

"The minute I get there."

Grace couldn't believe how much her mother's church had changed. But then again, maybe it was she who had changed. Or maybe it was a little of both. At any rate, there seemed to be a genuine spirit of love in their midst Sunday morning. Even the singing seemed to have a more honest and vibrant quality about it, to say nothing of the level of participation. Virtually everyone present appeared to be singing with gusto, whether on-key or off-key. When the time came for the sermon, Grace prayed that she would be open to receive whatever the Holy Spirit might lay on her heart. She had spent a sweet hour talking to her mother yesterday, sharing with her the decision she had made while in the mine. Grace also found the courage to talk to Nan about the shortcomings of the church and its members, Augusta in particular, who had, in effect, driven Grace away many years ago. But Grace was shocked to learn that things were not as they had seemed to her as a child.

Nan chided her, saying, "Why didn't you tell me about this, sweetheart? I could have explained it all to you then."

"But Momma, she snatched me out of that group of kids, and told me not to open my mouth. The preacher at that time, I don't remember his name, he just stared at us as she drug me out of the room. And another time, after Wednesday night supper, he asked me to come to his office. She caught me following him down the hall and told me to go sit down by you and not get back up. She seemed to be really angry with me. And ashamed of me."

"Grace, she was protecting you. She heard him talking about me, and about you, saying really hateful things about me not being married when you were born. He had already approached several members about revoking my membership and refusing to let us attend church. When Augusta found out, she put a stop to that nonsense. He was gone within the month."

Grace just shook her head. "I wish I'd known. All this time, I thought she didn't even like me. She seemed very harsh and bitter."

"When you were little, she was still grieving over Jesse. Then, for many years, it was an awkward situation. She knew who you were, but she just didn't know how to begin to build a relationship with you."

So here they were on Sunday morning, all four women – Augusta, Nan, Granny Annie and Grace – sharing a pew for the first time.

And now came the time for the sermon. Grace had never heard this man before, but recalled her mother and grandmother spoke highly of him. When he explained that he had made a last minute change of the sermon topic, to forgiveness and reconciliation, Grace was certain that God had been at work, to reassure her that there could finally be reconciliation now, in this place. When the invitation came, Grace was ready. With no hesitation, she went confidently to take the outstretched hand of the pastor.

Clare had been keeping a watchful eye out for Grace all afternoon, but when she finally did arrive, Clare had gone outside to give some scraps to the dog. When she stepped back inside through the back door, Grace was leaning against the stove, drawing in all the wonderful suppertime aromas.

Clare let out a squeal when she saw her. "Oooo, come here and let me hug your neck. It's been awfully quiet around here this week without you here keeping things stirred up! Don't you look wonderful, though, all rested up. And a little different, too. Did you get your hair cut? No? Oh, well, it doesn't matter. Tell me all about…everything!"

"It feels good to be out of that car," Grace said, rubbing the back of her neck. "Bugs are great on mileage, but not so hot for comfort on a long trip. All of the older ladies in my life were against me coming to Fairmount again so soon, and *alone*, but I finally convinced them how important it was to me to be here for James' release from prison. Oh, and by the way, my mom has spent the entire week going through her recipes and writing all the good ones down for you, so don't let me forget to give that to you."

"Mercy, I'm only half-way through going through mine for her. I'd better get busy on that. Would you like something to drink?"

"I'd love some tea – but I'll get it. Just go on with what you were doing, and I'll just sit here and talk to you. What is the reaction around town to James being released and Bo going to prison?"

"I'd say mixed. Bo has a few vocal friends who are trying to say he was coerced into confessing. Anybody who knows James though is thrilled for him. From what I hear, the official release is at twelve noon tomorrow. I think Ethan is trying to keep it very low-key, for his daddy's sake, at least for a few days. On Saturday night, there's going to be a little get-together at our church. To sort of reintroduce James to the community, give him a chance to see a lot of his old friends. I hope that's not too much for him, too soon, you know?"

"Yes, I hope so, too. Speaking of Ethan, I promised to call him as soon as I got here. I'll do that right now."

As she dialed the phone, Clare handed her a chocolate chip cookie, fresh-baked. "It's a good thing I don't live with you. How do you keep from eating everything you cook?" Grace asked. "Ethan? Hi, it's Grace…… Six o'clock? Sounds terrific. I'll be ready."

Forty

That evening was their first real date. Grace knew she would always remember it as not only the most fun date she had ever had, but also the night she fell into the aisle at the movies. They had gone out to dinner at a very nice restaurant, and the accompanying conversation had been just as satisfying as the dinner. It was later, at the movies, that Grace had embarrassed herself.

At several places in the theatre, it was necessary to step up as you entered the row of seats. Ethan and Grace happened to choose such a row. Going in was no problem, but going out, she completely forgot the step, so that when her foot moved into the aisle, there was nothing to support it. She toppled over like a bowling pin. Naturally, the theatre was rather crowded, so Ethan had to keep people from walking all over her while she attempted to rise. Grace was mortified, almost to the point of tears. On top of that, when she fell, she ripped the knee of her pants on a nail sticking out of the stairs.

When they reached the lobby and the lights, Ethan saw the single tear that had left a track down her cheek. "Oh, sweetheart, that's nothing to cry about," he said, wiping the tear away with his thumb. He teased her, "After all we went through last week, here you are crying because you tripped in the movie theatre. Do you know, you are beautiful even when you're falling? I notice these things. Truly. You fell with great grace and style. Why, in generations to come, when they want to discuss falling with style, your name will be spoken with awe."

"Oh, hush. I'm over it now. I just wanted tonight to be really special, unmarred by anything mundane or spastic."

"Tonight was not marred by anything, because we were together." When they reached Ethan's truck, he opened the passenger door for her, but she didn't get in immediately.

"You're right. It was special because I'm with you." She stood on tip-toe and kissed him on the cheek, then turned and hopped in the truck.

When Ethan arrived to pick Grace up the next morning, she and Clare were lingering over coffee in the dining room. Since he was early, he accepted Clare's invitation to sit down and share a cup with them.

"Ethan, I've been wanting to ask you if you had already planned your supper for tonight," Clare said.

"Well, not exactly. I've had several offers of dinner invitations, but I think I'd like to keep it quiet and simple and private tonight. Just Dad and I at home, you know?"

"I agree that that would be best. But, you know, I cook enough to feed an army every night. Could I bring enough for you and James for supper? I won't even come in. Or maybe I'll get Grace to bring it to you," she said, looking for confirmation to Grace, who nodded her head.

"And I'm not coming in either, Ethan. Not tonight. This should be just you and your dad," Grace agreed.

"Well, in that case, I accept, and I thank you very much, for the meal, and for understanding about tonight."

Grace changed the subject. "Why is it that we're going so early this morning? Will the paperwork take that long?"

"Oh, no. Nothing to do with the paperwork. They've arranged for Dad to have a final service in the chapel at ten this morning. I think they're even going to have refreshments afterward. It will give Dad time to say goodbye to some of his friends."

"But, you did say he plans to continue his ministry in the prison?"

"Oh, sure. It'll just be a little different for the other inmates, relating to him as a free man rather than as a fellow inmate. Anyway, Dad asked if we wanted to come early and be there for his final service as an inmate."

"I'm ready if you are," Grace said.

Grace had to admit she was slightly intimidated as they sat in the back of the chapel while James conducted the simple worship service. As she studied the backs of the inmates' heads, she wondered of what crime each had been convicted. Were any of them innocent as James was? Probably not, was her honest opinion, but it was within the realm of possibility. Regardless, she was moved by their apparent desire to search for God, even in this place.

As the service came to a close, many of them approached Ethan, who faithfully assisted his father each Wednesday morning with a communion service. With pleasure, she noted that one and all spoke to Ethan with complete respect, but also genuine openness and affability. Even the two guards who stood against the walls seemed to relax and enjoy the unusual camaraderie within those four walls. The warden himself popped in for a few minutes, mixing and talking to visitors and inmates alike.

Eventually, the time came to move the inmates back to their sections. One by one, James gave a manly hug or a warm handshake to each one, giving a few last words of encouragement, with promises to see them soon. After their departure from the chapel, a single guard was left to escort James, Ethan and Grace to the intake and release center. As they walked slowly down the hall, their footsteps echoing through the passageway, Ethan and Grace took up places on each side of James, putting their arms around him. Grace could sense the emotions raging through the normally peaceful man.

"Are you all right, Dad?" Ethan asked, squeezing Grace's hand on his father's back.

James straightened and seemed to gain new strength. "Yes. Yes, son. I'm ready. It has been a long time, though, since I've been outside these barbwire fences. It's going to take me some time to adjust. But, I will. I will."

When the three of them crossed the dividing line drawn across the concrete at the gate, the line between imprisonment and freedom, James turned and took a long, thoughtful look back at what had been his home for the past twenty-five years. Finally, he turned back around. With the huge smile on his face overpowering the tears in his eyes , James said to Ethan, "Let's go home, son!"

Forty-One

"Okay, sweetie, come on and spill the beans. You can tell your old, decrepit, practically ancient friend what's going on between you two," Clare teased. In a more serious tone, she added, "My 'many years' of living have made me very wise, little one! If you want to talk, I can promise you I'm a very conscientious confidante. I don't reveal what's shared with me in confidence." She and Grace were piled up among the soft pillows on the couch in Clare's sitting room. Hot chocolate with marshmallows was being consumed while B.J. Thomas sang from the hi-fi.

Grace smiled dreamily. Making a quick decision, she concluded that Clare was actually someone to whom she would choose to disclose some of her more private thoughts.

Sensing that Grace wanted to talk, Clare persevered, "Something has changed since the last time you were here, hasn't it?"

"Mmm-hmm. You're very observant, Clare. Your eyesight must not have completely deteriorated yet, in your old age," she joked. "Does it really show? I've tried to keep my feelings from being too obvious, but at the same time, I feel so happy. I can't hide it!"

"Oh, yes! It shows. To me, anyway. But you know men. They're usually a little obtuse about these things. So, I wouldn't worry too much about appearing, you know, as if you're coming on too strong. Only someone who's looking for it would notice. You just seem very happy, and glowing with love."

"I am."

"So, tell me the good stuff. Since you're trying not to reveal too much, I guess you two haven't actually talked about how you feel?"

"We've only agreed that we'd like to get to know each other better. I don't really know how he feels, beyond that. It's sort of hard to tell, because I'm sure that even if he wasn't intensely interested in me, he would still be the same kind, generous person he is to everyone. Does that make sense?"

"Perfect sense. But, speaking from my own point of view, I think you're worried over nothing, honey. The mere fact that Ethan wants to get to know you, tells me there's something serious going on on his side, too. Ethan has managed to escape the clutches of the sneakiest young ladies in this town," Clare giggled, "*and* their mothers, so I think he's smart enough to only get caught if he *wants* to get caught!"

A few blocks away, James and Ethan were having a somewhat similar discussion. James was saying, "There's something quite special about that young lady. She has a bright, shininess about her. No guile in her. One of my favorite qualities."

"I recognized that about her right away, too. She's not like anyone I've ever met before, Dad. She's strong and smart and beautiful, and she looks at life as filled with joy and fun."

"It's good for you to be around someone like that. I don't want to intrude on this subject if you don't wish to discuss it, but after you expressed to me your initial feelings about Grace, and the concern you had for her, both her physical safety and her salvation, I seemed to sense first a coolness between the two of you, and then a definite warming. I can surmise why the physical protection around Grace was needed, but, I thought I also detected a spiritual awakening in Grace after you came out of the mine?"

Ethan smiled. "As usual, Dad, you've discerned correctly. Grace accepted Jesus while we were in the caves. It was beautiful. I was so glad I was there."

"And what about any personal feelings for Grace? Is that part of the package, too?"

Ethan laughed uncertainly. "I'm not positive yet. I have very strong feelings for her. And I feel an assurance that God would give his blessing on us. But, I'm just not sure about making a lifetime commitment."

"Do you love Grace?"

"What should it feel like, Dad?"

"Well, I would say it is definitely a yearning for the other person, but balanced and controlled by a desire for the other person's happiness and well-being above your own. If you've already considered the instructions God has given us about marriage, and the practical common sense concerns – compatibility, similarity of goals and values, similarity of Christian beliefs – then, it's time to contemplate your feelings. Whether there is a feeling toward the woman that makes you ache to be with her, to protect her, to comfort her, to laugh with her, and, if need be, to cry with her." James stopped and studied his son's face. Ethan appeared deep in thought.

The silence had stretched into several minutes when James continued. "You had to take on such big burdens and responsibilities at such a young age, son. I wish I could have been there to keep that off of your young shoulders."

"Dad, don't be hard on yourself about that. You had no part in it. You did nothing wrong. Nothing. And, as we've both agreed many times before, God used all of those circumstances for our good."

"Still, after all of the years you took care of your mother, and worked to help support the two of you, it brings me a lot of comfort to see you laugh and have fun. We always need the laughter in our lives, too, son, to keep it in balance." James patted his stomach. "Tell me that it wasn't the years I went without home-cooked food that made that meal so good to me."

"It wasn't. Clare is a terrific cook. And, if you think you're up to it, she's invited us over to eat tomorrow evening, with her and Grace. Grace has to leave early the next morning."

"Son, even if I wasn't looking forward to meeting Clare, and spending time with Grace, I would jump at the chance to have another home-cooked meal like the one we had tonight!"

Forty-Two

"Grace, you've got a visitor," one of the older boarders called out from the front of the house.

Clare waved her on her way. "Go on, sweetie. I need to get busy anyway," she said, as she stacked empty breakfast plates.

"See you later, then," Grace said as she headed toward the living room. By the door stood Billy Lucas, looking extremely awkward and uncomfortable. Feeling a surge of pity for the boy, Grace smiled and went forward with her arms outstretched. After hugging him, she stepped back, but continued to hold his hands. "Billy, I'm so sorry about Sadie and Beamon." She could see the tears forming in his eyes, and his valiant effort to blink them away before they could fall. "Have you been able to talk to your Dad this week?" she said, guiding him into a small sitting area, away from the always blaring television.

"Yes, ma'am. I get to see him twice a week, and he calls me just about every night. He's different now. We can talk to each other better than we used to. I think it's because my grandpaw's not here anymore."

"I bet you miss Miss Sadie a lot, though. How's it working out living with Thelma?"

"It's good. You know, I'm eighteen, so I don't have to have a legal guardian, or even have anybody live with me, but I like her being there.

It makes things seem a little more normal, for both of us." Billy grinned, almost like his old self. "I've even gotten her to talk more than she used to. She's laughed at a few of my jokes, too. We're sort of taking care of each other, you might say."

"What are you planning to do this fall? Are you going on to college?"

"I am. Thelma wouldn't hear of me staying around, getting under her feet, she said. Hey, did you know I've got a little sister?"

"No..how..?"

"You know my dad has a girlfriend, and, I never knew about it before, but they had a little girl together. She's four years old. My dad told me about her after he went to jail."

"Well, have you met her? What's her name?"

"Her name is Sophie. I met her the other day when I visited Dad. Sophie and her mom were there, too. They're going to come up to the house Sunday after visiting hours. She's a sweet little kid. And her mom is pretty nice, too."

"I'm sure you'll be a great big brother, Billy."

"Grace, I came by here today to apologize to you. For the lies I told you, and for getting all of us into that mess at the mine. You could probably say it was my fault that my grandparents died."

"No, no, Billy. Don't ever think that. You shouldn't have lied to me, though. Why *did* you lie to me?"

"It doesn't matter now. Just something I had all mixed up in my head. Do you forgive me?"

"Yes. It's all forgotten. Now, you wanna be friends again?"

"Yes, ma'am!"

"If you've got a few minutes, I think Clare has some red velvet cake left over from last night. Want some?"

"Hey, I'm a growing boy. I can always eat!"

Ethan and James were sitting on the bench at the cemetery gate waiting for Grace. It was a warm, balmy June morning, with a promise of more penetrating heat to come later in the day. For now, though, the sun's rays on James' back couldn't have felt any better if they had been the knowing hands of a masseuse. Such pleasures to be enjoyed from the smallest details in this new life of freedom! He was grateful for the contentment he had felt during his years in prison, and now, thankful again for the restoration of so many parts of his life. It seemed that every breath taken since his release yesterday had risen on a sigh of thanks to God for such blessings.

Touching James on the shoulder, Ethan broke into his thoughts, with "Here she comes". And they watched as the VW bug rolled to a stop across the street from them. After greetings and hugs all around, they all three strolled through the gate, heading toward the center of the park.

When they reached the World War II monument, Grace pointed out to James the engraving of Floyd Lucas' name. After spending a few moments in silence, Ethan motioned to the left and said, "The Lucas family plot is over this way."

Beneath a lovely dogwood tree, two graves were obviously freshly covered, as evidenced by the bright red clay not yet grown over with grass. The large granite stone spanning both graves simply gave the usual dates of birth and death, with no hint of the turmoil and trauma surrounding their deaths. To the right, beside Sadie, was a much older grave with its own tombstone, marked with the symbol of the Purple Heart.

Grace had brought three bouquets with her to lay on the graves. James came around behind Ethan and Grace, and placed an arm around each of them. "I wish I could talk to Floyd, and tell him how proud I am of him. He was a good boy, and he grew into a good man. From what I hear, he saved the lives of several men in the Battle of the Bulge, one of the longest and fiercest battles in Europe. We lost seventeen thousand boys in six weeks in that battle."

Though his voice was quivering with emotion, James continued, "And even in the middle of that chaos, he wanted to make sure he did the right thing. He gave that letter to your father, Grace. If Floyd had kept it in his own hands, his personal effects would have been sent home, and Beamon would certainly have destroyed the letter. If your father had lived, and mailed it to the sheriff, who at that time was Beamon's uncle, it would still have been destroyed, because the sheriff would have protected Beamon, for sure."

Ethan picked up the story from there. "God's hand was definitely on that letter. Once the letter came home in your father's effects, it could easily have been discarded as simply a piece of trash. But even if your family had mailed it, it was only about five years ago that Beamon's uncle died, so it would still have been to no avail. Even the fact that you didn't know about your father, and didn't have access to his belongings until recently, played a part because only now, at this point in your life, as a professional journalist, would you have been able to recognize the letter as the beginning of a story."

"The story of a man who deserved to be free," Grace finished for him.

"Never doubt the timing of God," James admonished them. "It's always perfect."

Grace handed a bouquet to each of the men, and, as one, they laid them on the three graves.

Forty-Three

*G*race spent most of the afternoon in the kitchen assisting Clare, who was preparing not only the usual hearty meal for her boarders, but also a smaller, more elegant dinner for the four of them. They would wait and eat a little later in Clare's rooms, around eight o'clock, allowing Clare and Grace time to clean up the earlier sitting for the boarders.

Though Grace's skills were not in the same league as Clare's, she tried to relieve her friend of as much of the mundane work as she could. It hardly seemed like work, anyway, when Clare was singing and dancing and making wisecracks all afternoon. With a carrot stick or a stalk of broccoli for a microphone, the woman had all she needed to go into a full-scale imitation of Karen Carpenter or the Beatles. The best part was when she couldn't remember all the lyrics, though.

She had crooned sweetly, "Lo-ove, look at the two of us…Stranger with every day.…We'll take your lifeline away.….And though you smell… You know I'll ne---ver tell you so..…." And then, showing no mercy at all to Grace who was bent double giggling on the floor, Clare drew the mop close and went right on when the next song came over the radio.

" 'Ba-ba-ba, ba-ba-ba-ren,' sing it with me now, 'Ba-ba-ba, ba-ba-ba-ren'" Reaching down, Clare pulled a breathless Grace up to harmonize with her. Getting into the groove now, Grace leaned into the "mike" with Clare. "Went to a dance, lookin' for romance, saw BarbraAnn......" Their voices trailed off as they turned slightly toward the back door and saw James peering in with a strange look on his face.

While Grace was trying to get her giggles under control, Clare was opening the back door. Having never actually seen James before, she assumed the man at the back door was a delivery man or a utility service guy. "Can I help you?" she asked in an almost normal voice.

"Well, actually I was going to offer to help you and Grace, but, since I can't carry a tune, I may not be much help." James said, with tongue in cheek.

"Oh, my! Are you...? James?" At his nod, Clare immediately offered her hand, and drew him through the back door. "Come in, come in. I'm a nut, I admit it! Don't blame this shenanigan on Grace, James. She's basically an innocent bystander who got drawn in against her will."

Grace stepped up to give James a hug and contradict Clare's assessment. "Hey, I was a willing participant! James, you look great! Where's Ethan? I figured you two would be catching up with old friends, old places, that kind of thing today."

"We did some visiting this morning. But, Ethan needed to work at his office this afternoon, so I decided to take a walk, and see how the town has changed. I saw your sign out front. I hope you don't mind me dropping in on you unannounced," he added.

"Not a bit," Clare said graciously. "Not if you aren't traumatized by the little rock concert you happened upon."

"Are you kidding? I love to see people having a good time," James grinned. "I'm not averse to having fun myself, either. Although, I'm not sure I'm familiar with that "barber" song. I guess it doesn't have anything to do with haircuts, does it?"

"No," Grace laughed. "Next time, we'll let you choose the tune, all right?"

"Deal!" James said. "Now, I can see you're in the middle of cooking and baking. I'm actually a pretty good hand in the kitchen. If you could use the help, and don't mind me hanging around, I'd be delighted to join the band!"

"The more the merrier!" Clare chirped. She scurried around, pulling out pans and utensils, and got James situated at the counter with a pile of vegetables to peel and cut up. With admiration, Grace watched her two new friends, one bravely attempting to fit into a new world, the other extending a welcoming hand to ease the transition. "Here, Grace, you can layer the lasagna, then the meat, then the cheese, in this dish."

"And just what are you going to do, now that you've got all this free labor to boss around?" Grace teased.

"I'm going to 'oversee' this operation, as well as provide the entertainment," Clare giggled, walking over to the radio, turning it back up a notch, and retrieving her mop.

Forty-Four

Though she knew there was no good reason for it, Grace felt a tiny bit anxious at the prospect of spending another relatively normal evening of food and conversation with Ethan. She had to reassure herself that the feeling must be due to the fact that so much of the time they had spent together thus far had been far from normal. Still, she took particular care with her make-up and clothes, wanting to appear at her best for this wonderful man, whom she loved. Whom she *loved*, she thought with awe. It would be so unbelievably fabulous if he loved her back! But, she reined in her wayward thoughts, she would leave that up to God, whom she trusted to do what was best for her.

Later, downstairs in the kitchen, with their nice clothes safely covered by huge aprons, Grace and Clare served the boarders their meal at six-thirty sharp. Then, while that group was eating, Clare kept them both busy in the kitchen and her dining area adding the finishing touches to their own meal.

Standing outside the front door at a few minutes before eight, Ethan noticed a funny feeling in the area of his stomach. At first, he thought it might be hunger pangs. After all, his light noon-time lunch was hardly enough to carry him over to his regular dinner hour. That must be it, he thought, and dismissed it from his mind.

He looked over at his father. Except for the gray hair, he could have passed for a much younger man. Amazingly, he had kept the harshness of prison life from invading his body, mind, and soul. An overwhelming joy swept over Ethan, and he had no choice but to grab his father and give him a manly bear hug – again. "Thank you, Lord, for my dad," he said fervently.

"It's so great, isn't it, son?" James agreed.

"Yes, sir. Sorry I keep grabbing you with no warning; the blessing just catches me up before I know it." Ethan pulled his jacket straight, and touched up his hair.

"Me, too. Me, too," James murmured. "Is it eight yet? Ready for me to knock?"

"Go ahead." James knocked firmly on the front door.

That funny feeling was there again, sort of fluttering around in Ethan's stomach. Butterflies? Did he have butterflies over tonight's dinner with Grace? He wasn't nervous or anxious, but he was excited, he admitted to himself. Being with Grace was such a pleasure. He admired her loving spirit, and her zest for life. And she made him laugh and have fun. It's not that he was unhappy otherwise, but his was generally a calm, easy-going manner of living. Grace seemed to complete something in him, filling a spot he hadn't even realized was empty.

And there she was, opening the door, sparkling from head to toe, smiling just for him, with such love in her eyes…! He was taken aback by the force of the feelings rushing through him. Did she love him, then?

"Ethan, do you want to come in?" Grace asked for the second time.

"What? Oh, yes, thanks." The world shifted to a more normal state, he gathered his wits again, and walked through the door.

The excellence of the food was exceeded only by the conversation. There was so much to talk about; James was still catching up on all the changes in town over the last twenty years, Clare wanted to know more about the murder in 1940 and the recent events in the mine, Ethan inquired about Grace's childhood, and Grace, with her reporter's inquisitiveness, would have happily delved into all their lives until she had dug up every smidgen of information about them all. Fortunately, time, and the required courtesy of allowing everyone a turn to speak, allowed the others to come away with a few of their secrets intact.

Despite her certainty that she had prepared enough food for ten normal people, Clare had to say the dreaded words, "I'm sorry, that's all there is," not once, but several times before they reached the dessert course. Offering them a choice of coconut cake or blueberry cobbler with vanilla ice cream, she refused to even be surprised anymore when both of the men wanted "a little of both, please!"

At long last, everyone seemed to be sated, and Clare whisked away all the dishes, to be dealt with later, and served coffee in her sitting area. The room reflected Clare's personality: warm and happy, stylish, but comfortable. The conversation continued to flow naturally, punctuated by frequent laughter.

Grace addressed James, "What would you like to do with the rest of your life now, James?"

James gave her his usual peaceful smile. "Well, I'm not going to rush into anything. I believe I'll want to continue my ministry in the prison. I think I still have a lot to give there. I'm going to visit my mother's family who still lives near Dahlonega. Try to locate some of my cousins on my father's side. I might try taking my son fishing," he said with a grin at Ethan.

"I'm all for that!" said the son.

"And then, after a few months of catching up, I'm sure I'll need something more productive to do. For one thing, I need to support myself! I know, son, I know, and I plan to live with you for a while. But not forever."

"Do you think you'll want to pastor a church again?" Clare asked.

"I've thought about that. It has a certain appeal, I admit. But I'm just going to wait and see what the Big Guy has planned for me."

"Anybody up for a game of Scrabble or checkers?" Clare asked.

"I love Scrabble!" James exclaimed. "Couldn't ever get anybody to play it with me in prison."

"Uh-oh. Is that because they didn't enjoy playing the game, or because you were so good at it no one wanted to play against you?" Clare wanted to know.

"Hmm. Well. I really couldn't say for sure," he replied.

"Okay, I'm dead. I'll play you one game, pardner. I don't necessarily have to win, but if you start using words like paramecium or palindrome, that'll be the last game."

Ethan jumped in, "But you know those words yourself! You just said them."

Clare explained, "Yes. I know those words, but I can't spell them. I'm a terrible speller, always have been."

"Ah, but you can cook, which is infinitely more important," James said, rubbing his stomach with a contented sigh.

"Grace, would you like to take a walk while they're scrabbling?"

"I'd love to."

James and Clare were already squabbling good-naturedly over the scrabble board when Ethan and Grace slipped out into the fragrant night. Ethan was still feeling not quite himself. He couldn't keep his eyes off of Grace, and it felt like he was sitting on the edge of his seat all night, waiting to hear each word that fell from her mouth, not wanting to miss even one lovely syllable. Now, alone with her, his legs and arms didn't seem to be bending in the right places anymore, and his voice came out either too loud or in a whisper. This was all wrong, he thought. He remembered feeling this way on his first date in high school, junior-senior prom night. He wasn't supposed to react this way now, as a thirty two year old man. But here he was, acting like a love-sick teenager.

Later, he had no idea what they had talked about as they strolled around the block. But he remembered walking back up on the porch and pulling her into his arms for a slowly swaying embrace. He remembered that she had leaned against his chest as if she belonged there, and had then turned her face up toward him for several minutes as he returned her gaze, amazed at what he saw in her face.

There ensued a moment, or a lifetime, or some indefinable unit of time, of delicate, caressing, then loving and passionate, kisses. Reluctantly and breathlessly, they subsided once again into a tender embrace. Still, no words were given by either.

Grace finally whispered, "It's getting late. We'd better go in."

And they went back inside to join the others.

Forty-Five

"You sure you don't want to come, Clare?" James asked.

"I'd like to, but I need to stay here and do some cleaning and cooking. You guys go on and have fun," Clare said, a bit wistfully. "If you get back by lunchtime, come in with Grace and eat lunch with us."

"Only if you'll let us pay your regular lunch price," Ethan insisted.

"Okay, okay. You win. See you later." She waved goodbye as the men and Grace drove away. They had decided the night before to visit the old Heaven's Mountain Church this morning; Grace had postponed her departure until after lunch so that she could accompany them. Right now, she was wedged companionably between father and son in the front seat of Ethan's truck. It was a gorgeous sunny day, and the short ride up the mountain was pleasant.

Just before they rounded the last curve, knowing that James had not seen the church in more than twenty years, Ethan tried to prepare his father for the rather sad and shabby disrepair the once lovely structure had fallen into. "Just don't be too disappointed, Dad."

James was leaning forward slightly as the vista opened up before them. Though his shoulders drooped just slightly, it was hard for Grace to tell if it was from sadness or nostalgia. As they got closer, he reassured them both, "It still looks beautiful to me. So many of my happy memories, and a few not so happy, are centered around this church. Let's get out and look around."

After circling the building and ambling through the somewhat overgrown cemetery, they went back to the front of the church and walked into the vestibule through the unlocked front doors. It was obvious James was taken back to another time, as he moved slowly, touching each wall, each window and door molding. Ethan and Grace exchanged looks of understanding, and were quiet, letting him go at his own pace, through the foyer and on into the sanctuary. Grace sat down in the front pew, joined a moment later by Ethan. Occasionally James would ask a question, Ethan would answer, and then silence would return. After a long time kneeling at the prayer rail and surreptitiously wiping a few tears away, James slid into the second pew and appeared ready to talk.

"So. How about it, Dad?" Ethan asked.

"It's like the end of a long journey. It started up here, and it's ending here. Closure, I think they're calling it nowadays. I thought I had dealt with all the grief over your mother, too, and maybe I have, but I'm feeling a lot of sorrow right now over the time we lost while I was in prison, and grief that I couldn't have been with her when she got sick and when she went on to be with Jesus. Sorrow, too, for little Floyd Lucas and what he had to bear all by himself.

"Sometimes I'd work on my sermons up here at the church. Even though it was more comfortable at home at my desk, somehow I felt a little closer to God here. I'd sit here, just where I'm sitting now. Floyd came whenever he noticed I was here, and in fact, he came a lot even when I wasn't here, just to get away from his daddy. He'd sit on the front pew, leaning against the side like you are, Grace. If I was busy, he was always considerate, talked for just a minute, and then would go on off by himself, usually up to the belfry. He told me that sometimes Bo or Beamon would come looking for him, and he'd be in the belfry. He said he'd just stay quiet as a mouse and not move a muscle, and pretty soon, they'd give up and go away."

Grace's mind was racing. "Do you think that Floyd would have considered the belfry to be his own special place, James?"

He considered a moment. "Probably so. Why?"

Ethan had picked up on Grace's line of thinking now. "Because in his letter, Floyd said he hid the knife somewhere. We thought he took it home, but maybe he just went back up to the belfry and hid it."

Grace grinned and said to Ethan, "Let's go find out!"

Running out to the vestibule, Ethan pushed open the hidden door to the belfry, then stepped back and allowed Grace to precede him. Once in the bell tower, Grace directed Ethan to look on one side while she searched the other. Finding nothing, they swapped sides and looked behind each other. Still nothing. Ethan even felt all over the bell itself, and all the pulleys, ropes and carpentry connected to it. Finally they gave up and sat down with their backs against the wall.

"Oh, well. It doesn't really matter," Grace sighed.

"No, it doesn't. Bo already confessed, so it doesn't matter at all."

"It would have been a great little ending for my story, though," Grace grumbled.

"Are you finished with it?" Ethan asked.

"Yep. I've already sent in the rough draft and they want to put it in next week's edition of the Sunday magazine. I gave James his copy yesterday afternoon, and he said he was completely satisfied with it, too. I guess he forgot to tell you. Ask him to let you read it."

"I will. I'm sure it's perfect though."

"Well, not perfect. But I believe it's good."

They sat in comfortable silence for a few moments, then Ethan picked up Grace's hand and began to caress it. "Something's different about you, Grace, since you came back. Did anything happen while you were at home?"

His touch on her hand felt wonderful. "Only good things. Augusta and I spent some time together, and, Ethan, she showed me her photo albums of my father and even gave me some of the pictures!"

"Wow. What a change – for both of you. I'd love to see the pictures of your dad sometime."

"Another good thing happened. I went to church with my mother and both of my grandmothers."

Ethan stopped rubbing her hand and was listening intently. "And?"

"And – I made a profession of faith and joined the church." Grace turned toward Ethan and smiled, like the cat that swallowed the canary.

Without a word, he took her into his arms and kissed her soundly. All that happiness bubbling around inside of her made it impossible for Grace to sit still. Feeling suddenly full of energy, she stood, stretched and leaned out the window, taking in the full panorama of the mountain ranges surrounding the church.

Feeling bereft now on the floor by himself, Ethan unwound his long legs and joined her at the window. "Grace, will you look at me, please?"

Reining herself back in from the window, she gave him an expectant look. "Of course." Seeing the seriousness of his demeanor, she quieted immediately.

Taking both her hands in his, Ethan spoke. "Grace, I know we haven't known each other very long, and I don't want you to feel rushed into anything. You don't have to answer me in any way if you don't want to. But I know how I feel. It became crystal clear to me last night, and I'm just about to burst to tell you. I love you, Grace. I love everything about you. I love the way you share your joy with me. I love the way you stand by your convictions. I love your kindness. I love the way your mind works, and how you can take charge of a situation when the need arises. I love your beautiful face and body. I love the way you laugh…"

Grace put her fingers on his lips and whispered, "I get the picture. I'm so glad you figured out that you love me. Because I didn't tell you the very best thing that happened to me while I was home."

"What was it?"

"I figured out that I absolutely love and adore you, too."

"You did?"

"Mmm-hmmm."

As Ethan moved to kiss her, he teased, "I knew there was something different about you!"

Grace slid to one side so she could lean her head against the side of the window. Ethan wrapped one arm behind Grace's neck and used the other to brace against the window frame. Leaning in to kiss her again, he suddenly cried out, and pulled his hand away from the window. Seeing that he was bleeding, Grace grabbed his hand and applied pressure, while Ethan, unconcerned with the blood, was using his uninjured hand to search for whatever had caused the wound.

While he was examining the window, Grace managed to rip the bottom two inches off of her shirt and began binding up his hand.

"Grace, hand me that old nail over by the door. I think I can pry this out."

"What is it?" she asked as she handed him the large rusty nail.

"Just wait. I've almost got it," Ethan grunted. "There! Look at what we have here, Grace, my love."

Grace gasped. There in Ethan's hand lay a dirty, frayed piece of cloth wrapped around a small object. As he gently pulled aside the cloth, revealed was an old rusty knife, with the initials "B.C.L." engraved on the ivory plated handle.

With her hand over her mouth, all Grace could say was, "I can't believe it. I can't believe we found it." She reached and carefully picked up the knife out of Ethan's hand.

"Look at the cloth, Grace. There's something written on it."

As they gently spread the cloth flat in Ethan's hand, they made out the words at the same time. "Bo Lucas killed Amos Canfield with this knife. Daddy made him do it. Signed, Floyd Lucas."

They stared at each other in amazement, slow smiles gradually spreading across their faces, replacing the looks of disbelief.

Grace began to sputter excitedly. "This is a perfect way to end my story! It ties it all up together with a great big bow like a Christmas present!"

"My dad needs to see this!"

"You know, we've got to turn this in to the sheriff. But, he'll give it back to us, won't he, Ethan?"

"I think so. But he'll have to wait. This knife has been hidden for twenty eight years. A little longer is not going to hurt anything."

"What are you talking about?"

"I'm talking about some serious courting that was about to take place before we were interrupted. Remember?"

Grace raised her eyebrows and nodded seriously. ""Yes, I do seem to remember that we were quite busy with other things a few minutes ago."

"Shall we resume where we left off?"

"By all means. Where we left off." With joyful abandon, they fell into each other's arms, secure in the knowledge that their love was a blessing from above, a treasure to embrace for eternity.

Epilogue

It was the middle of the morning, but on the northern face of Heaven's Mountain where the sun had only now begun to reach into the shadows, the dew still lay heavy and glistening. As the fingers of light reached the open spaces of grass, the reflection was blinding. The air was crisp and clean and damp; someone had cut the grass in front of the old Heaven's Mountain Church yesterday evening, and the resulting aroma of "almost cinnamon" was sweetness itself.

Inside the newly white-washed church, an unusually large crowd was gathered. A little earlier, the tones of the church bell had rung out across the vale and into the surrounding hollers, a melody of the past come to life again. Within, all were hushed and listening as Preacher James prayed from his old pulpit.

"What a joyous, happy day, Lord. We dance and sing and praise you on this glorious day. All that was lost has been brought back to life by you. All things are fresh and clean, unblemished, unbroken, poised for a new beginning. Dear Father, grant your children wisdom as they begin their own journey of joy and life and love together. Ethan and Grace have pledged themselves to you and to each other. Walk close beside them each day, Lord, and, as each day ends, remind them to raise their eyes to Heaven's Mountain, to seek your face, and to cling to you and to each other for eternity. In the name of our blessed Savior, Amen.

"My dear friends, may I present to you Mr. and Mrs. Ethan MacEwen."

Ethan bent down to kiss Grace, and the congregation erupted into clapping and laughter and patting one another on the back. The newlyweds were glowing as they looked out over the familiar and beloved faces of those who had come to share this day with them. Nan, Granny Annie, and Augusta were there on the bride's side, of course. And on the pew behind them sat Clare and Ed. Across the row, Thelma was sitting beside a grinning Billy, with Martin Sawyer just behind. Joe Wilson's family filled up an entire pew all by themselves. Closer to the back, Grace spotted Diggy and his wife, who had been kind enough, at Grace's request, to bring Mrs. O'Dell, who was sitting beside them.

As they made their way slowly down the aisle, hugging friends and shaking hands, the first strains of a familiar air could be heard. The guitarist and the fiddler got the melody going, but soon everyone was clapping in time and singing a hymn that had not been heard in this place for nigh onto thirty years..

Up on Heaven's Mountain, sitting by the throne,
With my blessed Savior calling me His own.
O, to be so happy, not a tear I'll see.
Up on Heaven's Mountain for eternity!

A note from the author

I hope you enjoyed reading "Heaven's Mountain", the first book in the Heaven's Mountain Trilogy. The second and third books, "Mountain Girl" and "Mountain Song", will continue the story of the Heaven's Mountain characters. Can you guess who will be the main characters in the next book?

Thanks for reading! And may God richly bless you!

Jackie Wilson

Made in the USA
Lexington, KY
27 March 2019